I0690142

DEEP MAGIC

A WITCHES OF CLEOPATRA HILL NOVEL

CHRISTINE POPE

DARK VALENTINE PRESS

DEEP MAGIC

Copyright © 2017 by Christine Pope

ISBN: 978-1-946435-07-1

Published by Dark Valentine Press

Cover design by Lou Harper

Ebook formatting by Indie Author Services

PROLOGUE

LUCINDA SANTIAGO SAT HUDDLED ON AN uncomfortable antique chair in a corner of her bedroom. The day outside the sheer curtains that framed the window was dark, dank, and gray. A little early for Southern California's stereotypical June gloom of clouds and low fog, since it was only the start of May, but the weather matched her mood perfectly.

No, actually, if it was going to accurately reflect her mental state, then rain should be pouring down, the skies torn apart by thunder and lightning. This part of California didn't get that kind of weather very often, though.

Muffled voices drifted up to her from downstairs, although Lucinda couldn't make out whose they were. Joaquin Escobar must be one of them; the dark warlock from Central America never seemed to leave the house, forced everyone to come and pay him court here in the home that had once belonged to Lucinda's parents, the Santiago clan's *prima* and her consort...before Joaquin murdered them.

Not for the first time, Lucinda wondered why no one in her clan had tried to fight Joaquin, hadn't tried to get some kind of vengeance for their dead *prima* and for Simón Santiago, who had been the true head of the clan for as long as Lucinda could remember. True, the magic of her fellow clan members was useless against a warlock like Joaquin, since he was capable of nullifying the powers of anyone who got within ten feet of him, but a bullet could travel a lot farther than ten feet. Or did Joaquin Escobar's strange and terrible roster of talents include protection against civilian —nonmagical — weapons as well?

Lucinda didn't know. She also didn't know why she was even still alive. Unlike her cousin Marisol, who had become *prima* of the Santiago clan with the death of her Aunt Beatriz, Lucinda had no real value to Joaquin Escobar. She supposed she should be glad that the only fate she'd suffered so far was to be confined to her room. Marisol was a glassy-eyed shell of her former self, a pretty doll who appeared to exist only to do Joaquin's bidding.

This behavior frightened Lucinda more than

almost anything else, because she'd seen it before. She'd seen it in herself years ago, back when Matías Escobar decided to make her his toy in an attempt to gain true power in the Santiago clan, rather than being forever dismissed as someone adopted into the witch family only because Simón Santiago had needed the healing gifts Matías' mother possessed. Lucinda and her father had had their differences, but she could only thank him and bless him for being strong enough to expel Matías from the clan, thus freeing her from his influence.

But Joaquin wasn't interested in Lucinda. Not in that way, at any rate. True, he had seemed to be in a very good mood these past few days, although she wasn't sure precisely why. One time when Marisol brought up a dinner tray for Lucinda, Joaquin had come along for some reason, stood off to one side as the *prima* handed the tray over to their captive. After Marisol was done with her task, Joaquin had bent down and pressed his lips against her neck, had put his hands over her stomach in a gesture both possessive and significant. The new *prima* might look as slender as ever, but Joaquin seemed to be making it very clear that she already carried his child.

That little scene had effectively killed what scant appetite Lucinda possessed, but she'd made herself eat anyway. She needed to stay strong, stay focused. So far she hadn't been given a single opportunity to escape, but surely that state of affairs couldn't last forever. If nothing else, wouldn't the neighbors be wondering what had happened to her, to her parents? True, Simón had never been what you could call social, especially with civilian neighbors on every side in this upscale neighborhood, but he had liked to go out and tend his roses, had been seen leaving the property in his big black Mercedes S-Class from time to time.

Then again, if Joaquin had somehow managed to subjugate every member of the Santiago clan, then Lucinda guessed keeping a few nonmagical neighbors out of his business probably wouldn't be all that difficult.

It had been a shock to learn who Joaquin really was, that Matías was his son. In a way, it made sense; they were both the kind of monster who didn't care that they were using their magical gifts for the very worst purposes. She could only be relieved that at least Matías was locked up for life in a maximum-security prison somewhere in Arizona, his talents forever stripped from him by Angela McAllister and Connor Wilcox. If Joaquin had come here to Southern California to save his son, he was too late. No power on earth could restore the gifts the *prima* and the *primus* had taken from Matías. Besides, Joaquin hadn't left the house since he'd returned here, a blank-faced Marisol in tow. When he'd disappeared right after murdering Lucinda's parents…was it only a week and a half ago?…she'd thought about running— only to find every door and window locked against her. The minor talent every witch possessed when it came to opening locked doors couldn't help her. Clearly, Joaquin had laid a powerful spell on the house to keep her captive within.

Why, she still didn't know. Even though she wasn't of much use—she possessed minor gifts when it came to predicting and controlling the weather, which was why her cousin Marisol had been the *prima*-in-waiting instead of Lucinda, as the *prima*'s daughter—she could still be seen as a symbol to rally around, the only surviving child of the murdered *prima* and her consort.

Unfortunately, it didn't seem as if any of her fellow Santiagos appeared to care. Lucinda wanted to hate them for being complicit in her captivity, but she knew in their own way, they were just as much prisoners as she was.

Footsteps on the stairs. Although the house had been well-maintained, it was still now almost a hundred years old, since it had been built in the 1920s, back when silent film stars and East Coast tycoons constructed lavish mansions in Pasadena's Linda Vista neighborhood. Because of the house's age, the stairs creaked, which Lucinda now counted as a good thing. She'd hated those stairs when she was younger and wanted to sneak out to be with her friends, but at least now she always knew when someone was coming.

The clock on her nightstand told her it was a little past three-thirty. She'd had lunch several hours ago, and it was far too early for Marisol to be delivering her dinner. Besides, the footsteps on the stairs sounded heavier than her cousin's. Joaquin? It had to be, although Lucinda couldn't think what he might want. He'd spoken very little to her after he'd taken command of this house, of the clan. She'd gotten the distinct impression that he thought interacting with her was a waste of his time.

The footsteps paused just outside her door. Lucinda got up from the chair where she'd been sitting, not because she really knew what she intended to do, but because she refused to let Joaquin see how frightened she was of him. It didn't matter that he hadn't hurt her so far. She knew he could hurt her, could kill her, if he decided there was no real reason to keep her alive.

And if she was going to meet her fate at the hands of this dark warlock, then she was going to do it standing on her own two feet, like the daughter of the Santiagos that she was.

The knob turned. The door swung slowly inward. A man stepped into the room.

Not Joaquin, although she knew this man's face immediately. Younger, and handsome, with sharp-drawn features and piercing black eyes. Lucinda froze where she was, blood like ice in her veins.

It couldn't be....

"Hello, Lucinda," said Matías Escobar. "Miss me?"

1

HAYLEY MCALLISTER TURNED THE KEY SHE held over in her hand. Technically, she didn't need it, because all witches and warlocks possessed the ability to open locked doors without the help of a key, but not using one when it was given was generally considered to be in bad taste, if not downright rude. Besides, Brandon had texted her to go ahead and get herself settled in, since he wouldn't be home from work for a few more hours.

Going inside seemed so…final, somehow. She still wasn't sure she even needed to be here in Jerome, but her parents had been so unsettled by all the craziness of the past few weeks—the *prima* of the Santiagos murdered, some sort of psycho-pathic wizard from Central America taking over the Santiago clan—that they'd insisted she leave

Payson, where a small branch of the McAllister family had lived for a hundred years, and come to the mountain town that was the main settlement of their witch clan.

"You'll be safe there," Hayley's mother had told her. "It's much better than being here in Payson, where there might not be enough of us to protect you."

Hayley really didn't think she needed to be protected. But her parents wouldn't stop worrying that somehow the warlock who'd usurped the leadership of the Santiago clan might be able to sniff out her talent, might try to steal her away for his own nefarious purposes. So in the end she'd agreed, mostly because she couldn't put up with the nagging any longer.

Her brother Brandon was three years older than she, and had been living in Jerome for the past six months. His talent was for all things mechanical, and he worked in a custom car and motorcycle shop down in Cottonwood. The shop was owned by civilians, so they didn't have a clue that the newest member of their team just happened to be a warlock. All they knew was that he could smooth out the world's most crumpled fender, could bring his engine-whispering skills to bear on the most complicated transmission rebuild.

And since the flat he'd been renting had two

bedrooms, it seemed logical enough to have Hayley come stay with him. Of course, he'd confided to her that he hadn't been home much lately because he and the guys at the shop were working on a car they hoped would get them on some cable TV show, but he figured she didn't need to tell their parents that.

"Anyway," Brandon had added, "it's not like I'd be of much use saving you from this big, bad warlock anyway. It's more likely the other witches and warlocks in town would be handling that part of the deal."

Which, Hayley had to admit, was only the truth. Brandon's skill was a super-handy one, but it wouldn't exactly provide much in the way of magical defense.

She pulled in a breath and inserted the key in the lock, then picked up her bags and walked into the flat. The air smelled slightly stale, and she wrinkled her nose. Brandon hadn't been kidding about not spending much time here.

Right next to the door and placed up against the wall was a battered-looking table with chipped milk-wash paint. It looked like it might be original to the flat, and Jerome's former mining days. Hayley set the key down on the table, and put her bags on the floor under it before going to the window so she could pull up the blinds and open it, letting in a warm, fresh breeze.

That was better. The day outside was bright and clear, and from the third-story apartment, she could see all the way down the hill, out to Sedona, and on to the purplish outlines of the San Francisco Peaks, more than fifty miles away in Flagstaff.

Of course, she realized as she turned away from the window, all the extra light coming in also helped to illuminate what a mess the flat actually was. All right, Brandon had made a slight effort in the living room area, where the only thing really out of place was a pair of scuffed work boots lurking under the coffee table and a couple of controllers for the Xbox that sat on an entertainment center made of plain pine boards and some cement blocks, but the kitchen was a disaster—empty pizza boxes from someplace called Grapes sitting on the countertop, a pile of dishes cluttering the sink.

"What, did you think you were getting a live-in maid with me staying here?" she grumbled.

Problem was, she guessed that Brandon had been counting on exactly that. He might have a big heart and not a mean bone in his body, but he was also one of the world's biggest slobs...just as he knew that his little sister tended to be something of a neat freak.

Lips pressed together, she went into the kitchen and opened the cupboards under the sink, praying that her brother at least had some cleaning supplies on hand. Yes, she could always drive back down the hill into Cottonwood to buy what she needed, but since she'd just spent two hours getting here, she really didn't feel like sliding back behind the wheel of her car.

That had been her one small victory. She'd agreed to come here, but she'd insisted on driving herself, wouldn't be brought here by her parents like some kid getting dropped off at summer camp. After all, she was almost twenty-three, more than old enough to handle a simple drive of a hundred miles or so. Her parents hadn't been thrilled with that idea, but in the end they'd relented, mostly because they could tell she was willing to call off the whole plan if they wouldn't budge on this one small detail. Besides, Hayley doubted the boogeyman from El Salvador or wherever it was really had the time to drop everything to try to grab her during that one window of opportunity.

Actually, she doubted he was going to come after her at all, but she was tired of trying to argue that point with her parents. Her gift might be powerful, but so were the talents of a lot of other witches and warlocks, many of them in the de la Paz clan, making them much more accessible to someone in Southern California than a single witch holed up in the northern part of Arizona.

All that mess with the woman whose ex-husband was killed had been down in the Phoenix area, not up here.

At least Brandon had his act together enough to have liquid dish soap and cleanser and disinfecting wipes in the cabinet under the sink. Hayley got out the soap and a dish brush, and grimly started in on the mess her brother had left behind. Not exactly how she'd planned to spend her first day here in Jerome, but she knew she wouldn't be able to relax until she had all this cleaned up. Also, truth be told, she'd rather wait until her brother got home before she ventured out into the town. That way, he could handle the introductions. The witches and warlocks here were her distant relatives, true, but she hadn't visited Jerome since she was in junior high. The Payson McAllisters always kept themselves a little aloof; it had been something of a departure for Brandon to move here, although, given his talents, Payson didn't have much to offer.

Not much to offer her, either. Hayley knew her parents had been expecting her to settle down, but the thought of marrying a cousin—even a second or third cousin—didn't much appeal, and the civilian population in Payson hadn't presented any interesting prospects, either. She didn't want to marry some guy who cared more about the lift kit on his truck or his gun rack than he did his wife. Better to be single than second fiddle.

As to whether she'd meet anyone here in Jerome, well, she'd just have to see. She wouldn't have admitted it to her parents, and definitely not to Brandon, but somewhere in the back of her mind she'd had the thought that this extended stay in Jerome might not be such a bad thing after all, if she ended up finding someone who caught her interest.

He'd have to be pretty out of the ordinary, though. She'd had enough ordinary to last her a lifetime.

Levi stood off to one side in the McAllister *prima*'s living room, trying his best to be unobtrusive as Angela and her husband Connor and the warlock named Robert Rowe did their best to comfort Danica Rowe, Connor's cousin. She sat on the couch, a balled-up tissue in one hand, Robert's arm around her.

"How could this happen?" she demanded, managing to sound simultaneously furious and scared out of her mind. "You took his powers away! He was in a goddamn *prison!*"

"I know," Connor said. He stood next to Angela, clasping her hand. Levi had noticed that about them, how they often held hands, or briefly reached out to touch one another, as if to reaffirm the bond between them. It was an interesting thing to watch, this love between the *prima* and *primus*, so strong that Levi could almost see its energy shining between them, like a river of golden light.

He wondered what it was like to love someone like that. By now he was able to ponder their relationship in an almost abstracted way, for the months he'd spent here in this world had shown him that he apparently was not destined to be as lucky as the McAllister clan's leaders. The affection shared by Robert and Danica Rowe also seemed strong but did not have quite the same intensity, possibly because they were only an ordinary warlock and witch, not clan leaders like Connor and Angela. During the time Levi had spent here in Jerome, he had seen much affection shared by its inhabitants, from the youngest of newlyweds to couples married for fifty years and more. They were a loving lot, these McAllisters. They had also done their best to make him feel at home here, to make it seem as if he belonged to their clan, right down to a false driver's license that gave his name as Levi James McAllister and his current address as Jerome, Arizona.

Perhaps it would take a few more years to make this place begin to feel like home. He hoped so. He knew he could never go back to where he'd come from…not that he wished to. This plane of existence was so much more pleasant, had so much more to offer, even with all the recent developments in California.

"We're dealing with something none of us has ever encountered before," Angela put it. Her sharply delicate features were strained, her skin pale, making her emerald-green eyes that much more brilliant in contrast. "I mean, even just discovering how to take Matías Escobar's talents away was a real leap. The last thing we ever thought was that he'd somehow find a way to get them back."

Levi cleared his throat. "To be precise, he didn't get them back by his own efforts. It was the spirits conjured by his sister's spell that accomplished the task."

Danica shifted on the couch, her gaze seeming to bore into him. With her dark hair and hazel eyes, she appeared as though she could be a close cousin of Angela's, even though Levi knew the two were only distantly related. "Then tell us about these spirits, Levi, since you seem to know so much."

He did his best to ignore the anger in her voice, since he knew it was only born of fear. "I'm not sure I can tell you very much at all. There are many, many spirits that exist on planes other than this. There are many planes, some dark, some light, some in perfect neutral balance. Jack Sandoval has sent me images of the sigils used to summon these spirits, but they haven't been of much help, for those sigils are human constructs that have their origins here, on this plane, and I have no real knowledge of how they came to be devised in the first place."

"I'm fairly certain the planes where these particular spirits originated had to be dark," Robert Rowe remarked, his tone dry. His blue eyes, a startling contrast to his near-black hair, looked flinty. "So that should help to narrow things down a bit."

Levi wouldn't allow himself to sigh. These people, although brilliant and kind and gifted in their own ways, simply didn't understand the complexity of those other worlds. Even though Levi himself had come into being there, he could only speak for the place whence he had come, and planes similar to it. Certainly he had never encountered anything like these spirits—these demons, as humans referred to them—before.

"Not as much as you might think," he said. "I have been working on the problem, and I'll continue to work on it. But I think for now, vigilance is the most important thing. Also, the usurper has been in power in Santiago territory for almost two weeks now, and he has made no move against us. There is every possibility that he only means to consolidate power in Southern California, and will leave the Arizona witch clans alone."

"I'm not so sure about that," Connor responded, his tone grim. Even from across the room, Levi could see the way his tanned fingers tightened on his wife's hand. "He didn't have a problem with sending his daughter to murder people as sacrificial lambs down there in de la Paz territory. That witch is dead now, but with Matías escaped and his powers returned to him, it may only be a matter of time before father and son decide they want a bigger piece of the pie."

True enough. Or rather, Levi could just begin to force himself to make an attempt at comprehending the motives behind such evil. Humans, even witches and warlocks, did tend to have a regrettable fascination with power, with taking more than the universe had seen fit to give them. Had the usurper, this Joaquin Escobar, grieved at all over the loss of his daughter, Matías' half-sister? Or had he shrugged and moved on, glad that at least his son had been returned to him, a son with a magical gift which could bend everyone around him to his will?

While Levi found himself continually fascinated by human behavior, he was not quite certain whether he wanted to know the answers to those questions.

"Possibly," he admitted. "I can't say for sure whether they're merely biding their time. However, even if they plan to make some kind of move, it's one that will have to be carefully plotted out. The Santiagos are a large clan, but all of them put together—even if every single one of them has been somehow suborned—are not enough to take on the combined forces of the McAllisters, Wilcoxes, and de la Pazes. They will have to get some kind of help to accomplish such a thing."

"What kind of help?" Robert Rowe asked.

"I don't know for sure. Possibly from the other witch clan in California…?" He trailed off there, because he didn't know the name of the family in question.

"The Ludlows," Connor said. "They tend to keep to themselves—from what I've heard, there's a sort of no-man's-land in Central California that keeps them separated from the Santiagos. The Ludlows started out in San Francisco around the time of the Gold Rush and then spread out in all directions. Eventually they bumped up against the Santiagos, and that was when it was decided it would be better to have some kind of a buffer zone between them."

"Like the Neutral Zone," Angela remarked,

and Levi tilted his head at her, not understanding the reference.

"It's from *Star Trek,*" she said hastily. "It's not important."

Ah. A television show, he thought. Or was it a movie? Either way, he supposed it didn't matter all that much. "Right. Well, it's possible that Joaquin Escobar might attempt to use his son to get the Ludlows allied with the Santiagos, even if they've been enemies in the past."

"How big is the Ludlow clan?" Danica asked. Some of her earlier panic seemed to have retreated, but she was still hanging on to her husband's hand the way a drowning swimmer might cling to a life raft.

"Pretty big," Connor replied. "About as big as the Wilcox clan, I think. So if they join up with the Santiagos, that's like putting our clan together with the de la Pazes. It could get ugly very fast."

"It's already ugly," Angela said. For a moment she went silent, as though remembering those who had died because of the Escobars' machinations. "But it's also been quiet, at least so far. The Scottsdale P.D. hasn't discovered any actual supernatural elements in the deaths of Kate Campbell's ex-husband or her father, thanks to Jack Sandoval doing his best to bury as much of it as he could before he resigned. But we can't keep everything covered up forever. That's impossible."

Everyone in the room went quiet at that statement. Levi might not have been born into this world, but even he knew how important it was for the witch clans to keep their magical natures secret from civilians—people born without magical powers, that is. Actually, now he felt vaguely ashamed of the chaos he had created down in Phoenix and its environs as he'd vainly pursued Zoe Sandoval, who'd summoned him onto this plane of existence in the first place, and who had seemed like a lodestone to him, drawing him to her with her mere presence. In the end, he'd realized his mistake and had stepped back, allowing her to be with her true soul mate, Evan McAllister. However, in the meantime he'd created quite the mess for Zoe's Uncle Jack to clean up.

"Well, we'll have to worry about that when the time comes," Connor said. "Right now, I think the only thing we can really do is stay vigilant, stay together, stay strong. The wards here in Jerome have been reset, right?"

"Yes," Angela said. As Levi tilted his head at her, not quite sure what they were talking about, she went on, "Up until recently, the clan elders would put wards on the town to let us know if a Wilcox crossed over into our territory. Now, of course, we don't have any reason to keep the Wilcoxes out"—she flashed a quick grin at her husband, the tension in her features disappearing for one brief moment—"but we definitely have every reason in the world to take precautions so we know as soon as possible whether we have any Escobars or Santiagos skulking around."

"How is such a thing accomplished?" Yes, the wards sounded like a very good idea, but it seemed to Levi that keeping away people they'd never met might prove challenging when the time came to cast such a spell.

"A few drops of blood, or strands of hair, are the most effective," Angela said, "although we can do without if we have to. This time, though, thanks to the de la Paz clan's connections in our state's criminal justice system, they weren't as hard to get as you might think. Matías might be long gone, but the blood samples he had to provide while he was incarcerated aren't. Same thing for his partners in crime, Jorge and Tomas."

"The wards won't keep them out, though," Connor added. "They'll just let the elders know that we have intruders in the vicinity."

"You've done the same thing in Flagstaff?"

"No," Connor replied, his jaw tight with worry. "The area we'd need to cover is way too big. Jerome is unique in that it's very small, with only one road in and out. It's a lot easier to keep an eye on things. But Robert here has the talent of being able to detect when magic is being used—and within a fairly wide radius—so that will help us out. And I have to assume that Luz Trujillo down in Phoenix probably has someone with similar skills. Joaquin Escobar may be evil, but he's not stupid. He has to know that we're waiting for him."

Levi nodded. *An accurate assessment,* he thought. Still, the Escobar warlock had also shown a brazenness that indicated he was willing to take chances, as long as the payoff was large enough. He most likely would not hold back if he detected a weakness he could exploit.

Which meant Levi had to refocus his efforts on these demons that Escobar's daughter had summoned. Were they still here, or had they departed this plane with her death? Jack Sandoval's description of his and Kate Campbell's confrontation with the witch made it sound as though the demons had left upon her death, but Levi wasn't so sure. Much depended on the spell she had used to summon them. There was always the chance that they remained on this plane, waiting for the right person to come along and press them into service.

He decided it was better not to reveal his concerns to the people assembled here. They had enough to occupy them, and for the moment, all Levi had were idle speculations, nothing more. Certainly no real proof.

And if that person did come along? The

Santiago clan was large, after all, and it was possible that Joaquin Escobar might convince one of its members to explore a talent which had been previously ignored, or suppressed.

If that happens, Levi told himself, *then we will find a way to destroy them. We must.*

He wouldn't allow himself to think what might happen if his confidence turned out to be misplaced.

2

THERE. EVERY INCH OF THE KITCHEN HAD been scrubbed, and since she'd found some microfiber cloths in a drawer in the kitchen, Hayley figured she might as well dust, too. The living room sparkled in a way it probably hadn't since her brother Brandon moved in, and she'd dusted the room that was to be hers and wiped down the bathroom, too. They'd have to share, it appeared; the flat might have two bedrooms, but it boasted only a single bath—one that, luckily, appeared to have been updated in the past couple of years, with warm faux-granite tile in the shower enclosure and on the floor.

The bedroom she'd be using wasn't big, but it also had a beautiful view, and a closet with more storage space than she'd expected. And because it looked as if Brandon had never used the space at all, the room didn't require too much of her attention.

She put her things away, glad that her brother had at least left her a drawer in the bathroom for her use. Once she was done with that task, she wandered back out to the living room, went to the window to look outside again. The landscape had begun to take on warmer tints as the afternoon lengthened and the sun prepared to slip behind Mingus Mountain—because of the tall peaks looming over the town, it would be something of a reverse sunset here, with the most obvious effects of the sun going down seen in the east.

Her purse was still sitting on the little side table where she'd left it; Hayley got out her phone and checked for any messages. Another one from her mother, even though Hayley had already texted to let her parents know she'd arrived here in Jerome safely, right before she got her things out of the car and came up to the flat. Apparently a text message wasn't good enough, though—her mother probably wanted to hear the sound of her voice.

Sighing or rolling her eyes seemed like a waste of effort, since she was alone here in the flat. Instead, she pushed the button to return the call.

Her mother picked up almost immediately. "You got there okay?"

"Mom, I texted you right after I parked the

car." And thank God the flat came with two parking spaces behind the building. Jerome's streets seemed awfully crowded for such a small town. Probably all the tourists, but still.

"But you didn't call."

"I'm calling now." What was it about conversations with her mother that always made Hayley feel as if she was regressing to her junior high days? "I needed a little time to get settled in."

"Is Brandon there?"

"No. I was just about to text him."

"He should have been there to meet you."

Well, Hayley couldn't argue with that remark, but she also wasn't about to throw her brother under the bus by saying so out loud. "He's really busy. It sounds as if they're going to get one of their builds on some TV show. Anyway, he left me a key, told me where to find everything." Which was a complete lie, of course. However, just because Brandon tended to be absent-minded about such niceties, there was no reason to point out his shortcomings. "Anyway, I was about to go out and explore a little."

"By yourself? Maybe you should go over to Rachel's, let her know you're there."

Rachel McAllister, although a distant relative like almost everyone else in Jerome, wasn't quite as distant as some. Her great-great-great-grand-mother—or something like that—was Hayley's great-great-great-great-aunt…or something along those lines. The genealogy of the witch clans could get complicated, and she'd never had the patience for such things, leaving it up to the more analytical minds in the family to keep track of who could marry whom and that sort of thing.

Not that she'd yet run across a cousin who interested her enough for her to care. Most of the time she was able to convince herself she was just fine with the current state of affairs, even though she knew in her heart that she was damn tired of being alone.

"I will. I mean, I was planning to stop by her store, since it's just next door. Anyway, shouldn't it be perfectly fine for me to go wandering around Jerome by myself? I thought that was the whole point in sending me here, so I'd be someplace safe."

A pause, and then her mother said, "Well, yes, that was the idea. It still doesn't hurt to be careful."

"I'll be careful. But really, everything seems fine here. Quiet." Hayley decided it was probably better not to mention the row of Harley-Davidson motorcycles she'd seen parked in front of one of the bars out on Main Street. She had a feeling the local witches and warlocks made sure the bikers behaved themselves, but still, it was the sort of detail that would give her mother palpitations.

"'Quiet,'" her mother repeated, sounding dubious. But then she apparently decided it was better to let that subject go, and instead return to the topic of Hayley's absent brother. "Don't forget to text Brandon. He'll just keep working and working if you don't remind him to come home."

"I will." The last thing she wanted was to be a nag, but she figured one short text couldn't hurt. "But really, it's fine. I like the flat. And I think I'm really going to like it here."

"Well, good," her mother said, although she didn't sound as if she thought that was such a good thing. No, she sounded almost hurt, as if it wasn't fair for Hayley to warm up to Jerome so quickly, that it was somehow disloyal to her hometown of Payson.

But Hayley knew better than to get into that subject. At some point, she might miss the expansive forests that surrounded the town where she'd been born—although Brandon had told her you only had to drive a few miles up Mingus Mountain to get plenty of ponderosa pines and other foresty stuff, so she shouldn't be too deprived. Again, better to keep quiet on the subject.

"I should text him now," she said. "You know, just in case he gets up to his elbows in a transmission or something, and I miss my chance."

"All right. But you let me know if you need anything."

And if she did, what would her parents do about it—drive all the way out here to Jerome to bring her a spare phone charger or something? Not happening. This was her chance to break free, to prove she wasn't their little girl anymore. It would have been different if she'd gotten married and moved out to start her own life that way. But her mother seemed determined to treat her like a child, even though she hadn't been one for years… in the eyes of the law, anyway.

"I will, Mom. I need to go."

A long pause. "All right, sweetie. You take care of yourself."

"I will. Goodbye."

Hayley ended the call there, and began to set the phone down on the coffee table before realizing that she still needed to text Brandon.

Hey, I'm here, she typed. *You coming home anytime soon?*

She watched the display. It showed that the message had been delivered, but there was no response. Well, he could have the phone shoved in his pocket and might not have heard the notification—or he really could be elbows-deep in rebuilding a transmission.

A minute went by, then another. She'd just decided it was stupid for her to sit there and stare at her phone when it *binged.*

Oh, sorry, Brandon had responded. *We really*

need to get this primer coat on before I leave tonight—it needs to set up before we can start laying down the paint tomorrow.

Hayley had expected as much, but she couldn't keep herself from experiencing a twinge of disappointment. Yes, she was a big girl now. Even so, it would have been easier to run the gauntlet in Jerome with her brother at her side.

How late? she typed back, and wondered if the question sounded as pathetic to her brother as it did to her.

Maybe 8 or 9. Get yourself some pizza at Grapes—they'll take care of you.

Brandon, trying to be helpful, although, speaking of pathetic, Hayley couldn't think of anything much worse than sitting and eating alone in a strange restaurant on her first night here in town. Well, she'd just thrown out a bunch of takeout boxes from that very same restaurant, which meant she could order pizza to go and eat it by herself here at the flat. Still kind of a dreary prospect, but better than smashing herself into a corner of a booth somewhere and pretending she didn't exist.

Sounds good, she replied. *I'll try that.*

Sorry. Once I get this project done, it'll be better.

Right. As soon as he finished this car, something else would be waiting for his attention. She couldn't even be angry with him, because at least he was doing something he loved. Following his bliss, as they liked to say. Whereas she still hadn't figured out what the hell she wanted to do with her life.

No prob. I'll see you when you get home.

K. Bye.

That seemed to be that. Hayley made herself get up from the sofa and go over to where she'd left her purse, then dropped the phone in an inner pocket of her bag. She knew she needed to force herself to go outside. Otherwise, she'd probably just sit here on the couch, watching Netflix or channel-surfing and ignoring her empty stomach until Brandon came home. It seemed like the best thing to do would be to go over to Rachel's store, say hi. Hayley had met her distant cousin years ago at a reunion, but because the event had been so overwhelming, so full of witches and warlocks she'd never met before, she didn't remember much about her except that she had reddish hair and was plump, and wore the kinds of boho-looking outfits you might expect of a modern-day witch. Anyway, it was nearly five o'clock; if she didn't get moving now, Hayley knew she ran the risk of the store closing before she even got there.

She'd just finished locking the deadbolt and had begun to turn around to head down the stairs when a pair of piercing blue eyes met hers. The sight surprised her so much that she took a step back, and managed to drop the keys to the flat at the same time.

"I'm so sorry," said the apparition. He bent and retrieved the keys, then handed them to her. "I didn't mean to startle you."

"It's fine," she replied, regaining enough control of herself to focus on the man who stood before her. And holy hell, was she glad she'd focused on him, because he was insanely good-looking. At least six foot two, fair hair, those amazing blue eyes, and the face and body of a male model, or maybe an actor. In fact, he was positively Hemsworth-ian in the looks department.

"Are you Brandon's sister?"

"Yes." So her brother had actually remembered to mention her to his neighbor? At least, she assumed the man standing there must be the person who lived in the flat opposite Brandon's; there wasn't much point in coming up here otherwise. "I'm Hayley. You live next door?"

"Yes. I'm Levi—Levi McAllister," he added after a brief pause, as though he wasn't used to introducing himself in such a way. Well, that made some sense. Being a McAllister in these parts was kind of a given.

Yet another cousin, of course, but since he was a Jerome McAllister, it meant they were distantly enough related that it didn't really matter. A flush rose in Hayley's cheeks. All right, so the guy looked like a Greek god. That didn't mean she should automatically be contemplating whether they were genetically compatible.

"Brandon said you would be coming to stay for a while," Levi went on, and Hayley found herself mentally forgiving her brother for ditching her. At least he'd had the presence of mind to mention her to his hunk of a next-door neighbor.

"Yes," she said. "My parents thought it might be safer here."

"Safer?"

"From—" She stopped there and gave a nod in a vaguely southerly direction. "You know."

"The Escobars and the Santiagos."

"You know about all that?"

"Oh, yes." Levi's handsome blond head tilted to one side. "Was there a particular reason why your parents thought you would be at risk? Your brother didn't say anything, except that you'd be coming to stay in Jerome for a while."

Hayley shifted her weight from one foot to the other. In general, witches and warlocks didn't discuss their individual talents at first meeting. And she especially didn't want to talk about that sort of thing while standing here on the landing outside her brother's flat. Even though she and

Levi were the only people here, it felt somehow…exposed.

"Well…." she hedged.

"Ah, of course. I should not be asking you about your talent on such a brief acquaintance. I apologize."

"It's fine," she said quickly. At the same time, she couldn't help but give him a sideways glance of her own. There was something about the way he talked—much more formal than what she was used to, with a certain carefulness that made her think of someone whose native language wasn't English. But that didn't make any sense. He'd said his name was Levi McAllister, and he was certainly fair enough in coloring to be one of their clan. "I mean, I would rather not talk about it here, but…."

"But you would speak someplace else? Maybe…someplace where I could have a drink with you?"

A drink? This Greek god was offering to buy her a drink? All right, just so he could talk to her, but she didn't mind. It had been a while since a guy had seemed this interested in talking…or anything else. Besides, the truth about her gift was going to come out sooner or later. She might as well spill the beans to Levi.

Things in Jerome were definitely looking up.

～

Levi tried not to stare at Hayley as she ordered a glass of pinot grigio, then set down her menu. It was difficult, though; Brandon McAllister had somehow neglected to mention that his sister just happened to be a goddess.

Her long hair spilled over her shoulders and down to her waist like a veritable river of gold. Her eyes were…not the bright blue of a summer sky, but the cool, serene blue of a mountain lake. And her mouth was full and yet delicately shaped, quick to smile or purse itself in thought.

If asked, he probably would have automatically replied that Zoe Sandoval was his ideal woman. After all, she was the one who had brought him here, the only female in his universe…at first. But she belonged to another, and although giving her up had hurt him more than he'd thought he could bear, he'd also told himself that in time there would be someone else. He'd just always assumed she would be as darkly lovely as Zoe herself. Looking on Hayley McAllister, though, Levi realized that the perfect woman had literally stumbled onto his doorstep.

But he was getting ahead of himself. They had only just met, after all, and she had no way of knowing anything about his origins. The McAllisters here in Jerome were in on the secret, of course, but they had not allowed that secret to spread to the other branches of the family, the ones in Payson and Prescott. In fact, Hayley's brother Brandon still didn't know, either, although that was more because everyone thought it was Levi's place to reveal his origins, and he simply hadn't yet thought of the best way to broach the subject. It didn't help that Brandon was hardly ever around, making it difficult to come up with a reason for such a discussion that didn't feel completely contrived.

Levi ordered a glass of malbec for himself, and a faintly awkward silence fell, during which Hayley picked up the menu again and appeared intent on perusing its contents. The hour was still somewhat early for dinner, but possibly she was hungry after her drive. And wine did seem to go better with food. That was one human custom he'd taken to readily.

"Get anything you'd like," he said. "My treat."

She looked up from the menu, surprise clear in her amazing blue eyes. "Oh, no, you don't have to do that."

"It's fine. I asked you here, after all."

For a moment, she hesitated. "Well…if we share something?"

"Of course. But choose whatever looks good to you. I've had almost everything on the menu here, and enjoyed all of it." Which was only the truth. He hadn't yet attempted much in the way of cooking—Rachel fed him several nights a week, and the rest of the time he went around Jerome, sampling the wares of the various restaurants. While he enjoyed them all, he did seem to end up at Grapes a good deal of the time, possibly because it was closest to the flat where he now lived.

"All right. How about we start with the artichoke dip and go from there? It's a little early for dinner."

"That sounds fine."

Tina, the waitress, came back with their drinks, and Levi requested the artichoke dip. She took the order with her customary smile, but it looked a little tight around the edges, and he couldn't help but notice the way her glance flickered over at Hayley and back at him before she left. Was she jealous? He'd thought several times during his arrival here that Tina might be flirting with him, but even after more than a year of living in Jerome, he still wasn't completely certain of human emotions and reactions. Everyone had been friendly, true, but there was friendly...and then there was *friendly*.

Hayley lifted her glass of pinot grigio to her lips and took a sip. Again Levi had to prevent himself from staring, because even the simple act of drinking wine somehow appeared glamorous...

sensual…when she did it. He cleared his throat. "Is there much concern in Payson about what's been going on?"

She lifted her shoulders, but there was something a bit too studiedly casual about the movement. "It depends, I guess. My parents—especially my mother—are pretty freaked out. Other people in the clan…they seem to think it's not going to affect us, that whatever's going on in California or even down in Phoenix isn't going to reach Payson, since we're kind of under the radar, if you know what I mean. When people think of the McAllisters, they think of Jerome, not Payson or Prescott."

"I suppose that's true," Levi said slowly, considering her words. "But the clan is still connected, even with branches in far-flung places."

"That's what my parents think…which is why I'm here." Hayley swallowed some more pinot grigio, then set down her glass. "I was going to say that it's strange Brandon has never mentioned you, but then I realized if it's not related to a car or a motorcycle, he doesn't pay that much attention."

"Your brother seems like a nice enough person," Levi told her. "Possibly a bit preoccupied, but it appears as if he's very good at what he does. I've seen him bring some of his project cars here to Jerome, if he was delivering them to a client in Prescott."

"Well, that's his talent. And it really isn't just cars and motorcycles. He can fix anything. I think you could give him a jet engine in pieces in a box, and he'd still be able to put it together."

Yes, those talents, big and small, that appeared in all of witch-kind. Some useful, some rather obscure, but all serving to show that the people who possessed them were not ordinary humans. Hayley's words seemed to give Levi the opening he needed, and so he said quietly, "And your gift?"

She gave a quick glance around the restaurant, but although it was somewhat crowded, no one seemed to be paying much attention to them. The booths were filled with a mixture of McAllisters and tourists, everyone chattering away. When he'd first entered with Hayley, a few people had sent them curious glances, but that was probably because they wanted to get a look at the newcomer. Levi had heard through the McAllister grapevine that one of the Payson cousins was coming to town to stay for a while, but he'd been so preoccupied with what was going on in California with the Santiagos that it had slipped his mind.

Until he saw the beautiful woman standing on the landing in front of his apartment, that is.

"My gift is a pretty rare one," Hayley said at

last. Her fingers played with the stem of her wine glass, but she didn't appear in any hurry to lift it to her mouth and take another drink. "According to my parents, no one else in the clan has it—and neither does anyone in the Wilcox or de la Paz families." Voice lowering, she went on, "Basically, if I'm close enough to another witch or warlock—like, around two feet or so, although it works even better if we're touching—my gift enhances the power of their gift. So if you're a weather-worker who normally can only summon a very minor rainstorm, my talent could make you powerful enough to call a hurricane."

Levi felt his eyes widen. No wonder Hayley's parents had thought it better to have her here in Jerome, where she would be surrounded by those better equipped to protect her. He'd noticed how Angela and Connor, who normally would have been preparing to move their family to their second home in Flagstaff now that summer was approaching, had made no mention of leaving Jerome. Clearly, they knew of Hayley's gift, had realized that they needed to stay here to make sure the clan's strongest witch and warlock were nearby to offer whatever protection might be necessary.

"Is it an effect that occurs without you having to invoke it?" he inquired. To tell the truth, he didn't feel any different being near her. Or rather, he did feel somewhat different, but he could attribute those troubling physical reactions to pure biology. He might have come into being on a different plane of existence, but now that he was here in this world, his body was as human as that of anyone around him. It had felt strange at first, as though he wore a set of clothes that didn't belong to him, but over time he'd become used to his new form, couldn't really imagine existing as anything else.

Hayley shook her head. "No. I have to concentrate, to think of the person's talent. But once I do, it just…grows, I guess." Those sapphire eyes met his. "What's your talent, Levi? Maybe I could give you a little demonstration."

"Oh, not here," he said hastily. "It's far too public."

"You actually wouldn't have to wield your power, you know. Everyone says they can feel it working without having to do anything. Sort of like taking a shot of espresso."

Perhaps that was true. However, Levi didn't want to get into the subject of his own magical talent, because that was where he still remained fundamentally different from the rest of those with supernatural abilities. Unlike an ordinary warlock, he didn't have one singular talent, along with the grab bag of lesser abilities, such as opening locked doors, bringing flame to a candle, or invoking minor spells of protection, that all witches and warlocks shared. No, because his nature was inherently magical, despite his human body, he could summon a wide variety of abilities, from conjuring flame to laying on hands to heal the sick.

And, he hoped, dispelling demons, although he hadn't yet had the opportunity.

"Perhaps later," he said quickly, and took a gulp of his malbec.

Hayley's brows lifted, but she didn't say anything. Possibly her quiet was due more to the appearance of Tina with the bread and artichoke dip; newly arrived in Jerome, Hayley probably didn't know that the civilian residents of the town shared in the secrets of the witch population here, unlike basically every place else where witches and warlocks had to rub elbows with the nonmagical portions of the population.

They were silent for a moment as they both helped themselves to the appetizer. Levi realized he wasn't all that hungry, but made himself eat enough of the bread and the rich dip that his companion wouldn't notice, or at least comment on it. She did seem to have more of an appetite than he did, possibly because she'd spent a portion of the afternoon driving on mountain roads, and then still had to get settled once she was here.

When she spoke again, she seemed to have realized that the topic of his own talent was off-limits, because she inquired about ordinary enough subjects, such as which other restaurants in town were worth going to, whether it was safe to go down into Cottonwood. He gave a few recommendations on the former, and then said, "Cottonwood is in McAllister territory, but it isn't warded the way that Jerome itself is. It's probably better if you don't go down there alone, just to be safe."

"Are you offering to escort me?" she asked with a faint smile.

Levi experienced a sudden heat in his cheeks and wished that Zoe Sandoval's ideal man—the one in whose image she'd created him—had been olive-skinned like her, rather than so blond and fair. It made certain physical reactions much more difficult to conceal. "I could," he said. "That is, if you'd like me to."

"If you wouldn't mind. I don't want to inter-rupt your work or anything like that." She sent him an inquiring look. "*Do* you work? I mean, I know none of us really *have* to, but…."

"I do odd jobs around town," he said hastily. That was close enough to the truth. Once the McAllisters had discovered he possessed a wide range of talents, he'd been called to help with a variety of tasks, everything from summoning a much-needed rainstorm to refreshing the illusions

Margot Emory had laid to keep civilians out of the more sensitive areas the clan members really didn't want discovered. And healing, since the McAllister family currently didn't possess anyone with that particular gift. "But I can set my own schedule."

"If you're sure…." Hayley said, the words trailing off, as if she was worried she had somehow overstepped some boundary.

"Oh, yes," Levi cut in. The last thing he wanted was for her to think she was imposing on him, when inwardly he was thrilled that she'd made it so easy for them to spend some more time together. "I mean," he went on, "Cottonwood isn't a very large town. There isn't that much to show you. But I suppose it always helps to have someone familiar with a place give you a bit of a tour to get started."

A smile touched her full mouth. Levi realized he was staring again, and looked down at his plate so he could pretend to be interested in breaking off a piece of bread. Although he already could sense his own attraction to her, he didn't want to frighten her off by acting too aggressive. *Was* he acting too aggressive? It was so difficult to gauge these things. But he did know that he wanted to behave in a way that would make her want to spend time with him.

"Well, remember, I'm from Payson," she said.

"I totally get the whole small-town thing. Still, I appreciate the offer."

"Of course. Maybe we could start with lunch in Old Town Cottonwood, and go from there?"

She had the most delicious dimples. "Sounds like a plan."

What neither of them said—although it seemed implied—was, *It's a date.*

3

Levi got a text message from someone partway through their shared meal, and said he had to walk up the hill when they were done rather than going back to his flat. Hayley didn't ask who or what was "up the hill," since it felt too much like prying. They might have shared an appetizer and a glass of wine, but it wasn't as though she was suddenly entitled to learn all his secrets.

So she'd smiled and said that was fine, and would see him tomorrow. And even though she'd only had the one glass of wine, she still felt as though she was floating down Main Street when she went back to Brandon's place, even after climbing up two flights of steep, narrow stairs.

Still no sign of her brother, which fine. Hayley wanted some time alone to bask in the afterglow of her time with Levi. He really wasn't like anyone else she'd ever met—serious enough, but kind, and with a sort of subtle humor that seemed to catch her when she least expected it.

And she was going to see him again tomorrow. Could she really be that lucky? Was a change of scenery really all she'd needed to get her love life out of the doldrums?

For a moment, she almost forgot about the grim reason for her being in Jerome. She wanted to forget. So much better to think about Levi, about his bright blue eyes, and the lock of hair that seemed to always fall over his forehead. The strong lines of his jaw, the breadth of his shoulders. How such a hunk could've been hidden away in Jerome all this time, Hayley really didn't know, but the Goddess must have decided to smile down on her by allowing their paths to cross.

She pulled out her phone and looked at the time. Just past six-thirty. Most people with normal nine-to-five jobs would've been home by now, but she knew it would still be a few hours before Brandon decided to grace her with his presence. The cheesy bread and artichoke dip she'd shared with Levi would hold her for a while, but she wasn't quite sure whether it would serve as a complete meal replacement.

An inspection of the refrigerator told her there

wasn't much hope there, since all she found was some coffee creamer and a long-expired bag of salad. She put the salad in the trash, then planted her hands on her hips and looked around. The way Brandon had set up the living room really didn't make much sense, because when you sat on the couch, you were staring at a wall without a window, which was a total waste when you considered the gorgeous view outside.

And if her brother was going to force her to amuse herself for who knows how long, then he really deserved what he got.

Witches and warlocks didn't have to work the way nonmagical people did, since all the old witch clans had investments going back generations, investments that provided all the members of the family with a stipend that covered the usual expenses as long as they didn't get too extravagant. Actually, from what Hayley had heard, the Wilcoxes did tend to throw money around, probably because back in the day they hadn't scrupled at using their powers to make sure their investments grew at a rate no normal portfolio manager could explain. Even so, most of witch-kind took up some sort of avocation or career, depending on their interests and talents.

And Hayley had always entertained thoughts of being an interior designer, had even taken some online courses, although if she wanted to get serious about having that kind of a career, she knew she'd have to go to Phoenix and attend school there. She'd actually opened up that line of discussion with her parents, who weren't thrilled but who had seemed as if they were about to cave and give their blessing—and then the whole thing with the Santiagos blew up, and she knew there wasn't a snowball's chance in hell that they'd agree to her going off to school in Phoenix now, not when a bunch of people had apparently been murdered by demons down there.

Anyway, even though she hadn't gone to design school formally, she knew enough to recognize that her brother's apartment needed some serious rearranging. Since she was going to be living here for the Goddess knew how long, Hayley figured she might as well try to make the place a bit more aesthetically pleasing.

Moving everything around took about an hour, and she was sweating by the time she was done, even though a delicious evening breeze had begun to steal in through the open windows. Certain finishing touches would have to wait until tomorrow—the couch needed some throw pillows, and the walls were sadly bare of art—but just shifting the layout was enough to make the flat appear much more welcoming. And since she'd be spending her own money on whatever pictures and other trinkets the place needed, she couldn't see that Brandon would mind all that much. He was hardly ever here anyway.

But he did come home, a little before eight, and stopped dead after he'd taken a few steps into the living room. Expression disbelieving, he looked around, then apparently caught sight of Hayley, who by that point had settled onto the couch and was drinking a glass of water and texting with her friend Becca back in Payson.

"What the hell did you do?"

He didn't sound very happy. Hayley typed a quick, *Gotta go, B's home,* and put her phone down on the coffee table. "I just rearranged things a little. I can't believe you were okay with having your back to the window."

"It was fine the way it was."

"I don't know about that." She got up from the couch. They weren't a very huggy family, and she certainly wasn't going to try to hug him now, with the way he was frowning. Besides, his T-shirt was smeared with axle grease and the Goddess knows what else. "You'll get used to it. Anyway, I had to do something, considering I was sitting here, bored out of my mind."

His expression softened a bit. On Brandon, Hayley's bright blonde hair was darkened to a sort of dishwater color, and his eyes were gray rather than blue. "Sorry about that. I left as soon as I could."

Hayley didn't know about that—he was wrenching cars, not performing brain surgery or piloting a jet. Still, even though her brother tended to be easygoing, she really didn't feel like getting into an argument with him. "On the upside, I met your next-door neighbor. You might have told me you had a hottie living across the landing from you."

"I do?"

"You know, Levi?"

"Oh. Yeah, he seems like a nice guy."

Typical. A few years earlier, Hayley had honestly wondered whether her brother might be gay, just because he never seemed to show much interest in the opposite sex or having any kind of a real relationship, beyond a few girls he'd dated in high school. Now she realized he was just so focused on his work, and on using his magical abilities to enhance that work, that he simply didn't have any room in his mind for women. She supposed that same preoccupation had prevented him from noticing anything about Levi, except that he was a) a guy, and b) breathing.

"He is nice. We had a drink, and we're going to have lunch tomorrow."

Brandon raised an eyebrow. "That was fast."

"Well, what else was I supposed to do? It wasn't planned or anything. I was on my way out, and we sort of bumped into each other on the landing."

For a moment, her brother didn't say anything. Then he shrugged. "Well, like I said, Levi's a nice guy. If you have to go running around with someone, I suppose he's a good choice."

Hayley almost retorted that having lunch with someone wasn't exactly "running around," but she realized that since Levi was going to give her a guided tour of Cottonwood and its environs, then those kinds of activities could possibly be classified precisely as running around. "I'm glad he has your approval," she said primly.

"Like you'd stay away from him even if he didn't. Anyway, I came home early so we could get some dinner. Just let me change my shirt and get cleaned up a little, okay?"

Since she'd been starting to feel distinctly peckish, dinner sounded like a good idea. "Okay."

He inclined his head slightly by way of acknowledgment, and began to head toward his room. Just as he entered the short hallway where the bedrooms were located, he paused and said, "Oh, and Hayley?"

"Yes?"

"I do kind of like what you did to the living room."

He disappeared into his room, and she couldn't help smiling.

Yes, Jerome seemed to be working out just fine.

Although Angela's text hadn't been completely unexpected, Levi did wish it had come through just a little later. If it had, maybe then he would have had the chance to walk Hayley home, to say a proper goodbye. As it was, he'd only been able to hurriedly reaffirm their lunch plans for the following day before he headed up the hill to the big Victorian house that was the *prima*'s residence while she was here in Jerome.

And what do you think would have happened if you had been able to take Hayley home? he asked himself as he trudged up the steep incline. No street in Jerome was perfectly flat, but the one that led up to Paradise Lane and Angela's house was more sharply pitched than most. *Do you think she would have invited you inside? Kissed you good evening?*

Probably not. It was her first day here in town, and she did share the flat with her brother. Besides, while Hayley seemed friendly and open enough, he hadn't caught any of the signals he'd begun to recognize as signs of attraction, of a woman inviting him to do something more than simply talk.

Not that he'd ever pursued any of those invitations. A good deal of his hesitation stemmed from simple fear that he wouldn't get something right, that the woman he was with would recognize his utter inexperience when it came to any kind of intimacy. Yes, this world provided ample instruction on the physical act of love, and Levi thought he'd familiarized himself with the basics, and yet, he didn't know if that would be enough when the time finally came. Also, he'd found himself holding back because he thought he should have deep feelings for a woman if he was to be intimate with her, and so far he simply hadn't had that kind of reaction to anyone he'd met.

Except Hayley, it seemed.

He came to the white picket fence that surrounded the house where the *prima* lived, opened the gate, and headed up the flagstone walkway. As he climbed the steps on the porch, the front door opened, and Angela smiled out at him. "Hi, Levi."

"Hello, Angela." Over the past year and a half, he'd gotten a little more used to calling her by her given name, although some part of him found the practice too casual, as though she should be called by her title. Then again, there wasn't much about Angela that was very formal. If he hadn't known she was the leader of the McAllister clan, he would never have guessed it to look at her—today she wore faded jeans and a short-sleeved peasant top, her dark, wavy hair pulled back into a barrette.

"Come on in," she said, then opened the door and ushered him into the house. "Connor took Emily and Ian down the hill to the store, so we can chat for a while without having to worry about all hell breaking loose."

Levi offered her an uncertain smile as he followed her into the living room. The *prima*'s twins were somewhat legendary for their ability to cause havoc, although they seemed to have calmed down a bit in the last few months. Perhaps they'd just begun to realize that the approaching summer was the last one they'd be able to enjoy before starting school, since they would be old enough to enter kindergarten this coming August.

"Go ahead and sit down. Can I get you something?" Angela asked. "I don't have much except water or lemonade, but—"

"Nothing, thank you," he replied, then seated himself on one of the leather couches as she followed suit. "I just had a light snack with Hayley McAllister."

Angela's green eyes glinted. "So I heard."

Was Hayley the reason Angela had texted him and requested this meeting? Levi supposed he should have known that one of the town gossips would have sent word that he hadn't wasted any time in getting acquainted with Jerome's newest inhabitant. But really, he and Hayley had been bound to trip over one another sooner rather than later, considering that she now lived just across the landing from him.

"Was that wrong of me?" he said. "I thought it might be a good idea to make her feel welcome."

To his relief, Angela let out a chuckle and shook her head. "Of course it wasn't wrong. You're both adults—you can do whatever you like."

Was he an adult, though? For all intents and purposes, he appeared to be a normal adult male in his late twenties. However, he'd only been living in this world for a year and a half.

No wonder he couldn't quite figure out how he was supposed to act around women. They both fascinated and intimidated him, to some extent. And, although he did not like to admit it to himself—for he knew that Zoe had found her consort, and was therefore lost to him forever—the thought of being with someone who wasn't the woman who'd summoned him to this world had felt like a betrayal.

Until now. For whatever reason, daydreaming of a possible future with Hayley did not seem like an act of faithlessness.

"Actually," the *prima* continued, "I'm glad that you and Hayley met up. You like her?"

"She seems like a very nice young woman," Levi allowed, not wanting to commit himself to more than that. Somehow he couldn't quite allow himself to wax rhapsodic about Hayley McAllister, even if she was the most beautiful woman he'd ever seen.

"Good to hear," Angela remarked, a dancing light in her green eyes telling him that she knew he wasn't giving her the whole truth. "Because I want you to stick to her like glue."

Levi frowned slightly, not sure he'd heard her correctly. "You want me to what?"

"Did she tell you about her talent?"

Ah, now he saw where this was heading. He nodded.

"All right. Then you have to know how important it is that we keep her safe. There's a very good chance that we'll need her magical gift before this is all over, and the last thing we want is Joaquin Escobar or anyone in the Santiago clan getting their hands on her."

Now the *prima* looked dead serious, the glint gone from her eyes. Her hands tightened on the knees of her faded jeans.

"I'll do my best," he promised. "Who else here knows about her talent?"

"Not many. Obviously, her brother, and I've

told the elders, but they've been sworn to secrecy. The fewer people who know, the better. So you should impress that idea on her, in case it looks as though she's making friends here in town and might be inclined to share that information."

"Surely you don't think that anyone here in Jerome would betray her."

Angela's full mouth tightened, and she glanced away from him for a moment, her gaze fixed on something outside the window, although what, Levi couldn't tell. Perhaps nothing at all, except the shadow of new leaves fluttering in the breeze.

"I don't want to think that," she said at last. "I'm pretty sure no one would do anything on purpose to give her secret away. Problem is, when you're dealing with people like the Escobars, it's so hard to know what they're capable of. Matías Escobar's gift of coercion alone is bad enough. We still don't have any real idea as to how far his father's talents extend."

"But the wards—" Levi began, and Angela shook her head.

"A delaying tactic, nothing more. We can do our best to protect Jerome itself, but we can't tell people that they have to stay here, that they can't go down into Cottonwood to shop, or over the mountain into Prescott to run errands there. And it's more than that—I thought it was a good thing that the clans had opened up over the past few years, that McAllisters were going into Wilcox territory and Wilcoxes down into de la Paz territory or whatever, but now it just makes us that much more vulnerable."

"I'm not sure I understand."

The *prima*'s fingers played with the turquoise ring she wore on her right hand. Her father's work, Levi thought; Andre Begonie was a silversmith of some note. "If the Escobars try to come here, I'll know—Connor will know, and so will the elders, because of the wards we've set out. But if, say, someone from the clan decides to go shopping down in Scottsdale, then that person runs the risk of bumping into one of the Escobars' agents—and there's no guarantee they wouldn't be forced into giving up any valuable information they might have. We McAllisters are all over the map when it comes to our talents and abilities, so it's not as if I can count on everyone to be strong enough to withstand that kind of assault."

"But surely the de la Paz clan will be on guard against such things."

"Yes, they will be, of course. Problem is, the Phoenix area is huge. There are a lot of de la Pazes, but not so many that you could possibly expect them to police the entire area."

True enough. Phoenix and the smaller towns clustered around it made up a huge urban sprawl, a place that still felt bewilderingly oversized to

Levi. Although he knew there was no reason for him not to return, he'd stayed away ever since he'd come to live here in Jerome. Connor himself had taught him to drive, and Boyd McAllister had sold him his old truck, so it wasn't as though Levi had been confined here the entire time. He'd gone to Sedona, driven up and over Mingus Mountain to visit Prescott, had even rattled along the back roads that connected Jerome and Williams so he could eventually take the I-40 east into Flagstaff and walk in its pine forests. But he'd consciously stayed away from Phoenix, and Scottsdale.

Avoiding Zoe, doing his best to prevent himself from seeing how happy she was with her consort Evan?

Perhaps. Possibly a coward's move, but it seemed to make the situation easier for everyone.

"Then maybe it's best if you did tell everyone to stay close to home, at least for now," Levi said. "Given the situation, I don't think anyone could blame you. Just until we can get all this figured out."

Her eyes met his, troubled, haunted. "But when will that be? We're facing something that none of us has ever dealt with before. On top of that, we're all relatively new at this. I mean, I've been *prima* for almost five years now, and Connor has been head of his clan for about the same. But Luz has only been *prima* for three years. The ones who came before us—my Great-Aunt Ruby was *prima* for more than fifty years, and I think Maya de la Paz was the head witch of her clan for nearly the same length of time. They knew what they were doing, while we—"

Levi couldn't help but be moved by her obvious distress—and worried as well. Yes, Angela was young, but in the eighteen months that he'd known her, he'd seen how she appeared to be confident enough in her position, a strong woman who also had a strong man at her side. Now, though, he was witnessing the first cracks in that façade, the worry that she wasn't equipped to handle the crisis that had been dropped in her lap.

"We will figure it out together," he said quietly. "As we discussed at our meeting yesterday, together the three Arizona clans are very strong. Joaquin Escobar will think twice about taking us on. I am certain of that."

Angela gave him a tired smile, but the doubt was still clear in her eyes. "I hope you're right, Levi. Goddess, do I hope you're right."

4

ALTHOUGH LEVI HADN'T SPECIFIED AN EXACT
time for their lunch date, Hayley figured it must
be sometime around noon, and made sure to be
ready with time to spare. Actually, to be honest,
she was ready by nine-thirty, since Brandon was
already up and out the door before eight o'clock
even rolled around.

Well, if nothing else, that gave her plenty of
time to stew over what to wear, although she also
didn't want to seem as if she was trying too hard.
From what she'd been able to tell, Jerome was
even more casual than Payson, although the vibe
here seemed to be more latter-day hippie/bo-
hemian rather than ranch hand.

In the end, she decided on her favorite pair of
jeans, some flats, and a drawstring top in a blue
that nearly matched her eyes. Loose waves in her

hair from her biggest curling iron, and just enough makeup to make her look finished but not "done," so to speak. Even so, as she surveyed herself in the mirror, she wondered if she should have put on that second coat of mascara, or whether she should've gone with clear lip gloss instead of the faintly pearlescent pink she wore now.

And then she told herself to stop obsessing, because she still didn't have any clear sign that this lunch was anything except a friendly gesture on Levi's part. For all she knew, the *prima* had told him to be nice to her because her brother was too preoccupied to play the part of tour guide, and Levi was handy because he just happened to live next door.

Still, she couldn't keep her heart from beating faster as she heard a knock at the door. *Don't blow this,* she told herself, then turned the knob.

Oh, good Goddess, was he gorgeous. It wasn't as though he looked as if he'd gone to any particular effort—he wore faded jeans and a white button-down shirt with the sleeves rolled up, and had a dusting of dark gold stubble across his cheeks and chin—but he was still the best-looking guy she'd ever seen in her life.

"Hi," she said. Oh, definitely brilliant.

"Hello, Hayley," he replied, in the charmingly serious way he had. "Are you ready for lunch?"

"Absolutely." She grabbed her purse from where it sat on the table by the door, then came out onto the landing and locked the flat's door behind her. Sort of a pointless gesture when you thought about it, since any witch or warlock could get in without a key, and she kind of doubted any of the tourists milling around on the street would bother to walk up two flights of stairs in what was—on its exterior anyway—a slightly shabby building, but better safe than sorry.

Levi led her down the stairs and then to the rear of the building. Parked next to her hand-me-down Nissan Rogue SUV was a big Ford pickup, older but meticulously maintained. After opening the passenger-side door of the truck for her, Levi went around to the driver's seat and got in, then backed out. Once he'd expertly inserted the truck into the traffic on Main Street, fairly thick even though it was a Thursday and summer vacation was still weeks off, Hayley felt as though it was safe to ask, "So where are we going for lunch?"

"A little café down in Old Town Cottonwood called the Red Rooster. They have sandwiches, things like that." He cast a quick look over at her, as if attempting to gauge her reaction. "Is that all right?"

"Sounds great." To be perfectly honest, she really didn't much care what they served, as long as she got to be out somewhere with Levi. "I drove through Old Town on my way up the mountain. It looked cute."

"Yes, they've done a lot to restore the old buildings, get businesses and restaurants and wine tasting rooms in there."

Wine tasting rooms. Now, that sounded like fun. Did she dare suggest that she and Levi go wine tasting after they were finished with lunch? Probably better to wait and see how the meal went first. And besides, it wasn't as if they had to do every single thing today. She was going to be living here for…

…well, she honestly didn't know how long she'd be in Jerome. A few days ago, such an uncertain prospect would have made her anxious. Now, with the notion that she might get to spend a good chunk of that time with Levi dancing in her head, thoughts of such a future only sent a little thrill of anticipation through her.

They wound their way down the mountainside, through tiny Clarkdale, and on into Cottonwood. Although it seemed fairly busy here, too, Levi was able to find a parking space on the street just about a block from their destination. Hayley couldn't help but look around from side to side, trying to take in all the cute little shops and their various wares, the restaurants…and, as promised, the tasting rooms. She had a feeling she could kill quite a few hours here with some leisurely shopping and wandering.

The café where Levi took her was small but nicely decorated, with a sort of farmhouse motif —which made sense, considering it was named the Red Rooster. And after they'd placed their order at the cash register and gotten their drinks, they were able to snag a table off in a corner, thus guaranteeing that they'd be able to talk without having to watch every word they said.

He set down their iced teas as Hayley took the seat with her back to the window. The sun coming in through the plate glass was warm but not hot, soothing and pleasant. In the background, the chatter of the other patrons of the café were also somehow relaxing, providing a nice unobtrusive hum without getting in the way of her conversation with Levi.

"Do you come here a lot?" she asked, recalling the way the girl at the cash register had smiled at Levi. Then again, it seemed as if he tended to have that effect on people.

"A few times a month. It depends on whether I have a reason to come down the hill."

"Those odd jobs." He lifted an eyebrow at her, and she added, "You said you did a lot of odd jobs for people in Jerome?"

"Right. Yes. And sometimes down here— there's not enough room for everyone in Jerome itself, so the McAllisters have sort of slid down the hill into Clarkdale and Cottonwood as well."

That made sense. Hayley knew that Jerome itself was teeny tiny, with fewer than five hundred permanent residents, about half of them witches and warlocks. The rest of them had to go somewhere. Over the years, some had moved all the way out to Payson to become part of that branch of the family, but it was more likely for them to stay closer to Jerome if they could.

"Maybe I should get a job while I'm in Jerome," she ventured, and surprise registered in Levi's bright blue eyes.

"Really? Why?"

"Just to have something to do, I guess. I can't exactly sit around Brandon's apartment all day, can I?"

"I suppose not, but...." Levi stopped there, a faint frown creasing his eyebrows.

"But what?"

He took a quick glance at the restaurant's other patrons, then seemed to decide it was safe to speak frankly. "I think Angela would prefer it if you limited your contact with outsiders. If you were working in a shop or a restaurant, it could be problematic. In fact, she wants me to watch over you, to help safeguard your talent."

A certain sick feeling began to bubble in Hayley's stomach, even though she hadn't eaten anything yet, had only taken a few sips of iced tea. "So that's why you asked me to lunch? Because the *prima* told you to?"

"No, of course not," he said at once. "I'd already offered to go out to lunch, to show you around, before Angela asked me to help keep you safe."

As quickly as it had come, the sick feeling subsided. Hayley wrapped her hands around her glass of iced tea, felt the cool condensation against the tips of her fingers. "Do you really think it's that much of an issue?"

"I'm not sure," Levi replied. "But Angela seems to think so, and since she's the *prima,* we should trust her judgment. Considering how valuable your gift is, it's better to be safe than sorry."

Hayley was about to reply when the girl who'd taken their order at the counter approached with their sandwiches. Since this was definitely not the sort of conversation she wanted overheard, she waited until the girl had returned to her post at the cash register before saying, "I never thought I'd need a bodyguard."

"I'm not sure that's the right term. Just… someone to keep an eye out."

"Have you dealt with any of them?" She didn't bother to clarify who she meant by "them"; she was sure Levi could figure it out.

"No. It was Jack Sandoval who had most of

the contact with…the others. He sent me copies of his case files, though."

That sounded odd. Was it normal for a detective—all right, a former detective, but still—to give someone unconnected to a case sensitive information like that?

Levi must have sensed her confusion, because he said in an undertone, "We can talk about that later. Someplace else."

She got the message. Maybe some topics were safe enough to be discussed here in public, as long as they kept their voices down, but other subjects needed to be avoided unless they were alone. Well, she was fine with that, if for no other reason than doing so would give them a reason to *have* to be alone together.

"Okay," she said. "Well, Mr. Babysitter, what do you want to do after lunch? Some wine tasting?"

His eyebrows lifted slightly at the "Mr. Babysitter" epithet, but he only replied, "I'm not sure that's a very good idea. One glass, like we had yesterday…that would probably be all right. Anything more, and we might not be sharp enough."

Hayley didn't bother to ask him what they needed to be "sharp" for. Clearly, he seemed to think the Escobars had rogue witches and warlocks hiding everywhere, just waiting for their chance to grab her. Or something along those lines.

"If you say so," she remarked, and picked up half her grilled chicken sandwich. "I assume shopping is okay?"

Most guys probably would have looked less than thrilled at the prospect of spending half their afternoon trailing from shop to shop in Old Town Cottonwood, but Levi only nodded. "Shopping should be safe enough."

Well, that was something. She wouldn't abuse the privilege, of course. But spending a few more hours in Levi's company could only be a good thing. Then again, if Angela wanted him to play watchdog, it really didn't matter what they did, although recreational drinking seemed to be off the table.

What else was there to do around here? She wasn't sure what their next destination should be, once they were done in Old Town, but she'd figure something out. The afternoon would stretch into the evening, and from the evening to…?

Something exciting. She'd make certain of it.

Levi had always thought of Cottonwood as small and quaint, but by the time Hayley had exhausted the shops there, it felt as if the whole day had gone by.

Which wasn't exactly true. While she looked at throw pillows, he pulled his phone out of his pocket and glanced at the time. Four thirty-six. They'd spent more than four hours together, so that was most of the afternoon, if not the entire day. The strange thing was that those hours had moved more quickly than he'd expected, given that shopping had never been one of his favorite pastimes.

Hayley, on the other hand, seemed to excel at it. Not that she was profligate; no, she considered every purchase carefully, didn't simply buy things because they were new and novel and set in front of her. But she did seem to have inexhaustible energy when it came to inspecting an item, whether it was a pair of earrings or a bowl or a scarf.

When she finally announced that she was done, they went back to the truck, which—fortunately for her and her purchases—had a locking cargo box in the bed. They secured everything and climbed into the cab, and then she looked over at him and smiled.

Already Levi had learned to be wary of that smile.

"Back to Jerome, then?" he said as he turned the key in the ignition.

"We still have lots of daylight left," she replied, her big blue eyes guileless. "Let's go to Sedona."

"'Sedona'?" he repeated blankly.

"Yes, the place with the red rocks. You've heard of it, right?"

"Well, of course. I've been there several times."

"And I never have. It should be gorgeous at this time of day, with all this warm afternoon light."

Levi couldn't disagree with that assertion, since he had been in Sedona in the late afternoon, and at sunset, and it was, in fact, gorgeous. However, he would have to make sure they didn't linger, and headed back to Jerome before the sun had truly begun to set. The last thing he wanted was to be caught out in the dark. Yes, Sedona was the place where the McAllister and Wilcox territories overlapped, and so it should all be perfectly safe…but he couldn't count on that.

These days, none of them could count on anything.

"For a few hours," he said, and hoped he didn't sound too grudging. It wasn't that he didn't want to spend the additional time with Hayley, only that he would prefer to do it in a more familiar place. "We need to be back in Jerome before sunset."

"Oh, that's fine," she replied. "That'll still give

me a chance to see some of it, and we can always go back later and make a day of it. That is," she added hastily, "if you have the time."

For Hayley, he would make time. Besides, his responsibilities to the McAllister clan weren't at all onerous, especially if one argued that his guardian duties with her were far more important than any of those lesser responsibilities. "I'm sure we can arrange that."

His answer seemed to satisfy her, because she smiled slightly before shifting in her seat so she could look out the window. Right then there wasn't a lot to see, since they were traveling along the highway that connected Cottonwood to Sedona, and this section was mostly rolling, dry scrubland until they got closer to the resort town's world-famous red rocks.

Actually, those rocks gave him an idea....

"Perhaps we should go to Red Rock Crossing," he said, and Hayley turned away from the window to face him.

"What's that?"

"A state park. Oak Creek flows through it, and if you hike up a little ways, you can get a good view of Cathedral Rock. It's quite beautiful."

"That sounds perfect."

Good. He would rather be with her in the relative peace and serenity of Red Rock Crossing than the bustling shops of Sedona's uptown section. If he wished to be honest with himself, he'd had quite enough of shopping for one day. Also, he knew he needed to talk to Hayley about who he really was, where he'd come from. The time they'd spent together so far today had shown him that she enjoyed being in his company…but would she feel the same way once she knew the truth?

No matter how that discussion turned out, it would be better to have it at the park, rather than while sharing another drink in a public place. Yes, the park was a popular tourist destination, but since the day was winding down and the park would only be open for another hour or so, he guessed that most of the people visiting there would already be gone, or would be getting ready to pack up and leave. He and Hayley should have the place mostly to themselves, especially on a weekday afternoon like this before the summer vacation season truly began.

He got off Highway 89A at Upper Red Rock Loop, then drove past the high school and along the winding roads that led to Red Rock Crossing. Hayley was quiet as she watched the ruddy-hued cliffs pass by, her expression growing slightly puzzled as they turned down what appeared to be a semi-rural road with houses on either side.

"Oak Creek goes through the flats here," he

said. "But you'll get to see plenty more red rocks, I promise."

"Oh, I wasn't worried," she said. "It's beautiful."

Which it was. They'd had a decent amount of early rain, and so the roadside was already studded with wildflowers in shades of pale, pale lavender and white and fresh coral. Oak trees crowded on all sides as he turned down toward the state park, then stopped at the guard shack.

The woman there, whose deep tan and laugh lines told a story of too many days spent in the hot sun, gave him a puzzled look. "We're closing in less than an hour."

"I know," he replied. "But I still wanted my friend to see it."

A shrug as she took the ten-dollar bill from him. "No problem. The gate closes at six, and we lock it fifteen minutes after that, so make sure you're out by then…unless you want a park ranger to come along and collect you."

"We'll be out before then."

"Have a good time."

Levi nodded and maneuvered the truck down the narrow lane and into one of the parking spaces just past the guard shack. At this hour, only a few vehicles were left, one of which was an SUV with the tailgate open. The people there, a man and a woman, were in the middle of trading out their hiking boots for some sport sandals. They smiled at Levi and Hayley as they got out of their truck, but didn't seem inclined toward any contact beyond that…which was just fine by him.

"You didn't tell me I needed hiking boots," Hayley said in an undertone.

"You don't," he replied. "At least, not for most of the hike. It's really just a trail that goes through the woods and follows the creek. If you continue upstream for more than half a mile, then yes, boots would probably be a good idea. But we won't have time to go that far anyway—we'll only be going to a spot where the trail meets a nice open area where you can see Cathedral Rock."

"All right." Her gaze shifted from him to the creek, which was about twenty yards from where they stood. Two men—well, barely more than boys, probably only around nineteen or so— appeared to be standing in the middle of the water. "What are they doing?"

"There are some rocks in the creek bed that you can use to cross from one side to the other. That's why it's called Red Rock Crossing. But you don't have river shoes, and it can be treacherous if you're barefoot. It's also something better left for another day."

Hayley didn't respond at first, as though she was trying to decide whether to contradict him and say she wanted to try the crossing anyway, even if she did have to do it in her bare feet. If she did, there wasn't much he could do to stop her. For all he knew, she was experienced at this sort of thing. Were there a lot of streams and creeks around Payson? He couldn't be sure. He'd had enough to occupy him, simply learning how to live in Jerome, learning enough about Cottonwood and Sedona and their environs so he wouldn't make a mistake which might brand him as an outsider, that he hadn't had the time to study up on places like Payson. Sometimes it had been exhausting, keeping up appearances. And yet, he felt far more relaxed around Hayley than he thought he had any right to be.

"All right," she said at last. "Next time. Good thing I do have hiking boots—and river shoes. It looks like fun, though."

"It is," he agreed. "But we should probably start on the path, or we won't have enough time to get to the spot where you can see Cathedral Rock."

"Lead on." She wore dark glasses, so he couldn't tell whether that glint had returned to her blue eyes. Her voice had sounded somewhat amused, however.

He began to walk to the far end of the parking lot, and then to a path that followed the border of what used to be a pasture of some sort. This was his third outing here, and he had yet to see any animals grazing on the grass there, but it was clear enough from the pasture's well-maintained fences that visitors to the park were supposed to stay out.

Almost immediately, though, they were down among the trees, fresh and bright with their new leaves. The air smelled good here, damp and laden with the scents of growing things. Damp air was something of a luxury in Arizona, and so he breathed in deeply, glad that they had come here, glad that with the trees on every side and the birds calling overhead, he could almost forget the grim reason why Hayley was here with him at all, and not back home in Payson.

She was quiet, looking from side to side, taking in her surroundings. Possibly these woods of oak and sycamore and willow were very similar to the ones where she'd grown up, or perhaps they were just enough different that they provided something of a novelty. Either way, she seemed happy enough to simply be in his company, to walk at his side, or, if the path narrowed enough that they couldn't walk abreast, drop just behind him so he could continue to lead the way. He liked that about her, liked that she was willing to be silent, to absorb what she observed without having to endlessly discuss it. There were several McAllister girls in Jerome that he'd liked well enough, but the way they seemed compelled to chatter constantly made his head start to ache after a while.

They emerged from the woods into an open area where a large expanse of red sandstone, smoothed by millions of years of rain and wind exposure, spread out before them. Off to the right was the creek, not as bright as it might be at the height of day, its sparkle somewhat subdued but still lovely. All around were little towers, or cairns, of smooth river rocks.

Hayley looked around, apparently impressed enough to remove her sunglasses. Now that the sun was dipping behind the trees, she really didn't need them that much. "Where did they all come from?"

"People build them," he said. "I'm not really sure why. Possibly to see how high they can stack them, or to find out how many rocks of different shapes and sizes they can get to fit together."

"Ah." Smiling slightly, she went down to the water's edge and began gathering up an assortment of the smooth stones. She sent him a glance over her shoulder, eyes crinkled with amusement. "You want to help?"

Actually, he had thought it might be amusing to make a cairn of his own one day. This seemed as good a time as any, although they couldn't linger too long here if they wanted to get a glimpse of Cathedral Rock before they had to turn back. Besides, working together on the cairn might give him the opportunity he needed to broach the subject of his unusual origins.

"Sure." He came down to meet her by the creek's bank, began looking through the rocks she'd already gathered to see which ones would work best for the all-important base. "Do you want to start with this flat black one?"

She eyed it critically, then nodded. "I think that should work."

He found a spot a few paces away from where she was sorting stones and put the black rock down. "Hayley, there's something I should talk to you about."

Her head lifted, and she straightened up from where she'd been crouching. "That sounds ominous."

Although the words were almost flip, he could tell from her expression that she was anxious about what he intended to say next. Did she think he was trying to come up with a way to let her know that, while they might have had a good time together today, she shouldn't expect a repeat of the experience any time soon?

Nothing could be further from the truth, of course. He wanted very much to spend as many days like this as possible with her. His only fear was that she wouldn't wish to spend any more time in his company after she learned the truth.

"I'm not sure 'ominous' is the right word. Only that there is something you should know about me."

Expression deadpan, she said, "You're married."

Was that supposed to be a joke? He still hadn't quite learned all the ins and out of human humor. "No, I'm not married."

"Then what?"

"I—"

"Hey—" came a new voice, a male voice, and Levi stopped, annoyed that a stranger had interrupted him at such a critical moment.

A man and a woman emerged from the woods. They looked vaguely familiar, and then Levi realized that they were the couple he'd spotted in the parking area, the ones who had been trading out their footwear. Now it seemed that they had their hiking boots back on, although he couldn't quite figure out why. There was no way they could walk that far on the trail in the time they had left before the park closed.

"Hi," he said, his tone as neutral as he could make it.

Hayley set down the rocks she was holding, then smiled at the newcomers. "Hi."

"I dropped my phone," the woman said. "It had one of those bright lime green neoprene cases. Have you seen anything like that around here?"

"No," Levi replied. Not that he'd been looking, either, but anything lime green should have stood out fairly well against the red rocks where they stood.

Hayley sent a quick glance around, then shook her head. "Sorry—we haven't seen anything like a phone case."

"Damn," the woman said. She glanced up at her companion. They both appeared to be in their late thirties, dark-haired, with the kind of trim, athletic builds that indicated they probably hiked and participated in a lot of other outdoor activities. "I guess that means we'll have to keep going up the trail."

Levi pulled his phone from his pocket. He didn't get a signal out here, but the phone still displayed the time. "There's only about twenty-five minutes before the park closes."

"That's all right," the woman said. She smiled, and there was something strange about that smile, as if it was just slightly too wide, and possessed too many teeth. "That's plenty of time."

Before Levi could even blink, her smile stretched and stretched, her face shifting from that of an attractive woman to something out of a nightmare, all teeth and glaring red eyes. Black wings sprouted from her back.

Beside her, the man underwent a similar transformation, cargo shorts and hiking boots disappearing as they morphed into something monstrous, something that should never have been seen in this world.

Hayley's fingers dug into his arm. "What the hell are they?"

"Demons," he said.

The two hideous figures launched into the air, wings beating, stirring up dust and last year's dead leaves. "We want nothing of you, traveler," one of them said, its voice thin and sharp. Its baleful red eyes shifted to Hayley. "We only wish to take the girl from this place, so our master might have better use of her."

Of course. He didn't precisely know how the Escobars' demonic minions had managed to track him and Hayley to this place. Not that it mattered now. What mattered was getting away from them.

Hayley's chin lifted, and the wind moving down the creek bed caught at her long blonde hair, blowing it around her in a flurry of golden strands. In that moment, she looked more like a valkyrie than a witch of the McAllister clan. "You can tell Joaquin Escobar that I don't feel like being used, and that he can go straight to hell!"

The demons laughed, the sound like sharpened nails down a chalkboard. Despite himself, Levi couldn't help flinching slightly. "You can tell him yourself," one of the demons hissed.

And then they both dove.

Levi raised his hands. The power of the earth was strong here, so strong that he understood why the McAllisters and the Wilcoxes had agreed to leave this as neutral territory, so that none of them could use it to their advantage. Still, that power would serve him well now.

The shockwave burst out from him, catching the demons mid-dive so they both tumbled toward the rocky ground. Before they hit the earth, however, they somehow managed to pull out of their fall and burst skyward again, the frenzied beating of their wings stirring up so much debris that Levi could feel his eyes sting with it.

"You are strong," one of the demons said. "But not strong enough."

"Tell me," Hayley said in a fierce, urgent undertone. "Tell me about your talent. I can make you strong enough."

The moment was here, although it had arrived in a way he had never imagined. He didn't have time to tell her everything. Just enough. "My talent is…all of them. All at the same time. Just lend me your strength, so I might use it."

Those sapphire-hued eyes widened, but she didn't hesitate. She moved closer to him, appeared to take in a breath and let it out.

And it was as if—well, she'd said that other witches and warlocks had told her the boost from her talent felt like drinking a shot of espresso, but in his own case, Levi thought it was more like getting a syringe full of adrenaline straight to his heart, or perhaps grabbing hold of two downed power lines with his bare hands. The energy flowed through him, sparking along every nerve ending, waking his power.

In that moment, he felt as if he could do anything.

The sky was cloudless, but lightning rained down nonetheless, striking the demons in multiple places all over their dark, inhuman bodies. Foul-smelling smoke began to steam up from their wounded flesh, and they cried out, those cries so sharp, they seemed to tear at the very air itself, assaulting his eardrums.

But still they forced themselves forward, although the lightning strikes had made them earthbound, and they could only drag themselves toward their assailant on bleeding hands and knees, the rocky ground beneath them causing additional wounds. Hayley clamped one hand on his arm, and another wash of energy flowed over him, bright and brilliant as the lightning he'd just called.

A wall of flame roared out from him, engulfing the demons, so fierce, so hungry, that once it had passed, all that was left was a pitiful pile of strange, distorted bones, a pile which collapsed into dust even as he stared at it.

Thunder seemed to echo off the cliff walls around them, but he knew that was only the shock of the flame wall dissipating...or perhaps the pounding of his own heart.

A deafening silence fell. Then, very deliberately, Hayley lifted her hand from his bicep. Her face was pale but resolute.

"What in the Goddess' name *are* you, Levi McAllister?"

5

THEY DIDN'T SPEAK ON THE WAY BACK TO THE parking lot. The guard smiled and waved at them as they drove over the backup spikes at the park's exit, just as though she hadn't noticed anything out of the ordinary, that this was just the normal end of a normal day. The SUV that had belonged to the demons was gone, too. Had it disappeared in a puff of smoke the same time they were immolated by the wall of flame Levi had summoned?

You'd think the park ranger might have noticed *that*.

Hayley's thoughts bounced this way and that, refusing to settle on any one thing. The way Levi had been able to call down the lightning, the fire, to create shockwaves out of empty air. She'd never seen anything like it. Oh, sure, witches and warlocks had always been able to summon fire. Not like that, though. Enough to light a candle, or kindle logs in a hearth, or to touch a spark to the sacred bonfires at Samhain and Beltane. Not a raging wall of flame so powerful, it might as well have been napalm.

And never had they been able to call the fire to them along with everything else.

My talent is…all of them, he'd said. *All at the same time.*

It wasn't possible. And yet…she'd seen it with her own eyes.

Only after they were back on the highway, the late afternoon sun flaring out above Mingus before it sank at last behind the dark bulk of the mountain, did Levi speak. "I was about to tell you."

Her mouth was dry. She wished they had some bottled water in the truck so she might wet her throat before she replied, but its cab was empty, spotlessly clean. "What exactly were you going to tell me, Levi?"

That you have the powers of a god?

Another silence. His hands tightened on the steering wheel, knuckles pale against his lightly tanned skin. "I'm not really a McAllister."

That much seemed obvious enough. Hayley gave a dry little cough before she said, "I kind of gathered that. So who are you?"

"I'm...." He paused for a few seconds, then gave her a quick sideways glance, as though he needed to gauge her mood before continuing. Then he returned his attention to the road, although there weren't that many vehicles on the highway. A few people heading back to Cotton-wood after a day spent working in Sedona's gift shops and hotels, tourists going to their time-shares in Sedona after a few hours of tasting wine in Old Town. "I was brought here by Zoe Sandoval. She's the *prima*-in-waiting of the de la Paz clan."

"I know who she is," Hayley said. Actually, the only reason she knew anything about Zoe at all was because she'd married a McAllister, although it sounded as though she was still using her maiden name. Well, that made some sense. It would be sort of confusing to have a *prima* with the last name of an entirely different witch family. "You said she brought you here? Are you from a clan in a different part of the country?"

"I wish it were that easy." His gaze was now fixed on the road ahead of them, tension clear in the lines of his throat and jaw. "No, I'm not a warlock at all. I'm not exactly sure what I am. She brought me here from a place outside the world because she was getting desperate, because she hadn't yet found her consort."

A place outside the world. Hayley rubbed her

temple, which had begun to throb. Well, she supposed she shouldn't be too surprised that she was getting a headache, not after what she'd just witnessed. Her brain seemed to think this might be a good time to check out. "But Evan McAllister is her consort," she pointed out, fastening on the part of Levi's remark that seemed the easiest to unpack.

"Yes, she found that out after she summoned me. I couldn't return to the place where I'd come from, and so I came to live here in Jerome with the McAllisters."

"Why couldn't you go back?" she asked, then wondered why she'd asked the question. Yes, she was confused and still more than a little freaked out, but she knew she didn't want to give Levi the impression that she thought it might have been better if he'd gone back wherever he'd come from.

"I still don't know for sure," he replied. "The most logical theory I've been able to come up with was that, since Zoe was the one who'd opened the gateway between the worlds and brought me here, only she had the power to send me back."

"I assume she didn't want to."

"No. Actually, we spoke on the phone, about a month after I came here. I asked her why she hadn't sent me back to the place I'd come from, since it would have been simpler for her, for her family and the McAllisters. And she told me that she didn't even realize what she was doing as she was doing it. The spell she used—it wasn't as if she could simply reverse it and send me away. The magic didn't work like that."

He spoke so calmly of spells and gateways between worlds, as if he was merely talking about the commonplace activities they'd used to fill their afternoon. Hayley's fingers closed on the armrest built into the passenger-side door, feeling a little reassured by the sturdy plastic beneath her hand. At least it felt real, whereas it seemed as if the rest of the world had been tilted on its axis. She'd just seen Levi destroy a pair of demons. *Demons.* All right, buried in some of their clan's teachings were rumors of other worlds, of the beings that inhabited them, but she'd never really believed in any of that. Even after hearing about what the Escobars had done in Phoenix, of the beings they'd supposedly summoned to do their dirty work, she still hadn't quite believed. Not like this, not in her gut.

She had to believe now, because she'd seen those demons with her own eyes.

"But you're—*you're* not a demon, are you?" Goddess, it felt crazy to even ask the question. And yet she knew he couldn't be human, even though he looked like a man.

"No. I still don't know exactly what I am. A

being of one of those other planes, someone whose consciousness was shaped in another world. When I was brought here, I didn't look the way I do now. I was a monster."

He spoke calmly, as if he was talking about someone other than himself. Hayley found it hard not to stare at him, to analyze every feature, every limb, as though attempting to discover something that might give a hint of those monstrous origins. She saw nothing, though, except an extremely handsome man.

"What happened?"

"I changed. The process took a few days. I would say the damage had been done, but even if I'd appeared to Zoe as I am now, she still wouldn't have taken me as her consort. She would have kissed me, and known her summoning had been to no avail."

"Did that upset you?"

Voice still calm, he said, "Some. After all, I'd been brought here to be her consort, and without that, I had no purpose. But fate decreed that Evan should be her soul mate, and I'm not one to argue with the universe. Besides, I've enjoyed the life I've made for myself in Jerome. The McAllisters know what I am, and yet they've still accepted me, taken me in. They allowed me to become part of their world." His expression was almost too neutral as he spoke, as if he didn't quite want to reveal how important that acceptance had been to him.

A quiet life in a sheltered place, as far as she'd been able to tell. And yet he'd known exactly what to do to fight those demons.

"The demons…." she began, then stopped, mostly because she didn't know which question to ask first.

"It's troubling," he said. "We'll need to go talk to Angela and Connor. Do you think you can do that?"

"Of course," Hayley replied. Yes, she was feeling rattled, but not so much that she couldn't go with Levi to the *prima* and *primus* and do her best to give an accurate recounting of what had just occurred. She wasn't a child, after all.

"Good. Because I want to hear what they have to say about how those demons were able to locate you. I can't quite figure it out. Sedona is neutral territory, unwarded, but even so, I'm surprised at how quickly they pounced. They seemed to know exactly where to go."

That was for sure. And it wasn't even as though they'd been lurking in the woods in demon form, waiting for their prey to arrive. No, they'd managed to make themselves look like normal people. How did that even work? Were there demons everywhere, wearing the faces of regular humans? The thought made Hayley's stomach clench, and she did her best to push it away. If she allowed herself to dwell on that notion, then she'd end up jumping at every shadow.

"If this was a spy movie, I'd say they'd bugged my phone or something so they could listen in to everything I was saying." Hayley made herself shrug, although she was feeling anything but nonchalant at the moment. "But we're not talking about spies, are we?"

"No." Levi's fingers tapped on the steering wheel as he turned right on Mingus Mountain Road, cutting away from the highway and down to the heart of Cottonwood. "Also, the trip to Sedona was a spur-of-the-moment decision. It certainly wasn't anything we had planned."

That was for sure. It wasn't even as if they'd discussed going to Red Rock Crossing when they were still out wandering around the shops in Old Town, someplace where they conceivably could have been overheard. No, that discussion had taken place right here, in the cab of Levi's truck. The flesh on the back of Hayley's neck crawled. Did that mean these demons could hear every-thing she said, no matter where she might be?

To distract herself, she asked, "Does Brandon know?"

Levi gave her a quick puzzled look. "Does Brandon know what?"

"Does he know about you? That you're not really a McAllister?"

"No. At least, I haven't told him, and I don't think anyone else had any reason to mention it to him."

"Oh." She wasn't quite sure whether she should be angry with Levi—and, by extension— the Jerome McAllisters—or relieved that at least in this case, her preoccupied brother hadn't let an extremely important piece of information slide right by.

"That bothers you?"

"I'm not sure." She reached up and adjusted the sun visor; even though it had looked like it was about to set for at least the last fifteen minutes, the sun was doing a damn good job of continuing to blast right into her eyes. Sunglasses only went so far. "It just seems like it's something you might have wanted to tell him, since you're neighbors and everything."

"We live next door to one another, but we don't have much of an opportunity to speak to each other. Your brother isn't home much. I truly didn't think that my origins were an issue. And I didn't stop to think that you—" Levi stopped there, obviously pretending to be occupied with turning right onto Main Street instead of finishing the thought.

Maybe she should have left it alone, but Hayley had never been particularly good at that sort of thing. Besides, despite everything that had happened, everything she'd just learned about him, she couldn't deny that she still felt some sort of draw toward Levi. And that was probably even crazier than realizing she'd just been in a fight with a couple of demons. "You didn't stop to think that I what?"

He kept his attention focused forward. The streets were beginning to be more crowded now that they were approaching Old Town Cottonwood, but she didn't think that was the real reason. "I suppose I didn't stop to think that the sister Brandon had coming to stay with him might be someone I was interested in, and that the truth would have to come out."

There—he'd said it. She hadn't wanted to read too much into things, because all day he could have just been acting polite, helping out by showing the newcomer around, and yet she'd still thought—had hoped—that maybe he was attracted to her in the same way she was attracted to him.

Her heart was beating away like crazy, but she did her best to sound neutral as she asked, "You're interested in me?"

This time he did turn his head slightly. Those clear, sky-colored eyes met hers. "I thought it was obvious."

"Well…." Since she wasn't quite sure how to respond without sounding conceited, she settled for lifting her shoulders and giving a nervous chuckle. "To be honest, I don't know what to think. I mean, you just told me you're a being from another dimension. But you're interested in a human woman?"

"Of course I am." He shifted slightly in his seat, as though suddenly nervous. "That is, wherever I came from, I am human now, too. Scientists and doctors could run all sorts of tests on me and discover nothing out of the ordinary—except that I happen to have identical DNA to a man called William Levy."

"Who's William Levy?"

"An actor," Levi replied. "From Mexico."

Hayley couldn't help but shake her head at that response. "You don't look Hispanic."

"No. But he is a star in Mexico, in something they call *telenovelas*."

Soap operas. Mexican soap operas. And Zoe Sandoval had seen William Levy in one of them, or come across his image on the internet, and decided he was the perfect template for her ideal man. Well, Hayley couldn't exactly argue with her choice. Whatever the inspiration, Levi was insanely good-looking.

"Anyway," he went on, "my spirit might have come from someplace else, but this body is as human as yours is."

And a gorgeous body it was. Hayley knew she should be focusing on more important things than Levi's looks, but she couldn't help being relieved by his words. Physically, he was human. It wasn't as though he was going to turn into a monster when the sun went down, or something like that.

Even so, she couldn't exactly ignore how he'd driven off those demons. No ordinary human could have done something like that. So the spirit within, whatever it was that gave a witch or warlock their power, also gave Levi his own extraordinary set of talents.

Since she realized she was staring over at him, she forced herself to look away, out the windshield. By that point, they were past Old Town Cottonwood, approaching the curve that would take them up into Clarkdale and then the lonely, winding highway which led into Jerome. Thinking of that road, of the stretches that didn't have any houses or even streets branching away from it, she couldn't help but shiver slightly. What if more demons were lurking up there?

"Do you know where the wards are set?" she

asked abruptly. She knew about them because they were part of the reason her parents had thought she would be safe here, that the McAllisters would know if the Escobars tried to make a move.

Levi didn't show any reaction to this sudden change of subject. Maybe he was relieved they'd moved on from talking about his relative humanity...or relieved that she wasn't going to question him too closely about his supposed "interest" in her. "The one on this side of town is right at the first switchback, by the abandoned gas station."

Good. That meant they were almost there. Of course, those wards had been set to let the people in Jerome know whether any enemy witches or warlocks were in the vicinity. Could they do much to drive off demons, or any other ungodly creatures the Escobars might want to send their way?

Levi seemed to understand her unspoken question, because he said, "The wards won't do a lot. Maybe warn the elders. That's about it."

"Can they fight off demons?"

Levi lifted one hand from the wheel and ran it through his hair. Usually he didn't seem so distracted, which meant her question must have troubled him. "No. That's not where their skills lie. I don't think anyone in Jerome has that kind of ability, except maybe Connor and Angela...and me, of course." He didn't say it in a boastful way, his tone instead matter-of-fact. And Hayley couldn't argue with him on that point, because she'd seen what he'd done. "Still," he continued, "I can't help but think there's safety in numbers. Those demons didn't go after you when you were here in town, or even in Cottonwood. No, they waited until you were in an isolated place, with no one around."

"No one except you," she pointed out. "And that turned out to be all the situation needed."

"You and me, actually," he said, and this time he almost smiled. "I don't think I could have destroyed them without your help. Driven them off…maybe."

Never had she been more glad of the talent she possessed. In the past, she'd only used it for small things, realizing from an early age how destructive it could be, if employed the wrong way. But as soon as her gift made contact with Levi's raw power, it was like flipping the switch and sending a burst of nitrous oxide to give a sudden energy boost to an engine…to use terminology her brother would approve of. No wonder those demons had been blasted down into dust.

The truck went around the first switchback and began to climb into town, and Hayley couldn't help letting out a small sigh of relief. Maybe Levi was right, and the wards couldn't really do anything to hold back demons, but even so, passing the spot where they were located was like passing a psychological barrier. She felt better, even if it didn't mean much.

A few cars passed them going down the hill, probably the last tourists clearing out as the stores began to close. She checked the clock on the dashboard. Six forty-two. Around time to start thinking about dinner, maybe, and yet she couldn't recall a time in her life when she'd had less of an appetite.

They drove down Main Street and passed the building where both Levi's and Brandon's flats were located, heading farther up the hill. After making a second loop, Levi turned off onto a steep residential street lined with perfectly restored Victorian houses. He parked in front of the biggest of these.

"I probably should have called first," he said as he turned off the engine. "But there are some things better said in person."

Hayley nodded. "Once they hear what we have to say, I'm sure they won't mind, even if we're interrupting their dinner."

What the twins might think about that, she wasn't as sure. She knew that Angela and Connor had two small children, but Hayley wasn't certain of their ages. Four? Five? Not an age where kids enjoyed having a meal disrupted, but there wasn't much they could do about it now.

She followed Levi up the front walk, then stood next to him as he rang the doorbell. A long pause, and then the door opened.

Hayley had never seen Connor Wilcox before this, because of course the Wilcoxes were still the enemy with a capital "E" the last time she'd visited Jerome, some eleven years earlier. He was very handsome, his greenish-gray eyes a striking contrast to his sooty hair. Looking at his visitors in some puzzlement, he said, "Levi? What's up?"

"Something…happened this afternoon," Levi replied. Although he appeared unruffled enough, a certain tension underlaid his tone. "Hayley and I were hoping we could talk to you and Angela."

Immediately Connor's gaze flicked toward Hayley. "Oh, right—you just got here from Payson yesterday, didn't you?"

She nodded. "Yes. I'm staying with my brother Brandon, in one of the flats above the kaleidoscope store."

"Well, come in. Luckily, we eat early around here. Angela was just trying to get the twins to watch some TV so we could have a little quiet time." A quick flash of a rueful grin. "Judging by the expressions on your faces, I have a feeling that's not going to happen."

"We're really sorry to interrupt—" Levi began, but Connor shook his head.

"It's okay. Kind of goes with the territory

when you're the head of a clan. Why don't you two go ahead into the living room, and I'll go get Angela."

"Sure," Levi and Hayley said, almost in unison, and Connor gave them a half-smile as he headed down the hallway toward the back of the house, presumably in search of his wife.

The living room was a large space with leather sofas, a carved juniper coffee table, and what looked like oils from local artists hanging on the walls, since the scenes they depicted appeared to be from around the Verde Valley, or over in Sedona or even Flagstaff. It all looked very clean and neat, and Hayley wondered how Angela managed it with a pair of four-year-olds. Well, the house was fairly large; maybe she adopted the same philosophy as Hayley's mother, who'd always maintained that it was all right if your own room was a mess, and who didn't care too much about the TV room, but who would raise holy hell if that mess managed to creep into the living or dining rooms, or whatever else she deemed the "company" areas of a house.

From down the hallway came the sound of high-pitched kids' voices, and a woman speaking in what sounded like a reply, although Hayley couldn't quite make out what she was saying. Then what was clearly some kind of cartoon, complete with a soundtrack of bizarre noises and loopy music.

That seemed to be enough to keep the twins occupied, because a moment later, Connor reappeared with Angela. Her expression appeared somewhat frazzled, although she smiled as soon as she saw Levi and Hayley.

"Hi," she said. "Connor made it sound as if it was important."

The last word ended on a slight rising note, as though she wasn't entirely certain that the subject of their visit merited this kind of an interruption. Hayley found herself studying the *prima's* face without trying to be obvious about it. She'd only seen Angela at a distance, and that had been back when she was a high school girl of sixteen, not the young woman in her late twenties that she was now. The wavy dark hair was the same, and she was still slender and not overly tall, but now she was beautiful where she'd only been pretty before, as though the years had sculpted away all the adolescent awkwardness and left the beauty the Goddess intended behind.

"It is important," Levi said. "Hayley and I went to Sedona earlier this afternoon, to Red Rock Crossing. A pair of demons attacked us there."

"*What?*" Angela appeared genuinely shocked, one hand going to her throat even as she glanced over at her husband, who seemed to have gone completely still, his eyes fixed on Levi's face. "Demons?"

"Two of them. They looked like regular people at first, a man and a woman, but…they weren't."

"Levi destroyed them before they could do anything to us, though," Hayley said. "It was kind of spectacular."

"Because of Hayley's help," he put in quickly. "Her power strengthened mine, and yes, because of that, I was able to reduce them to dust. Still, it was an encounter I would have preferred to have avoided."

"I can imagine," Connor said, his tone dry. "How did they even find you?"

"Well, that's why Hayley and I wanted to talk to you. We hoped you might be able to offer some insights."

Angela looked pale, but she seemed to recover herself, saying, "Please, sit down. Maybe I should get you some water, or—"

What Hayley really wanted at that point was a drink, but she thought it would be rude to ask. Besides, maybe after she and Levi had had this talk with the *prima* and *primus,* they could go get some more wine, find a quiet corner in a bar or restaurant so they could talk.

Or, better yet, go up to his place. He must

have some wine squirreled away there somewhere, right?

"We're fine," Levi said after Hayley shook her head slightly, letting him know that she was all right for now. She'd been thirsty back in the truck, but now she just wanted this to be over with. Crazy as it seemed, what she wanted most was to be alone with him.

"Okay," Angela responded, looking almost disappointed, as though she wished she could have fled to the kitchen to get them some water—anything to delay discussing what had clearly been a frightening encounter.

Levi took a seat on one of the sofas, and Hayley sat down next to him. Shouldn't she have been more freaked out by his revelations on the drive over here? After all, he'd admitted to being from a completely different dimension. And yet, it felt good to have him sitting there beside her. Reassuring. He'd saved her from those demons. Maybe she shouldn't be having such a visceral reaction—relieved to be rescued by the big, strong man—and yet Hayley knew there wasn't a damn thing she could've done to protect herself from those otherworldly assailants. Her talent was a powerful one, but it only worked in coordination with someone else's magical gift. On its own, it couldn't do squat.

Angela and Connor also followed suit, settling

themselves on the couch across from the sofa where Hayley and Levi sat. They glanced at one another briefly, their expressions troubled. Or maybe they were silently determining who should speak first.

"You said the demons looked like regular people," Connor said. "Was that the first time you saw them? Is there any chance you might have run across them before you were in Sedona?"

Hayley did her best to mentally run through everywhere she and Levi had gone that afternoon, the people they'd passed on the street or seen in Cottonwood's various shops or restaurants. However, she couldn't recall noticing anyone who'd looked like the couple who'd approached them by the bank of the creek.

Judging by Levi's flummoxed expression, he couldn't recall them, either.

"I don't think so," Hayley said. Next to her, Levi nodded. "They were obviously dressed for hiking, so they would have stood out among the people we saw shopping in Old Town. I really think we first saw them in the parking lot at Red Rock Crossing. It looked as if they were getting ready to leave, but then they came up to us about twenty minutes later, with some story about how they'd lost their phone somewhere along the trail."

Both Angela and Connor were quiet for a moment, as though digesting those pieces of information. Then the *prima* asked, "Did you get any kind of a strange vibe from them?"

"No," Hayley said at once, even as Levi added,

"I didn't sense anything unusual. It wasn't until they began to change shape that I realized they weren't ordinary human beings."

"Well, that's just great," Angela remarked. She pushed a stray lock of wavy hair away from her face and let out a gust of breath, as though simultaneously annoyed and frightened. "Because if we can't even sense them, we're going to have a hell of a time fighting them."

"The wards won't stop them?" Hayley knew she'd already asked Levi more or less the same question, but she figured she might as well hear it from the people who'd actually set the things in the first place.

"No." Angela glanced over at Connor, as if for additional confirmation, and he shook his head. "They're really just an early warning system. They can't physically stop anyone from coming into town."

"It feels like a sharp tingle, stronger than what you might feel when you encounter a strange witch or warlock for the first time," the *primus* went on. "But the only real deterrent about them is that they ruin any chance at stealth an intruder might have. If the demons are bold enough that they would actually enter a town full of witches and warlocks, they're sure not going to care about stealth."

No, Hayley supposed not. At the moment, she could only be glad that there had been just the two of them. What if the Escobars—if that was who had summoned the demons in the first place —had sent four of them? Five? For all she knew, that was what they would do next, once they found out this particular attempt had failed.

"The only good thing," Levi said, "if you can call it good, is that they obviously were waiting for Hayley and me to be alone, away from civilian eyes. Otherwise, they would have attacked us as soon as they saw us in the parking lot. They must care about escaping notice."

"Well, Joaquin Escobar may be an evil bastard, but he's not stupid," Connor remarked. "I don't care how powerful he is—if he attracts the attention of civilian authorities, he's going to have a very big problem on his hands. So I'm pretty sure he's going to do what he can to operate in stealth." The *primus* paused there, his gaze moving from Levi to Hayley and back again, as if he was trying to determine what exactly had led the two of them to go off to such an isolated spot on their own in the first place. Under that brief but intense scrutiny, Hayley could feel the color flame to her cheeks. Of course she and Levi hadn't done anything except talk, but she knew it looked a little suspicious. All right, Angela had asked Levi to keep an eye on her, but Hayley had a feeling that the *prima* hadn't been talking about walks in the woods, far away from anyone else.

"Which means the two of you had better avoid any future field trips out in the wilderness," Angela said. "Jerome and its immediate environs are probably the safest place for you to be, but you should be okay in Cottonwood and Clarkdale, as long as you stay around other people. I wouldn't recommend any hikes, though."

"Even if we have others with us?" Levi asked.

"Even then." Angela hesitated, then continued, "The problem is, we just don't know what the Escobars might send against you next. You could head out to hike along the Verde River with every person in the clan who has decent offensive magic, and it might not be enough." Her gaze shifted to Hayley. "You amplify magic, right? Does it work on only one person at a time, or can you use it so it boosts the powers of everyone around you?"

"One person at a time, as far as I know." For some reason, she felt faintly guilty, as though she should have experimented with her talent more, although such explorations carried their own dangers. "I'm not completely sure, though."

"Well, it's not something we can count on. Maybe we should try working on it, though, while you're here in town."

Hayley knew better than to protest. The *prima* was only a few years older than she, but in the McAllister clan, her word was law. She nodded, not sure what she should say in response.

Anyway, if her movements were going to be curtailed, if she was going to be stuck in Jerome and its immediate vicinity for the foreseeable future, she might as well have something to occupy her time.

Connor added, "Because Hayley might be able to only give one 'boost' at a time, so to speak, then having four or five other people with you might not make that much of a difference. It's just too risky."

"So what next?" Levi inquired. His brows were pulled together in a faint frown, but otherwise he didn't look too worried. Was he simply relieved that he'd been able to pass some of the burden on to the clan's leaders?

"For now? Go home, try to relax as best you can. If you're not safe here, you're not safe anywhere."

"Wow, Connor, that's really reassuring," Angela remarked.

Her husband gave her a lopsided smile. "I wasn't trying to be reassuring. Just honest."

The *prima* shifted on the couch so she faced Hayley and Levi again. "Connor and I will get in touch with Luz Trujillo and see if she's heard or felt anything out of the ordinary down in her territory. Even if she hasn't, she needs to be on guard, too. These demons—the way they were able to disguise themselves—if that's what we're up against now, we have to take even more precautions than we already have."

Hayley really wasn't sure how much else could be done, but she didn't voice her misgivings. This was all for better minds than hers to deal with.

"Then I'll go ahead and take Hayley home," Levi said. "It's been a taxing afternoon."

"I can imagine," Angela replied. "Maybe you should get in touch with your brother, Hayley, let him know what happened."

"I will." She got up from the couch, adding, "He should be home from work soon anyway."

Which was a little white lie. She honestly didn't know when Brandon would appear, but if past behavior was any indication, he probably wouldn't be getting home for at least another hour. Possibly two. Fine with her. That would give her more reason to stay with Levi. She doubted he would allow her to be alone in the flat, even if he was just next door.

He rose as well. "If Luz has any words of wisdom, please pass them along."

"We will," Angela promised. "But for now, stay inside. It's starting to get dark."

A glance outside the living room window told

Hayley that the *prima* was only being literal—by that point, the sun had set behind Mingus Mountain, and blue-tinted shadows were stealing across Jerome's streets.

Still, she couldn't help shivering slightly. What would happen next, with darkness encroaching on every side?

6

Hayley seemed subdued—not that Levi could blame her. That encounter with the demons must have shaken her, and it probably hadn't helped that neither Connor nor Angela had any particular words of encouragement.

After he'd parked the truck behind the brick building where his flat was located, and after they'd begun to climb the steps, he said, "You'll come to my place."

Hayley shot him a faintly amused look from beneath her lashes. "Oh, I will?"

Damn. He hadn't phrased that correctly, had he? Although he'd done his best to master the intricacies of the English language during his time here, every once in a while, its nuances managed to escape him. "What I meant was, it's probably safer if you come to my flat. At least until your brother gets home."

"I was going to text him, tell him what happened."

"It's probably better to wait."

By that point, they'd gotten to the landing that separated the two apartments. Hayley tilted her head at him and asked, "Why? If he finds out I've been hiding something from him—"

Levi laid a hand on the doorknob and opened the door to his flat. "I'm not asking you to hide anything. I'm only saying that transmitting that sort of information by phone isn't a very good idea. Also, he works with civilians, correct?"

"Yes," Hayley replied, her expression still somewhat dubious.

"Well, it's better if he doesn't react negatively around them. They might ask what the problem is, and he would have to lie, cover it up. When he gets home, you can tell him then."

She appeared to weigh these arguments, then shrugged. "All right. It's not as if he could do much about demons, anyway. I doubt he can pick up an engine with his brain and throw it at them."

The mental image her remark conjured made Levi smile slightly. "No, I suppose not. But come inside."

Hayley followed him into the flat and gave a quick glance around—looking at the décor, curious, but trying not to seem too nosy. Since he always kept the place neat and clean, he doubted she would notice much. Disorder made him edgy, and so he always expended the effort to make his home as serene and uncluttered as possible. He'd never stopped to analyze precisely why he preferred things to be orderly, but he guessed it probably had something to do with his unorthodox arrival in this world. His surroundings were one thing he knew he could control.

"These photographs are really beautiful," she said, going closer to a set of low antique bookcases and the triptych of black and white images that hung above them—Sedona by moonlight, every outline defined, every contour of the rocks given an additional sharpness because of the high contrast of the images. "Everyone always talks about Sedona's red rocks, so I never thought about what they'd look like if they were shot in black and white. They're very…architectural."

Which had been his intent in taking the photographs, but he was surprised to hear her make such an insightful comment about them. "Have you studied photography?"

"No," she replied as she turned away from the photos and back toward him. "But I've taken some design courses. That's what I was thinking about doing—interior design. Unfortunately, the closest school was in Phoenix, and after the big demon incident down in Scottsdale, my parents weren't too interested in having me go to school there."

"That's unfortunate. But perhaps you can still go, once all this is settled."

Her mouth tightened, and he couldn't help but notice the way her gaze slid away from his. "If it's settled. Connor and Angela didn't sound too hopeful."

"That's only because we're at the very beginning of learning about these demons, how they're being controlled, the limits of their powers. It's far too early to give up hope."

"If you say so."

She sounded defeated. Levi couldn't blame her, but at the same time, he wanted to do what he could to cheer her up. "Go ahead and sit down. Would you like some water, something to eat?"

A sudden glint entered her blue eyes, and for a moment she didn't look at all worn down. "After what we just went through, I was kind of hoping for some wine."

He liked that idea as well, although he didn't want her to think that he was trying to take advantage of her. Then again, she was the one who'd made the suggestion....

"I've been collecting wine from the local wineries," he told her. "Pillsbury has a very good chardonnay."

"That sounds heavenly."

"And some cheese and crackers?"

"Even better."

"I'll be back in a moment."

As Hayley settled herself on the couch, Levi went into the kitchen and got out the items in question—cheese and wine from the refrigerator, crackers from the cupboard. During his time here, he'd done his best to sample as wide a variety of cuisine as was possible in the areas surrounding Jerome, but he did have to admit to an overwhelming fondness for cheese. In fact, he'd consumed cheese and crackers and cheese and bread as a meal many nights, not wanting anything else. Luckily, this human body his otherworldly soul inhabited didn't seem to care much what he put into it, as long as it got some sort of fuel; he had neither gained nor lost weight during his time in this world, no matter what he ate.

He arranged the cheese and crackers on a plate, and retrieved a set of glasses from the cupboard next to the one that held the plates. After he uncorked the wine, he put everything on a tray and took it out to the living room—or rather, he went around the low wall that separated the pocket-sized kitchen from the space that served as both living and dining rooms, and set the tray down on the coffee table.

Hayley leaned over so she could take a look at

the assortment he'd put together. "I had no idea I was going to get a gourmet cheese plate."

"The stores in Sedona offer some very good selections." For some reason, it felt strange to sit down next to her, even though he'd done the exact same thing at Connor and Angela's home only a few moments before. Perhaps it was merely that he and Hayley were alone here together, and so sitting beside her on the couch was fraught with certain implications which hadn't existed in that previous situation.

Still, since he thought it would look even more obvious if he took one of the armchairs that faced the sofa, he made himself sit down, then immediately busied himself with pouring wine into the glasses he'd brought. He set down the bottle of wine, and handed a glass to Hayley.

She took it, offering him a grateful smile. "Thank you. I have a feeling this is going to taste great."

"It is very good chardonnay."

Her smile widened. "That's not exactly what I meant. I mean, I'm sure it's wonderful, but it's more that I just really needed a drink after all… that." She waved with her free hand toward the window, apparently indicating Sedona and the ugly incident with the demons.

Levi could understand that sentiment. "Then let's drink to vanquishing demons."

"To vanquishing demons!"

They clinked glasses and both drank. Yes, that was better. He hadn't even realized how tense he was until the chardonnay slipped down his throat, cool and yet smooth and buttery at the same time. The muscles in his neck and shoulders began to relax slightly, even as Hayley let out a sigh.

"Oh, Goddess," she said. "That does help." She shifted on the couch so she was facing him and added, "I don't want you to think I'm a lush or something. Most of the time, I don't drink at all. But sometimes you just need a glass of wine."

"I completely understand that. Wine is one of the things I've enjoyed most about this world."

Some of her smile seemed to fade at his remark. Was she troubled by the reminder that he wasn't as human as she, that he had come from someplace else entirely? Well, he couldn't take the comment back, and he wasn't altogether sure he wished to anyway. She needed to accept who he was if…

…if what? If they were to have any kind of a future together?

Levi knew he was getting far ahead of himself. After all, he had only met Hayley the day before. He thought her beautiful, and he'd seen during the confrontation with the demons down by the creek that she was also brave. Even so, while those were both admirable qualities, he knew he needed to learn much more about her so he could make sure she truly was the woman he'd been waiting for all this time.

She sipped her wine, her eyes not quite meeting his. Was she really that uncomfortable with the reality of his origins?

At last she said, her voice low, not much more than a whisper, "Levi, I'm scared."

He blurted out the first thing that came to his mind. "Of me?"

This time she did look at him, her shock registering in those big blue eyes. "No, of course not!" she responded, her tone so vehement that he knew she must be telling him the truth. "Do I act like I am?"

"Well, not exactly, but…." He let the words trail off there. The last thing he wanted was to reveal to her how worried he'd been that she would never be able to look at him as anything except some kind of alien creature, one masquerading as a human but not quite good enough at maintaining the façade.

Hayley set down her wine glass, then reached over and laid one hand on top of his. Her fingers were slender, delicate, and yet he could still sense the strength within them. "Levi, you saved me back there. If it hadn't been for you, those demons would've taken me to the Escobars, and the Goddess only knows what would have happened next." She paused, then went on, "I'll be honest—it did freak me out a little when you told me about where you'd come from, that you weren't exactly the guy next door." The corners of her mouth lifted slightly. "So to speak. But then I realized that part didn't matter so much. It didn't change who you were, that you were someone who'd reached out to me, who wanted to help me feel at home here. And it didn't change how I felt."

"How do you feel?" Maybe he shouldn't have asked that question, but he needed to know. People so often cloaked their true sentiments in words they didn't mean, pretended to feel things they didn't. It seemed that Hayley liked him, but perhaps she only saw him as a friend, someone to spend time with. She'd just admitted to being discomfited by his origins. Perhaps those feelings were enough to preclude anything except friendship with him.

"'How do I feel'?" she repeated, then shook her head. "It feels strange to be talking about this at all. We've only known each other for two days. But I...." She seemed to stop herself, lifted her hand from his so she could nervously twist the band of silver knot-work she wore around the middle finger of her right hand. "I've never been very good at this kind of thing. I don't know what else to say. If I blurt out everything I've been thinking about you, it kind of takes the mystery out of it, don't you think?"

"Why would you want there to be any mystery?" he asked, genuinely confused. Of all the nuances of human behavior, the one he still had the most trouble with was people's inexplicable desire to play games with one another.

"Isn't that how it's supposed to work?" Hayley shook her head. "Like I said, I'm not very good at this. All I know is—" Again she paused. "All I know is that I've been wanting to do this all day."

Before he could even blink, she'd leaned forward, placed her lips against his. She tasted slightly of the chardonnay she'd just drunk, but sweeter and even more intoxicating. Her mouth opened, and he tasted yet more of her, felt the blood in his veins sing at the delicious savor of her. And he also felt how his body reacted to her, how he experienced a sudden heat and pressure in his groin. Wanting her.

Needing her.

His hands went up cup her cheeks. How soft her skin was, how smooth and perfect and warm. He could sense how her breathing accelerated, how her heart pounded heavily within her chest. Actually, he had to stop himself from thinking about her breasts, about the way he'd noticed the curve of them in the tight T-shirt she was wearing today, the enticing shadow that lay between them.

This was only their first kiss, after all—he could not expect anything more tonight, no matter how much he might want it.

After a long moment, she lifted her lips from his. Her eyes shone, and he could see a flare of color in her cheeks that had nothing to do with the time they'd spent outside today. "I hope that was okay."

"It was more than okay," he replied, every nerve ending in his body still thrumming from the effects of that kiss. "It was perfect."

Her cheeks flushed an even deeper red. "I'm glad. I mean—I didn't know what else to say, and you were sitting there looking like that, and it just seemed the right thing to do."

"Looking like what?" he asked, genuinely puzzled.

"Like a Greek god or something," she said. "I'd never wanted to kiss anyone like I wanted to kiss you right then. And I suppose I figured, well, this was one way to prove that I really wasn't frightened of you."

Levi couldn't help but chuckle slightly at that admission. "True enough."

Her head tilted as she watched him for a moment. "Was it your first kiss?"

"No," he replied, and her face fell slightly. He was actually glad that she'd reacted that way; he thought it charming that she'd wanted to be the first woman he kissed. "I did kiss Zoe, but it was more to prove to myself that I truly wasn't her consort. And I obviously wasn't, so that was the end of that. There hasn't been anyone since."

"Then the girls here in Jerome are falling down on the job."

He grinned. "I didn't say they didn't try."

Hayley reached for her wine and allowed herself another sip, then set it back down so she could finally help herself to a cracker and some cheese. Before she took a bite, however, she said, "You stopped them?"

"No, it was more that I didn't allow myself to be put in a position where things might take a turn for the intimate." Levi realized he was hungry, so he picked up a piece of cheese. Savoring the rich flavor helped him to organize his thoughts, because he could tell from the lift of Hayley's eyebrows that she was expecting an explanation as to why he'd been so dedicated at dodging Jerome's eligible female population. "Somehow I could tell that none of them were the right person for me. They're all very nice young women, but I wasn't interested in something casual. It didn't feel right."

She was quiet for a moment, apparently weighing his words. "But this…this does?"

"Yes," he said at once. She didn't respond, and so he went on, "Is this too much for me to be saying right now? I still haven't quite figured out how the timing of these things is supposed to work."

At that remark, Hayley gave him a rueful smile, and once again reached over to touch his hand. "I don't think there's a right or a wrong way. It's just…I guess I'm trying to deal with realizing that this thing between us is real. Is it okay to say that, when we barely know each other?"

"Witches and warlocks tend to recognize their attractions very quickly," Levi pointed out.

"Well, that's true," she said. "But you're not exactly a warlock, are you?"

"No," he replied. "And yet I have magic flowing in my veins, just as you do. So I would say I'm the equivalent of a warlock, which makes it close enough."

"A warlock who has access to all our powers at once," Hayley said. "I've never heard of anyone like that."

She had a point. Levi almost mentioned that Damon Wilcox supposedly could work all kinds of magic, that his talent, in a way, was magic itself. However, he realized that making comparisons between himself and that now-deceased worker of dark magic was probably not a very good idea. Hayley appeared to have accepted him—he knew she would have never initiated that kiss if she'd felt differently—but there was no point in saying something that might disrupt their new and fragile rapport.

"Yes. I can't say that I'm the same as all other warlocks, because that wouldn't be true. I suppose all I can do is ask how much it matters to you."

In response, she leaned forward and kissed him again. This time, he put his arms around her, drew her close. How exquisite she was, how warm and alive and so very, very real.

When they pulled apart, she shook her head. "It doesn't matter to me where you came from, or who exactly you are. Because I know you're Levi, and that's good enough for me."

He took her hand and pressed it to his lips. She could have no idea what a gift she'd just given him, how he immediately recognized the stirring in his heart, even though he knew now was not the time to give voice to those words. Not aloud anyway.

Instead, he settled for saying them in his mind, letting them echo in his thoughts. Hopefully, one day very soon he would be able to tell her exactly what he was thinking.

I love you, Hayley McAllister.

7

OF COURSE HER PHONE HAD TO GO OFF SOON after that. Hayley was tempted to ignore it, but with everything that was going on, it didn't seem very wise to ignore a text.

Her brother's number. *Leaving now,* the text said. *I'll be home in 20. Burgers at Bordello's OK?*

Shooting Levi an apologetic glance, she typed, *Sure. See you then,* and shoved the phone back in her purse.

"Your brother?" he asked.

"Yes. He's on his way home. I guess we're going out to eat again." She shook her head and added, "I really need to get to the grocery store and get some actual food so I can cook dinner. We can't keep going out to eat *every* night."

Levi appeared rather impressed by that comment. "You can cook?"

"Well, I wouldn't say I'm a gourmet or anything, but my mom taught me. 'A necessary life skill,' she said on more than one occasion." Hayley shrugged, adding, "Frankly, it probably would have been easier if my talent was cooking, but what do you do?"

"Your talent is a very important one," Levi said. He reached out to touch her cheek, and she thrilled all over again at the brush of his fingertips against her skin. Crazy how the smallest of caresses from him managed to light her up inside. "We will have need of it."

And with those words, the afterglow was abruptly gone. She didn't want to think about what had happened this afternoon, didn't want to think about the threat looming over the entire clan. Those kisses from Levi had helped to erase the terror of those moments, but only for a little while. Once again she could see those hideous, unearthly creatures advancing toward her, could see the wall of flame that rushed out to consume them. She supposed she should be relieved that they'd been dispatched with relative ease.

Next time might be much, much harder.

"I suppose so," she said, hoping Levi would be able to tell from her tone that she didn't want to discuss it anymore. "Anyway, I hate to kiss and run, but I guess I should get back next door."

"Are you going to tell your brother about us?"

he asked, sounding genuinely curious.

Oh, Goddess, that was going to be a fun conversation. "I'll tell him something," Hayley replied. *What, I have absolutely no idea....* "And I'll also have to let him know what happened this afternoon. Brandon doesn't have much of a temper, but that's one thing I know will upset him."

"It is better to be honest. Although you should also tell him to keep it to himself for now, at least until we know how Connor and Angela are going to handle the situation."

Hayley hadn't even thought about that. Would they make a general announcement of some sort, or were they going to keep things quiet for a while, hoping that they'd be able to come up with a solution that didn't involve invoking mass panic? "I'll make sure he knows to keep quiet about the whole thing. Besides, from what I've been able to tell, he doesn't seem to hang out much up here in Jerome because he's working all the time."

"That's true enough. It doesn't seem as if he's done a lot to get involved with the clan."

Was it her imagination, or had she detected a note of disapproval in Levi's voice? Well, as an outsider who had been embraced by the McAllister family, he probably didn't think much of Brandon's solitary habits. Hayley supposed she could try to explain to Levi that her brother's behavior didn't have anything to do with disliking the Jerome branch of the family—otherwise, he wouldn't have hung around as long as he had—and everything to do with the tunnel vision that descended whenever he was working on a project. Problem was, it did seem as if the shop where he worked had an unending stream of projects. Great for keeping busy and not having to worry about money, but not so great when it came to the socializing end of things.

"Brandon always was kind of antisocial," she said lightly. "But now that I'm here, I'll see what I can do to get him out a bit more. Anything coming up that I should know about?"

"There are always bands at the Spirit Room on Friday night," Levi replied. "That might be a good place to start, especially since he only has to walk half a block to get there."

That prospect sounded halfway promising. If there was beer involved, she might be able to coax her brother out of his flat. "I'll see if I can figure out a way to mention it." Then she went on her tiptoes, gave Levi a quick kiss, just to show that she would rather stay here with him, but that she needed to go meet her brother.

He seemed to understand, because he smiled as he walked her to the door. "I'll see you tomorrow, though?"

"Absolutely. I'll come over after Brandon's gone to work and I've gotten myself put together."

Levi touched her hand briefly, and then Hayley slipped out and hurried over to her brother's flat. It all looked exactly as she'd left it, but then, why wouldn't it? The place had been empty all day. She thought of everything that had happened—the demon attack, the kisses she'd shared with Levi—and reflected that it felt as though she'd been gone much longer than a mere eight hours or so.

With a start, she realized that everything she'd bought in Old Town Cottonwood was still locked up in the cargo boxes in Levi's truck. Well, she hadn't bought anything perishable; the accent pillows and picture frames and whatnot could wait until the next day. She just hoped Levi didn't plan to run down the hill to go grocery shopping or something, because he wouldn't be able to fit anything else into those boxes with all her stuff crammed in there.

No, she very much doubted that he'd be going down to Cottonwood tonight. Angela and Connor had made it pretty clear that they didn't want anyone going out at night alone...or alone in general. Those strictures suited Hayley very well, because they meant that she had a perfect built-in excuse for spending as much time as possible with Levi.

The half-smile that had touched her lips at the thought of being with Levi almost every waking moment faded abruptly, however, as she realized that her brother was driving home alone in the dark. A chill struck her, and she grabbed her phone from her purse and tapped out a quick text.

You almost home?

No answer right away, and the icy feeling in the pit of her stomach intensified. That road was so winding, and so dark. Anything could happen along its lonely twists and turns. Hayley tried to tell herself that her brother had driven the highway to Jerome hundreds of times and could probably do it in his sleep. Besides, what would demons want with her brother? Brandon had a powerful talent, true, but unless the Escobars suddenly got it into their heads to compete in an episode of *Dream Machines* or something, kidnapping a warlock who happened to be a mechanical wizard didn't make a lot of sense.

Unless, of course, they were really only concerned with causing as much mayhem as possible, in which case, the random murder of a McAllister warlock might perfectly suit their needs.

To her infinite relief, her phone buzzed then. *Just parking now,* the message read. *U must be hungry.*

I am, she typed back. *Just wanted to check.*

I'll be up in a minute.

She put the phone back in her purse and realized her hands were shaking. That wasn't good. She needed to look calm and collected, as though she'd just spent an ordinary day exploring her new home. Yes, it would come out soon enough that her day had been anything except ordinary, but better to approach this slowly. Too bad they were going out to eat again. That particular conversation would have been a lot easier to manage someplace where they could talk in private.

Well, she'd talk about the demon attack, and sort of ease into the whole Levi thing and see where things went from there. If she was lucky, maybe there wouldn't be a lot of outsiders at the restaurant. To be honest, once the shops closed, there didn't seem to be much to do in Jerome. With any luck, most of the tourists would have gone back down the hill and over to their hotels and condos in Sedona, and she and Brandon would be surrounded by locals.

Almost before she'd completed the thought, the door opened, and her brother stepped inside the flat. He tossed his keys on the table next to him and then paused, sending her a narrow-eyed look. "You okay?"

"I'm fine," she lied. "It's been kind of a long day. And there's some…stuff…I need to talk to you about."

He didn't look terribly thrilled by that reply, but at least he only said, "All right. Give me five minutes, and then we'll head down to Bordello's."

Crazy name for a restaurant, although Hayley knew that Jerome had been a pretty wild town back in the height of its copper-mining days. "Okay."

Another probing glance, and then Brandon shrugged and headed back to the bathroom. She heard water running, heard the wooden floor creak as he went into his room and shut the door. At least his job had apparently made him a master of the quick clean-up, because it probably was less than five minutes before he emerged wearing a clean T-shirt, his dark blond hair combed back from his face.

"Ready?"

"Yes." Hayley got up from the couch, retrieving her purse as she did so.

"You might want a jacket," Brandon told her. "It's getting kind of cold out."

"All right." A coat rack stood on the other side of the door, and she'd hung her brown suede jacket there the day before as she was unpacking her things. Now she paused to set her purse on the floor so she could slip into the jacket, then slung the bag over her shoulder.

She noticed that Brandon didn't put on a jacket, but refrained from commenting. He didn't play the protective big brother very often, although every once in a while that sort of behavior would slip out.

The Goddess only knew how he'd react when she told him about what had happened earlier that afternoon.

They went downstairs and walked down Main Street. As Hayley had thought, it didn't look very busy, although she heard the sounds of acoustic guitar and drum coming from inside the Spirit Room as they passed. So there was something going on up here. She wondered if the bar had live music every night, or just as it got closer to the weekend.

Bordello's was about two blocks away from her brother's flat. It wasn't very big, and looked fairly crowded, but a couple in their fifties—clearly tourists—got up from their table just as she and Brandon approached. The restaurant's sole waitress, who also seemed to be a civilian, smiled at Brandon and said, "I'll get that wiped down in just a minute. Hang on."

"No problem," he replied.

Maybe she was imagining things, but Hayley thought she saw something a little more than simple courtesy in the waitress's smile. Well, it wasn't really that implausible. Just because Brandon tended to act like he was oblivious to women didn't mean that women were oblivious to him.

The table got cleared and set with fresh silverware and napkins in lightning time. "Take a seat," the waitress said. "Here are some menus. Anything to drink?"

"Do you have merlot?" Hayley asked.

"Sure do."

"A glass of that, please."

Brandon lifted an eyebrow, but only said, "And I'll have a Lumberyard pale ale. Thanks, Mel."

"Got it," Mel said, and headed off to the tiny bar, which wasn't much more than an alcove set into the restaurant's wall.

Since it was impossible to ignore the way her brother was staring at her, Hayley remarked, "So I want a glass of wine. I am an adult, you know."

"I know," he said. "I'm just not used to seeing you drink. Rough day?"

"You have no idea."

Both eyebrows went up at that reply, but he kept silent, instead studying the menu Mel had given him. Hayley decided she'd better do the same, since it would be a lot easier to place her order as soon as the waitress returned with their drinks. Everything sounded great—she hadn't even realized how hungry she was until she started trying to decide what to have for dinner—but she decided she'd have a bison burger, just because it sounded exotic.

Mel came over with Brandon's beer and Hayley's wine, and took their orders after she'd set their drinks in front of them. "I'll get those out to you as quickly as I can."

Hayley smiled at her. "Thanks so much." Still, pleasant as the waitress seemed to be, it was a relief to have her gone, so she could take a sip of wine and mentally brace herself for what she needed to tell Brandon.

He drank some beer, then asked, "What's going on, Hayley?"

She set her glass down, wrapped her hands around its base. "A lot."

"Something related to why you're here in Jerome?"

Why such a question should surprise her, she wasn't sure. After all, just because her brother had his head buried in engines most of the day didn't mean he still didn't know what was going on in the world. "Yes, something like that." She glanced around, but her hopes from earlier seemed to be borne out, because, with the exception of the waitress, everyone else in the restaurant was clearly a member of the McAllister clan. While they might not know anything about the demons the Escobars had sent after her, they at least were privy to the general situation.

"Like that, or exactly that?"

Hayley swallowed some more wine. It felt warm going down her throat, gave her the courage she needed to answer her brother's question. "I guess exactly that. Levi took me around Cottonwood this afternoon, but then we decided to go over to Red Rock Crossing so I could see a little bit of Sedona." She paused there, trying to get a read on Brandon's expression. He didn't seem particularly disturbed by her spending an afternoon with his next-door neighbor, which she had to assume was a good sign. "We hiked along the creek for a little while, and then these people came along, saying they'd dropped their phone somewhere on the trail, and asking if we'd seen it. Only…they weren't people."

Brandon's brows, several shades darker than his hair, drew together. "Then what were they?"

She swallowed, then said in little more than a whisper, "Demons."

"De—" Her brother caught himself there, as if realizing that bursting out with the word "demons" in a crowded restaurant wasn't a very good idea, even if that restaurant happened to be filled with other witches and warlocks. "But—you're okay, right?"

"Yes, thanks to Levi. He was able to drive them off."

"With a little assist from you."

She should have known her brother would guess at that part of the story. Or maybe he didn't want to acknowledge that his neighbor was such a powerful warlock that he could banish demons all on his own.

Well, technically speaking, they hadn't been banished at all. They'd been annihilated.

"Yes, I used my power to help out. And…they were destroyed. But before that, they said they were there so they could take me back to their master."

"One of the Escobars?"

"Had to be."

Brandon was silent for a few seconds. Then he asked, "You're sure you're okay?"

"I'm fine. No harm, no foul. When we got back to Jerome, Levi and I went to talk to Angela and Connor, to let them know what happened."

"I assume they weren't happy."

There was an understatement. "Not really. I think they're going to make some kind of an announcement at some point, but they wanted to talk to Luz Trujillo first, just to see if anything weird had been happening down in the Phoenix area."

Again Brandon was quiet, apparently trying to absorb everything she'd just told him. "Our parents are going to flip out when they hear about this. I mean, they sent you here so you'd be safer than you were in Payson, and you're in Jerome barely a day before you're attacked by demons."

Hearing it stated so baldly made Hayley wince. "Do we have to tell them? I mean, I'm fine. Levi protected me. And I'll make sure not to go into Sedona again. Angela and Connor were wondering whether that had something to do with it—neutral territory, you know, something that doesn't belong to any one clan."

"If we don't tell our parents, and they find out —that's going to be even worse. You know that, right?"

Unfortunately, she did. All the same, Hayley didn't want the drama of listening to her mother go off about the demon attack, because she knew it would be followed immediately by a suggestion that maybe she should come home to Payson. That was something she absolutely did not want to do…not after those kisses she'd shared with Levi. Wild horses couldn't drag her away.

"All right," she said, not bothering to hide her reluctance. "But let me do it. I'll call when it feels right to call, okay?"

"Okay." He still looked doubtful, though, as if he wasn't entirely convinced that she'd actually make the call. Which wasn't fair at all. If she said she would do something, she did it…even if it might take her a while to work up the nerve.

Mel came over with their burgers then, and

asked if they needed anything else. Since there was enough food on the plate in front of her for at least two meals, Hayley shook her head and said she was fine, and Brandon echoed that sentiment. Once the waitress had gone over to check on a table by the window, he went on, "There's more, though, isn't there?"

It wasn't exactly a question. Hayley picked up a sweet potato fry and bit into it, glad of the excuse for stalling a little, even though she knew she wouldn't be able to avoid responding. Then she said, "I like Levi."

"He seems like an okay guy." Brandon seemed to check himself then, eyes narrowing as he stared across the table at her. "Wait…you mean like, like?"

"Yes. Like, like."

Expression wry, her brother said, "Well, that was fast."

Didn't she know it. All right, it was one thing to be attracted to someone, to think they were good-looking or whatever, and something else to have them seem to take over all your thoughts, to consume valuable head space that, what with everything else that was going on, might have been put to better use. "I didn't exactly plan it," she said, knowing how defensive she sounded even as the words left her lips.

"I didn't say you did." Brandon's mouth

turned down slightly, but then he shrugged and picked up his burger, took a large bite. Once he was done chewing, he said, "It's not because he saved you from the demons, is it? I mean, gratitude is one thing, but—"

"No," Hayley cut in. She didn't know exactly why it was so important to convince her brother that wasn't the case, but it was. "I—he's a good person. We had fun together this afternoon. Well, until…." Might as well stop there. They both knew what she was talking about.

"Am I supposed to give my blessing?"

"Of course not. I just—I just wanted you to know. Levi and I will probably be spending a lot of time together, and I didn't want you to be wondering about what was going on."

"Mmm." Brandon took another bite from his hamburger, and seemed to reflect on what she'd just said. "Maybe when you talk to Mom, you can tell her about Levi first. She'll be so thrilled that you've met someone you like, the whole demon thing might skate right by her."

Not a bad idea. Dynamics of love and relationships and life choices in witch clans tended to be slightly skewed, because everyone was guaranteed a stipend that would cover their living expenses, which meant that the quest to find a career to sustain you was not quite as important as it might be for a civilian. Although Hayley knew her mother thought she was trying to be patient, her dissatisfaction with the love lives of both her children tended to bleed into almost everything she said to them. Once Brandon had moved to Jerome, their mother had seemed to give up on him, and focus all her hopes for grandchildren on Hayley, which was more than a little irritating. It wasn't that she didn't want to have a family…eventually…but she thought she had plenty of time. More than once she'd cursed the tendency of witches and warlocks to meet their apparent soul mates early on, and therefore settle down and start having kids at an early age. If you didn't fit into that mold, you definitely felt the pressure.

So Hayley could see why her mother would be thrilled by her interest in Levi. But…what if he couldn't even father children, despite his human appearance? She knew she was getting way ahead of herself, but it was still a concern that would have to be addressed at some point if they stayed together. *Together.* She wanted to laugh at herself. Could she even say that they were together when all they'd done was share a few kisses? It seemed as if Levi wanted more, wanted to pursue a future with her, but….

"Maybe," she said, since she could see how Brandon was staring at her across the table, clearly expecting some kind of a response. "I'm kind of hoping that word of this demon attack doesn't make it to Payson for a while."

"I'm not so sure about that," he said as he reached for his glass of beer. "If Angela and Connor want to get the word out, then they will. That means all the branches of the family—in Payson and Prescott and even down in Wickenburg. I really don't think you'll be able to hide it from Mom…or Dad."

Probably not. That had just been wishful thinking. Hayley knew what she really wanted was to be able to spend some time alone with Levi, to figure out whether their connection was mere physical lust, or something deeper. Whether current circumstances would allow her that time was an entirely different proposition.

"I guess so," she admitted, picking up another sweet potato fry. "I don't want to give them the wrong impression, though. I like Levi…a lot… but still, we've just met each other." She paused there, wondering if she should tell Brandon about Levi's origins. Maybe not now. They had enough going on. Anyway, she honestly couldn't say whether knowing the truth would make that much of a difference to her brother. He'd lived next door to Levi for more than six months now, had made his assessment of him based purely on their interactions and nothing else. Wasn't that better? Did it really matter where Levi had come from? He'd admitted that his body was human, that physically he wasn't really any different from any of the other warlocks in the McAllister clan, even if he did have a far greater range of powers. "Anyway," she went on, trying to deflect the conversation toward something that didn't involve her and Levi, even as she knew that Brandon would detect such deflection from a mile away, "what about you? I know you're buried in engines twenty-four/seven, but have you really not met a single interesting female since you got here?"

He gave her a weary smile. "Besides getting hit on when I go out to eat, or to the grocery store? That's not why I came here. I figure…if the right woman is out there, then our paths will cross eventually. In the meantime, what's the point of obsessing over the situation? It's not like I don't have plenty to keep me busy."

Hayley couldn't really argue with that sentiment. At least he hadn't shut her down completely, which was what he'd tended to do whenever their mother tried to bring up that particular topic of conversation. He'd adopted a Zen attitude about the whole thing, which seemed healthy enough.

Unfortunately, she wasn't sure whether "Zen" would get the clan through an outright confrontation with the Escobars' demons….

8

LEVI FOUND IT DIFFICULT TO FALL ASLEEP that night. Perhaps it was only the lonely space in the bed next to him, the one that now felt so empty without Hayley occupying it. But he knew he was getting far ahead of himself. After all, they'd only kissed. From what he'd been able to tell, there generally seemed to be a span of time between a first kiss and the occasion of a couple getting into bed together, although he knew that span was predicated on a variety of factors, not all of which he completely understood. However, he was fairly certain that Hayley wasn't quite ready to make that next step.

Which was fine, because if he was forced to admit such a thing to himself, he didn't know whether he was ready, either. Oh, the surge of need in him as he kissed her was real enough, as were his body's physical responses to her nearness, to the sweet savor of her lips, and yet he knew it was probably better to wait. Something so pure and so precious shouldn't be rushed.

At the same time, however, he couldn't quite rid himself of the sense of time ticking past, of knowing that dark forces were massing, and if he passed up a chance to be with Hayley, he might not have such a chance again. As soon as he'd heard of the killings in the southern part of the state, of how Joaquin Escobar's daughter had summoned dark beings to do her bidding, Levi had known that he very likely would be the one to stand between the Arizona witch clans and the sort of violence many of them couldn't even begin to comprehend. They had lived at peace for many generations, the feud between the McAllisters and the Wilcoxes notwithstanding. Even at the height of that magical cold war, none of those involved would have ever contemplated drawing such evil beings into their conflict.

Unfortunately, Joaquin Escobar had no such scruples. He would take what he wanted, and to hell—perhaps literally—with everyone else.

Levi rolled over onto his back and stared up at the ceiling. The curtains in the flat were fairly thin, and so he could see the reflected light of a gibbous moon on the flat plaster surface, pale yellow, just bright enough to further interfere with his sleep. Was Hayley having the same difficulty in falling asleep? He ached for her in a way he'd never ached for anyone before, not even Zoe. Back then he'd been half-crazed, trying to come to terms with this new world in which he'd found himself, as well as the body he wore, a body that had been constantly changing. He'd wanted Zoe because he thought she was the key to coping in this strange and novel place... whereas he wanted Hayley simply because of who she was.

And it killed him to think that she was just across the hall, but might as well be a million miles away, thanks to her brother and bodyguard. If Levi got up now and went over to the other flat, asked to see Hayley, he doubted he would receive a very friendly reception, and not only because of the lateness of the hour. Yes, Brandon McAllister had seemed pleasant enough...but that was before Levi showed any interest in his sister.

The phone on his bedside table buzzed, and he immediately rolled over and picked it up, squinting at the display. Yes, it was later than he'd thought, nearly midnight. But because it was coming from Angela, he didn't even consider not pressing the green button to accept the call.

"What is it?" he asked.

Angela's voice sounded more strained than Levi thought he'd ever heard it. "Caitlin just called me. She's had a vision. Can you come up to the house?"

"Yes, of course." In matters of such urgency, the time of night made very little difference. "What did she see?"

"I'd rather not talk about it on the phone."

"I understand. I'll be up there right away."

"Thanks, Levi."

She ended the call, and he set the phone back down on the table. After climbing out of bed, he went and got a pair of jeans out of the dresser, a T-shirt, and a warm fleece hoodie, since even in early May, it could be quite cold in Jerome at this hour. He dressed quickly, then slipped the phone into his pocket. For a second, he contemplated driving up to the *prima's* house, since it would probably be faster. However, since she'd also seemed concerned about secrecy, he thought that walking would attract less attention, especially since his truck was parked directly below the back bedrooms of the two flats, which meant either Hayley or Brandon might hear him leaving.

Instead, he slipped out the door of his flat, and went as quietly as he could down the stairs that would take him to street level. There he had to undo the deadbolt to the door that opened onto Main Street, and lock it again behind him.

The waxing moon cast a ghostly light on Jerome's streets, nearly deserted at this hour.

Down the block, voices still carried from the Spirit Room, which would be open until two, but otherwise no one seemed to be out and about. Levi walked quickly, going past the fire station, following the hairpin curve that led up to the next terraced level of the town. From there, he cut over to the stairs that took him directly to Paradise Lane, a street of restored Victorian homes that had once belonged to the elite of Jerome's copper-mining days—the overseers and doctors and brothel owners.

Angela's house was the largest on the street, which only made sense. Two bronze fixtures flanked the large oak door with its beveled-glass insert, their light spilling onto the quiet street.

He hadn't even lifted his hand to knock before Angela opened that door, her eyes haunted, shad-owed in the uncertain light. "Come in," she said.

Without replying, he entered the house, stood uncertainly in the foyer. The *prima* was wearing only a tank top and some yoga pants, her feet bare, which led Levi to think that she'd been asleep when Caitlin called, and had gotten imme-diately out of bed without worrying about her attire. Past her, he could see Connor sitting on one of the living room sofas. Since he was wearing a T-shirt and a pair of flannel pants, it seemed that he also hadn't bothered to change before coming out to wait for their visitor.

"Caitlin called me about fifteen minutes ago," Angela said as she led him into the living room. Levi sat down on the unoccupied couch, while she took a seat next to her husband. "She was…upset."

Considering how often the clan's seer had visions of things that were less than pleasant, Levi didn't find that revelation too surprising. "What did she see?"

"She saw Matías Escobar…and Lucinda Santiago. Apparently, he decided to pick up where things left off when Lucinda's father banished him from California."

Yes, Levi had heard that the Santiago *prima's* daughter had been forced into some kind of a relationship with the young Escobar warlock. "That isn't entirely unexpected, is it?" he asked, even as he realized how cold the question must have sounded.

Angela's lips thinned. "No, but Caitlin and Lucinda had become sort of long-distance friends, so this vision was very traumatic for her, as you might imagine, especially when she'd had to suffer visions of Danica experiencing much the same thing several years ago. The question is…what are we going to do about it?"

"How much can we do?" Levi asked. "I assume that Matías has Lucinda trapped in Santiago territory, correct?"

The *prima* and *primus* glanced at one another. Connor reached over to take his wife's hand, although Levi didn't know for sure whether he had done so to comfort her—or to give her the strength to utter her next words. Perhaps one day, if he was lucky, he would have been with Hayley long enough to know what the correct reaction should be.

"Yes. From what Caitlin saw, it seems that Matías is still in the house that used to belong to Lucinda's parents, the former Santiago *prima* and her consort." Angela paused there, then took a breath before continuing, "We need to go to Southern California and get Lucinda away from Matías."

Levi didn't know why he should be so shocked. On the surface, of course attempting such a rescue seemed like the right thing to do. But it was very rare that members of one clan would interfere with the doings in another witch family's territory, no matter how nefarious those doings might be. "That will be…difficult," he said at last.

"We know," Connor replied. "We also know that we wouldn't be able to attempt that kind of a rescue without your help. You have access to powers that no one in either of our clans has."

"Well, possibly, but…." Levi had to stop himself there, because he saw little use in protesting what all of them already knew. There were many skilled workers of magic in both clans, but few with the sorts of abilities that would be of much help in such a mission. Whereas he—well, if a magical talent had once existed, then he could use it. He settled for saying, "That may be true, but such a mission will still be extraordinarily dangerous. Have you forgotten about Joaquin Escobar's powers as a null? I know I am not an ordinary warlock, but we also don't know whether I would be immune to his dubious talent."

"It's a risk," Angela said. Although the lighting in the living room wasn't very bright, Levi could still see the way her knuckles whitened as she clung to her husband's hand. "From what we've been able to tell, though, Joaquin Escobar's power has a fairly limited field of effect, so unless he's right in the same room with Lucinda, you should be okay. If his so-called 'gift' would even make a difference to someone like you." She hesitated, then went on, "Believe me, we know what we're asking of you. But what kind of people would we be if we just shrugged and turned away, tried to tell ourselves it was somebody else's problem?"

The kind of people who wouldn't be able to look at themselves in a mirror. At least, Levi realized that he couldn't live with himself if he knowingly abandoned Lucinda Santiago to Matías Escobar's brutal abuses. And how could he ever deem himself worthy of Hayley if he ignored the plight of another young woman?

"We wouldn't be McAllisters," Levi said firmly, then added, with a glance at Connor, "or Wilcoxes. But what do you propose? We can't quite stage a commando raid and go in, guns blazing."

"Which probably wouldn't work anyway, if the Escobars can summon demons on command," Connor remarked, his voice grim. "No, I was thinking of my family history. The talent hasn't appeared since then, not in my family at least, and never seemed to appear in the McAllisters, either, but my great-great-whatever grand-uncle Samuel had the ability to teleport—to send himself from place to place. So we were thinking if you could mirror that talent—"

"Then I could send myself into the Santiago house, get Lucinda, and come back out again, all in the blink of an eye," Levi said. At the same time, he recalled how he had instantly sent himself from place to place after first arriving in this world, although back then he had been acting instinctively, with little thought involved except a blind need to find Zoe. His control had been so poor, he'd actually chased after several young women who merely looked like her. What Connor was suggesting was something different, a controlled jump to a specific place. "That could work…and there would be minimal risk involved, since I could simply send myself there and come back here before anyone noticed anything wrong."

Apparently it wasn't that easy, though, because Angela and Connor exchanged another one of those meaningful glances. "Well, not exactly," Connor said. "From what I've been able to tell— and from what my cousin Danica told me, since she actually traveled back in time and met Samuel —his power wasn't unlimited. He could probably teleport himself a few miles at the most."

"It's a lot farther than a few miles from here to Pasadena," Angela added, her voice strained.

"Yes, but Samuel didn't have Hayley," Levi pointed out. "It's possible she might be able to amplify my abilities enough that I could still send myself all the way to Southern California."

"It's five *hundred* miles," Connor said. "It would require a hell of a magical boost. I know Hayley's powers are strong…but are they *that* strong?"

To be honest, Levi didn't know for sure. It was the sort of thing they'd have to test. Yes, having her there to add her powers to his had meant that he'd easily defeated those two demons, but when you got right down to it, there was a decent chance that he could have vanquished them unassisted, even though it would have been more difficult and very likely would have taken much more time. So he couldn't say whether Hayley would really be able to strengthen his powers to the point that he could blink himself from one place to another that was hundreds of miles away.

"I don't know," he said. "But there's only one way to find out."

Brandon left early for work, as he always seemed to. Hayley had barely stepped out of the shower before she heard someone knocking at the door. Startled, she went out into the hallway so she could catch a glimpse of the clock that hung on the living room wall. Seven fifty-five…way too early for a social call.

Biting her lip, she knotted her bathrobe a little more tightly around herself, and made sure the towel she'd twisted around her hair was secure enough that it wouldn't come loose and fall in her face as she walked over to answer the door. But when she opened that door, she almost wished she hadn't. Standing there was Levi, fully dressed, a worried expression on his face.

"I'm sorry to come over so early," he said. "But, what with everything that happened yesterday, I forgot to get your phone number. I suppose I thought it didn't matter, what with us being next door to one another."

"It's all right," she said automatically, although she didn't really know if it was. Even if she supposed at some point he would have seen her without makeup and with her hair a mess, she would have preferred to postpone that evil day until a little further in the future. "Um—Brandon left some coffee in the carafe in the kitchen. Why don't you get yourself some, and I'll put some clothes on."

"Oh, yes…sure," Levi responded, a slight flush under his light tan telling her that he hadn't really noticed her dishabille until then.

Hayley didn't know if that was better or worse. "Be right back," she said, and fled into her room and shut the door. No time for a deliberate consideration of what to wear—she grabbed her jeans from the day before, some clean underwear, and the first T-shirt that came to hand, an old gray number that was starting to get a little frayed around the edges.

Well, that was a good metaphor for how this day was starting out…a little frayed around the edges.

No time to do anything more than run a comb through her damp hair, and hope that it wouldn't frizz too much as it dried. She slipped into a pair of flip-flops, took a few seconds to smooth some tinted lip balm on her mouth, and then hurried back out to the living room. Levi had gotten himself a cup of coffee, as she'd suggested, and he stood by the window and stared down at the Verde Valley, brightly illuminated by the early morning sun. However, his expression was dark, distracted, a contrast to the sunny May morning.

"What's going on?" she asked.

He turned toward her. "Your clan's seer had a vision last night of Lucinda Santiago. She's being held by Matías Escobar."

"Oh, no." The words had come automatically enough to Hayley's lips, but she paused for a second to get a good look at Levi's face. He seemed worried, but also determined, which began to set off alarm bells in her head. "So… what are we supposed to do about it?"

"As much as we can." He moved toward the coffee table so he could set his mug down on it, then came over to her, took her hands in his. Was he always that warm, or was it only that her own fingers had suddenly gone cold? "Connor and Angela and I have a plan, but we need to see how much you can help with it."

"Me?" The word came out almost as a squeak, and Hayley cleared her throat. Yes, she'd kind of hoped battling demons would be the last of her dealings with the Escobars for a while, but apparently not. Still, that didn't mean she could start acting like a coward. She needed to be there for Levi, and for all of her clan. Besides, hadn't she just been complaining a few days ago about how nothing exciting ever happened to her? Locking her fingers around Levi's, she went on, in a much steadier tone, "What do you need me to do?"

"It seems the easiest thing for me to do is to teleport myself into the Santiago house, where Lucinda is being held. But I need to see what kind of range I have with your power amplifying my own."

"'Teleport'?" Hayley repeated. Damn it, the squeak was back in her voice. She drew in a breath, and said, "I mean, you can do that?"

"As far as I can tell, there's very little I can't do." He stopped there and shook his head. "That sounds like boasting, I know. But, as I told you, my powers are…all of them, so to speak. I used this power before, when Zoe first brought me to this world. However, I used it wildly, without thinking, and only in the area around Phoenix."

This all sounded completely crazy, but Hayley told herself she needed to be calm, needed to think about the situation with something resembling logic. "Do you know how far you were able to teleport yourself when you were down in Phoenix?"

"Perhaps…ten, fifteen miles? I know I went all the way out to Mesa from Scottsdale."

"And it's how far to where Lucinda Santiago is?"

"Angela said it was around five hundred miles."

Hayley flicked a strand of damp hair over her shoulder and told herself she needed to stay calm. "That's a lot farther than fifteen miles."

"I know." Levi let go of her hands, brought his fingers up to lightly cup her cheeks. She couldn't help feeling a thrill at his touch, even though she knew she should really be concentrating on the problem at hand. "That's why we should test it first, with places I know."

"Such as?"

He bent and kissed her, so very gently, as though he realized she needed that reassurance right then. "I'll try Prescott first. It's about forty miles, so a little more than twice as far as the farthest jump I performed in the Phoenix area. That should give me some indication of how much your talent boosts mine."

"Okay," she said. Prescott didn't sound that frightening. All right, probably because she didn't want to analyze what they were doing too closely. Because then she'd be trying to figure out how someone—even a being like Levi, who didn't necessarily have to follow the normal rules—could simply close his eyes, visualize his destination, and send himself to an entirely different place that just happened to be miles and miles away. "But...how will you get back? Because if you send yourself to Prescott, I won't be with you anymore. You won't have my talent to help get you back." She forced herself to say the next words, even though they scared the crap out of her. "You'll have to take me with you."

At once he shook his head. "No."

"Why not? If it's safe, then I should be able to travel with you."

"It's not simply a matter of safety while traveling in such a way." He hesitated before continuing, his voice gentle, "There's no way I could bring you with me into the Santiago house, the place where the Escobars now live. That would be dangerous, a risk I would never take with you. Also, I'll be stealing Lucinda away, when the time comes. If I had you with me, that means I would have to teleport the both of you, along with myself. I am strong...but I'm not sure I'm *that* strong."

Hayley wanted to argue, but she could see the logic in what he was saying. She reached over and took his hand in hers, needing the reassurance of his touch. "Okay. But you have to tell me how you're going to get back."

"With this test, that's simple enough. You'll help me travel to Prescott, and then I'll break up my return trip into two separate jumps. There's a campground in the National Forest that's about halfway between Jerome and Prescott. I'll stop there to get my bearings, and then come back here." His fingers tightened around hers. "You'll barely notice that I'm gone."

"I find that hard to believe." She swallowed, then said, "And if this test is successful?"

"Then we'll keep attempting longer and longer jumps," he replied. "After this, I'll try going to a place I know in Phoenix. That's a hundred miles."

"And you know enough places in between that you can still make small jumps to get yourself home?"

Levi offered her a reassuring smile. "Yes. I drove here with Zoe and Evan. They had to stop for gas in Cordes Lakes. Even without that, I paid attention to the towns and rest stops between here and there."

"Let me guess," Hayley said. "Photographic memory?"

"Not exactly, but similar in concept. If I've seen it, I can go to a place, even if I haven't physically been there before."

She didn't like it. She didn't like any of this. But she knew she had to help Levi, had to assist him so he could go rescue Lucinda Santiago. Maybe there were other witches and warlocks in similar dire straits—hadn't Joaquin Escobar basically made the Santiagos' new *prima* his captive wife?—but for whatever reason, Levi and Angela and Connor seemed to think Lucinda's plight was the more urgent.

Somehow Hayley managed to put on what she hoped was an encouraging smile. "Well, you did tell me you were a man of many talents, Levi. I guess that means we need to see how powerful your teleportation skills actually are."

"Yes." He went quiet for a moment, his body still, as though he looked inward to summon the powers he needed to send himself so many miles away. "All right, Hayley—lend me your strength."

She put a hand on his shoulder, felt the strength of his muscles beneath her fingertips. The energy flowed from her into Levi, and then…

…and then he was gone.

A startled gasp escaped her lips. She didn't know why she should be so shocked, except that maybe she'd expected to hear some kind of noise as he left, have some kind of warning. But she didn't. One second her fingers were resting on the smooth cotton of his T-shirt, and the next, her hand touched only air.

What to do now? Wait, she supposed. He hadn't really told her how long this would take. Not too long—after all, he'd blinked out of existence in less than a split second. But still, he'd have to send himself to that campground he'd spoken of before he could come back here.

More because she wanted to do something than because she really needed any more caffeine, Hayley went into the kitchen and poured herself the rest of the coffee in the carafe. Since she'd turned off the coffeemaker, the liquid inside the carafe was now barely lukewarm, but she didn't care. It was something to occupy herself.

She'd just begun to rinse out the carafe when Levi appeared a few feet away from her. Even though she'd been expecting him, she couldn't help startling. Luckily, she retained enough presence of mind not to drop the carafe. Instead, she set it down on the kitchen counter and went to him, put her arms around his waist.

"So it worked."

He held her tightly against him. "Yes. It was easy enough to send myself to Prescott, thanks to the boost you gave me."

Hayley let herself enjoy a few more seconds of feeling him hold her, of listening to his calm, regular breathing, before she stepped away a pace and sent him a questioning look. "So…where *did* you go?"

"To a stall in the men's room at Target."

It was too much. She felt the laughter begin to bubble up inside her and started to giggle. "The *what?*"

"It was a place I know. Besides, it was private.

I didn't have to worry about anyone seeing me materialize."

Well, that made sense, she supposed. Trying to repress the giggles that still threatened to rise up and choke her, she said, "I had no idea you were such a fan of Target."

"It is a very useful place," he replied, clearly mystified by her amusement. "I've purchased many helpful items there."

"Okay, I believe you." She pushed her hair back, glad that it felt like it was beginning to dry. "Do you need to rest? Or do you want to try the jump to Phoenix?"

"That jump wasn't very taxing. I'd like to attempt a longer one."

His words should have reassured her. At the same time, though, she wondered if he was allowing himself a false sense of security. Then again, he'd performed these jumps without help from anyone. He should be able to tell whether he was out of his element or not.

"All right." She reached over and laid a hand on his arm, but not tightly. The last thing she wanted was for her touch to somehow hold him back. Too much was at stake.

The energy flowed from her, and into him. Once again he disappeared…

…only to reappear a few seconds later, disappointment clear in his expression.

"It didn't work?" Hayley asked, worry surging through her. Yes, Levi looked all right, except for the concern she could see in his features.

"No. That is, I teleported…but only as far as Cordes Lakes. That is about fifty miles from here, so farther than Prescott, but not by much."

"Maybe I didn't lend you as much power as you needed," Hayley ventured. "Maybe if we tried again—"

"No," Levi cut in. "It wasn't you. Your gift more than doubled the distance I normally would have been able to travel. And still, fifty miles is a large distance. Even if the Santiago clan has someone with this same ability—and of course we can't know that for sure—I doubt they'd be able to go much further than the two or three miles that Connor told me his distant ancestor was capable of. It should be enough."

"Enough for what?" Hayley asked, although she had a sinking feeling that she already knew the answer.

"To free Lucinda Santiago. We'll have to go to their territory, of course, but I'll make the final jump to steal her away. All we'll have to do is set up a rendezvous point. You can wait for me there, and then we'll head home to Arizona. We'll have a fifty-mile head start. It should be simple enough."

Simple.

Right.

9

Normally, Levi would have said that Brandon McAllister seemed like a level-headed enough person, but at the moment his blue-gray eyes were practically shooting sparks. "You want to do *what?* Are you all out of your minds?"

They sat in the living room at Angela and Connor's home. After Levi had contacted the *prima* and *primus*, and given a report on his experiments from earlier that morning, they'd sounded cautiously optimistic, but said they thought it was probably a good idea to have a meeting that included Brandon, partly because he'd been tasked with keeping an eye on his younger sister, and partly because, as Connor added, an amused note in his voice, "There isn't anyone in the clan better suited to driving a getaway car."

Not that Connor looked amused now. No, he stood by the hearth, arms crossed, jaw set as Brandon stared back at him angrily. "No, we're not out of our minds. But common sense suggests that getting as large a head start as possible is required for this particular situation, and Levi can go more than twice as far if he has your sister to lend him her talent."

"I don't know why you're intervening at all," Brandon protested. "I thought you both said when you briefed the clan on the Escobar situation that this Joaquin Escobar had taken the Santiago *prima* as his own, and that we intended to stay out of it. Why is Lucinda Santiago's situation different?"

"Because we're doing what we can to avoid outright clan warfare," Angela said as she got up from the couch and went to stand next to her husband. "Matías Escobar thinks he has a claim on Lucinda, but he doesn't. Aside from being the daughter of the late *prima,* she doesn't have much of a position in the clan. Her magic isn't very strong, and her parents kept her hidden away because of her 'shame' in being coerced by Matías in the first place. He'll be angry that we've stolen her, but it's not like one clan kidnapping the *prima* of another clan, which is exactly the situation we'd find ourselves in if we tried to take

Marisol away. From what I've seen so far, Joaquin Escobar is much more cool-headed than his son. I don't think he'll try to come after Lucinda, whereas he most certainly would attempt to get Marisol back."

None of these arguments seemed to have much effect on Brandon. His normally pleasant features were pulled into a deep frown, and he sent a narrow-eyed look from Angela to Levi and then back again. "If Joaquin Escobar is so cool-headed, then what the hell was he doing, sending demons to try and kidnap my sister?"

"He probably thought it was an acceptable risk," Levi said. "The attack occurred on neutral territory, away from McAllister lands. Also, Hayley is not the *prima,* or the *prima*-in-waiting. He rolled the dice, thinking we wouldn't retaliate."

"And we're not," Angela put in. "We're rescuing Lucinda because it's the right thing to do. We've discussed the risks, and have decided they're acceptable."

"'Acceptable'?" Brandon repeated. He turned toward Hayley, who had been sitting next to Levi this whole time, face pale but resolute. "I can't believe you're going along with this. Don't let them bully you into doing something you don't want to do."

"Nobody's bullying me," she replied. Her chin went up. "You know me better than that. I want to help." She paused, and sent her brother a searching look. "What if those demons had been successful in kidnapping me? Are you trying to say you wouldn't want any rescue attempt to be made?"

A tense silence fell then. Brandon didn't reply at first, although Levi noticed how the other man wouldn't quite meet Hayley's eyes. At last he said, "No. Of course not. But—"

"There aren't any 'but's, Brandon. Not in this situation. We've got to get Lucinda out of there. I need to go along to help Levi." She clenched her fingers on the knees of her faded jeans. "And I really want you to come, because you've probably got the fastest car in Jerome. Or is that '68 Camaro you have parked out back behind the flat all show and no go?"

It was Brandon's turn to lift his chin. He crossed his arms and replied, "Hardly. It's got a 350 engine and nitrous, and a racing transmission. The Santiagos would have to have some pretty fast broomsticks to catch up with that car."

"Well, then," Hayley said, as if that settled it.

Perhaps it did. Levi noticed how Brandon didn't reply, went silent, as though mentally going over the car's specifications to make sure it was up to the task. When he finally spoke, he sounded resigned, if still somewhat annoyed. "Okay. All right. When do we do this?"

"Now," Angela replied.

Eyebrows lifted, Brandon said, "Now?"

"We don't want to waste any more time," Connor said. "It's roughly seven hours from Jerome to Pasadena, so you should make it there a little after dark. That's probably for the best—this is the sort of thing better attempted under cover of darkness. You'll get Lucinda, and come straight back. Is that going to be a problem?"

"I guess not," Brandon replied. He rubbed at his elbow, appearing to consider his options. "I'll have to call work, tell them a family emergency has come up and that I have to take the rest of the afternoon off."

"Probably tomorrow, too," Angela told him. "You won't be getting back here until the middle of the night."

Her suggestion only earned a shrug. "I've gone to work on only a few hours of sleep before. I'll be okay."

No one seemed inclined to argue, possibly because they knew that was Brandon's decision to make.

After a pause, Connor said, "Then do what you need to, but try to get on the road in the next half hour if you can."

Brandon shrugged. "It won't be a problem. I've got a full tank of gas."

Hayley glanced at Levi, and he nodded. For a lightning-fast trip like this, it wasn't as if they needed to pack much—some snacks for the road, jackets for when night fell and the temperatures cooled off. All their preparations needed to be mental, not physical.

Then he stood, and Hayley rose next to him. "We'll be back before you know it."

"I doubt that," Angela said. "Just…be careful, and be quick. The Escobars might be expecting something from us, just because of their failed attempt to snatch Hayley."

"They might," Levi replied. "But I doubt they have any reason to think we'd be going after Lucinda."

"And you have the photo I forwarded from Caitlin?"

"Yes."

Because he'd informed Angela that he needed some kind of visual reference for where he was "landing," so to speak, Caitlin had sent the *prima* a photo of Lucinda's room. She'd had it because the Santiago witch had been thinking of redecorating, and had sent an image of the bedroom in question to get her friend's input. This way, Levi could go straight to Lucinda. With any luck, the Escobars would barely have time to register that a strange warlock had entered the house before he'd safely escaped, and taken the young woman with him.

Or perhaps they wouldn't notice at all. Angela had once said that he didn't exactly register with her the way a witch or warlock who was a stranger might. The slightest twinge, possibly, but not the tingle at the back of her neck like she usually got.

"Then go with the Goddess," Angela said, her tone almost formal.

Levi nodded, and took Hayley's hand. They headed out to the front porch, Brandon a few feet behind them. He still looked less than thrilled by the entire situation, but it seemed he'd exhausted his arguments...for now.

"I'm going to head over to the deli, get some sandwiches for the road," he said as the three of them paused where the front walk to the *prima*'s house ended. "Do you want anything? It's probably better if we only stop for gas."

"Ham and cheese with Dijon," Hayley replied promptly.

"That's a good idea," Levi said. "Roast beef on rye, no mustard."

"Got it." Brandon headed off down the street, going to a steep staircase that cut between two properties and would put him nearly where the deli was located. As he went, he raised his cell phone to his ear, no doubt calling his work to let them know he wouldn't be returning from his extended lunch.

Levi and Hayley went in the opposite direction, walking down the hill to Main Street, and so to the building where both their flats were located. Neither of them spoke. Levi didn't know for sure whether her reticence was simply because she didn't want anyone overhearing what could be sensitive subject matter, or whether, now that the moment was upon them, she was beginning to wonder what she'd gotten herself into.

Hopefully, not much of anything. She would be far away, after all, some fifty miles from the scene of the crime. They would have to decide on a rendezvous point once they were within the proper range, but that shouldn't be too difficult— an obscure corner of a shopping center parking lot, or one belonging to an office building where the employees had gone home for the evening. All they really needed was someplace where they wouldn't be observed.

"I'll get my jacket," Hayley said as they reached the landing that separated the entrances to their two apartments. "And some bottled water."

"That's a good idea," Levi responded. As she touched her fingers to the doorknob, he reached out and put his hand on her shoulder. "Are you all right?"

At once she smiled, although her expression appeared somehow doubtful, as though she had smiled because she couldn't think of what else to do. "Sure. I mean, I'm not going to lie. This whole thing kind of scares me. But it's not like I'm even going to the Santiago house. I'll have Brandon there. I'm frightened for you, though."

"I'll be fine," he told her. "I know what I'm doing. The Escobars won't be expecting us. Remember that."

"I'll try," she said, even while her smile slipped, looking wavery around the edges. "I'm glad we're going now, though. That doesn't give me enough time to really let myself get frightened."

In response, he bent and kissed her, tasted her sweet lips. Not too deep a kiss, because they both knew now was not the time for that sort of thing. Just enough, though, enough to show her how much he cared, that of course he would be careful, because he wanted to make sure he survived this and came back to her.

Then they both went to gather up the meager supplies they might need, and by the time they were done, Brandon had returned, carrying a bag of sandwiches from the deli. He didn't seem inclined to speak, but only asked if they were ready. Since of course they were, there was nothing left to do except go downstairs and climb into Brandon's vintage car. The back seat seemed somewhat cramped, although Hayley declared that it was just fine when Levi asked if she would be comfortable there for such a long drive. He knew she was probably just trying to forestall an offer from him to sit there himself, which would have been even more awkward, since he was so much taller than she.

And then they were on the road, heading down the hill into Cottonwood so they could pick up the highway that wound its way into Camp Verde, where they got on the interstate and began to drive south. Levi could feel the power of the engine in the vehicle, its raw, brutal strength. Brandon hadn't been idly boasting when he said he doubted any of the Santiagos had a car like this. Perhaps they had something comparable—Levi had heard that people in Southern California enjoyed their cars—but he didn't think their vehicles could best this one.

Brandon drove fast, but not so fast as to attract the notice of any state troopers, something he was probably used to doing, considering how conspicuous this car was. If they were pulled over, Levi thought he most likely would be able to talk their way out of a ticket, but he would prefer to avoid doing so. That sort of thing sounded uncomfortably close to Matías Escobar's own dubious talent for mind control, and Levi didn't like the thought of exerting that kind of influence for such an illegal reason.

Otherwise, they drove without talking, music from the satellite radio doing its best to fill up the silence. Clearly, when Brandon restored this car, he made sure to put some modern conveniences in it, although Levi would have preferred something a little more soothing than the alternative rock station Hayley's brother had chosen. Still, Levi knew he could tune most of it out if he concentrated on the landscape passing by, on the dry, dusty desert, which began to be painted in hues of gold and orange as they continued west and the sun sank ever lower in the sky.

They stopped in Quartzsite for gas, and to eat the sandwiches Brandon had bought for them, and use the restrooms at the gas station. After that, it was back on the road, and on into California's desert, which seemed even more barren and empty than the desert lands that surrounded the Phoenix area. When they came down the mountain passes outside Palm Springs, Brandon spoke up.

"Maybe now we should try to figure out where we're going to wait for you?"

Hayley rooted around in her purse and pulled out her cell phone. "Let me check around. How far are we from Pasadena?"

"Still about seventy-five miles."

"Okay." She brought up the map application on her phone and started dragging it around, zooming in on likely spots. "There's a big mall in Ontario—Ontario Mills. I think we should be able to park there. It's about thirty-five miles to Pasadena, but I like it because it's right next to the freeway."

"That sounds fine," Levi said. "I don't think that extra fifteen miles is going to make much of a difference. And I should be able to jump back without having to find an intermediate spot."

"We can't count on that, though," Hayley said as she searched around on the map again. "Especially since you'll have Lucinda with you. There's a Walmart right where the 57 and 210 Freeways connect in a place called Glendora. Here's a street view." She held up her phone, angling it toward the front seat so Levi could get a good look at the image. "Can you work with that?"

"Yes," he replied. One Walmart parking lot looked very like another, but this one, with the embankment of the freeway off to one side and an imposing mountain range just ahead, was distinctive enough that he knew he could navigate his way to it if necessary.

"All right," said Brandon. "How far to Ontario Mills?"

"About another ten miles," Hayley told him as she inspected her phone again. "There's an exit at

Milliken Avenue, it looks like. Right after you cross the 15 Freeway."

"Got it."

They all lapsed into silence again. In the reflected illumination from the dashboard lights, Levi could see how tightly Brandon's fingers were wrapped around the steering wheel. He'd seemed very calm all during the long drive, but clearly his apparent cool was only a façade. Well, Levi couldn't blame him for being nervous. So far everything had gone smoothly enough—he'd been worried that some sort of alarm might have gone up when they crossed over into Santiago territory, and that they might be confronted before they got anywhere near Pasadena, worries that seemed to have been for naught—but he wasn't about to start believing that this would be a simple operation. False confidence only led to trouble.

Brandon eased the Camaro over to the right, then got off at the ramp Hayley had called out. As she'd said, this shopping center was vast, with acres of parking lots, and satellite feeder roads that led to smaller freestanding stores that weren't part of the mall itself. Those same roads also connected to a number of restaurants, which still had their fair share of patrons, even though it was now past eight o'clock.

Seeming to know it was better to avoid those spots, Brandon drove to a dark place between light posts, and set off enough from a mall entrance that these parking places weren't in great demand. He turned off the engine and looked over at Levi. "Now what?"

"Now I go to fetch Lucinda." Levi made sure he spoke calmly, so neither Brandon nor Hayley would be able to guess at any of the doubts that had crossed his mind on the drive here. "It shouldn't take very long. Stay with the car."

"Like we'd go anywhere," Hayley remarked. "Don't worry—we're staying put."

"And I'll be ready to hit the gas," her brother added. "Just don't take any crazy chances, all right?"

"I wasn't planning on it." Levi shifted in his seat so he could see Hayley more clearly. In the dim light, her face seemed pale, but it was also set, calm, as though she braced herself for whatever else might come next. Good. Once again he admired her strength, even though he guessed she hadn't bargained on any of this when she'd made the move to Jerome from Payson. For a second he paused, fixing the image of Lucinda Santiago's bedroom in his mind, the pale yellow walls, the filmy curtains at the windows, the antique furniture. Then he said, "Hayley, lend me your strength."

She put her hand on his arm. At once he felt the added boost from her particular talent, licking along his veins like a burst of strong coffee. He called his own power to him, the one that would send him across the miles to the Santiago house. As he went, he uttered a silent prayer to the Goddess the McAllisters believed in, that she might be looking down on their efforts and would grant them a little grace, just enough to have Lucinda be alone in her room, and not elsewhere in the house, or, even worse, to have Matías Escobar with her.

The world dissolved around him, and took shape again. Good. That meant Joaquin Escobar's powers either weren't affecting him because of his otherworldly nature, or he was far enough away from the usurping warlock that it didn't make a difference either way. Levi stood in the room he recognized as Lucinda Santiago's, now dimly lit by one lamp on the table next to the queen-size bed. The covers of that bed were rumpled, as if someone had just recently gotten up from it, but it was now unoccupied.

Off to one side, through an open door, he heard the sound of water running. At once Levi was able to detect Matías' presence, strong, but dark and somehow foul, like the odor of garbage drifting up from a trash can that should have been sealed shut.

But there was Lucinda, standing next to the dresser. She'd apparently just finished pulling a T-shirt on over her head, but otherwise she wore only a pair of lacy white underpants. An embarrassed flush rose to Levi's cheeks, even as he told himself that her clothing wasn't the issue here.

Her dark eyes widened slightly as she took in his sudden appearance, but he still noted how they looked dull and glassy, not entirely comprehending. Of course they wouldn't be. Danica Rowe had spoken of how Matías' powers of mind control left a person unable to do much on their own, able only to blankly absorb what was going on around them unless given specific orders by the dark warlock.

Because of this, Levi knew there was no point in trying to reason with her. The spell would wear off eventually, and now he had to seize the moment, while Matías was still in the adjoining bathroom.

Levi took two quick, purposeful steps toward Lucinda, wrapped his arms around her waist. Her mouth opened, perhaps to call out to the man she thought was her lover. But Levi wouldn't allow her that chance. At once he summoned his gift, visualizing the place where even now Hayley and Brandon waited for him.

And nothing happened.

Damn. He'd hoped that he could cover that mere thirty-five miles or so, but it seemed even that was too much of a stretch without Hayley's gift providing the additional strength.

"Hey, *chica,* you want to go to that club I was telling you about?" Matías stepped out of the bathroom, still rubbing his spiky black hair with a dark red towel. His eyes locked on Levi's. "What the fu—"

Levi didn't wait to hear the rest of the sentence, or to allow Matías the opportunity to use his powers on him…if they would have even worked. Instead, he visualized the parking lot of the Walmart in Glendora, the waypoint that would allow him to leave this place and get Lucinda safely away from the Escobars.

Darkness flashed around them. It must have begun to sink into her spell-muddled brain that Levi was taking her away from her lover, because she began to struggle in his arms, fighting to get away from his grasp.

"I'm trying to help you," he murmured as they materialized in the Walmart parking lot.

"Let go of me, *pendejo!*" Lucinda snapped, writhing with far greater strength than he might have imagined. Danica's accounts had made it sound as though she'd acted as if she was drugged, but the Santiago witch didn't appear nearly so lethargic.

"Hey—what are you doing to that woman?"

Levi's gaze tracked to the speaker, a heavyset man who'd just finished manhandling what appeared to be a box containing a flat-panel TV into the cargo area of his SUV. Wonderful. While Levi might have applauded the man's protective instincts at another time, now all he could do was stifle a curse.

No time to waste. He pulled in a breath, once again locked the image of the parking lot at Ontario Mills in his mind, the shiny black Camaro gleaming in the half-hearted light of the distant lampposts. Both the angry man and the Walmart disappeared, and Levi stood next to the car.

Thank the Goddess.

His relief was short-lived, however, because Lucinda seemed to sense the way he'd momentarily relaxed his grip on her, and wriggled her way out of his arms and began to run barefoot across the empty parking lot. He immediately gave chase, even as he heard a muffled curse from within the Camaro, followed by the sound of more running feet.

Lucinda was quicker than Levi might have guessed, but even so, her slender legs were no match for his longer ones. He caught up to her and snaked an arm around her waist, yanking her back toward him. She began swearing at him in Spanish, calling him a bastard and a demon and worse. The insults didn't concern him; at this point, he could only hope that no one here would notice her, or the way he began dragging her back to the car.

Brandon came up to them, the frown he wore visible enough even in the semidarkness. "What's going on? You'd think she'd be happy to be rescued."

"A magically advanced case of Stockholm syndrome, I think," Levi replied. "It will wear off in time. For now, we need to get her out of here."

"No shit." Brandon gave a quick glance around, clearly as worried that Lucinda might attract attention as Levi had been.

By that point, they were almost back to the car. Hayley crawled out of the back seat and held the door open so Levi could unceremoniously stuff their freed captive in the far corner and fasten the seatbelt. For good measure, he muttered a quick charm, one that would prevent her from undoing the belt until he released it.

Even so, she fought against the restraints, uttering guttural sounds like a trapped wild animal. Hayley gave the Santiago witch a resigned glance as she climbed into the back seat next to her. "It's going to be a long trip," she muttered as she fastened her seatbelt.

"I'm sorry," Levi said. He got into his own seat and shut the door. "With any luck, Matías Escobar's hold over her will begin to diminish the farther we travel."

"Which means we need to get the hell out of here." Brandon had taken his place in the driver's seat and started the engine. It came to life with a reassuring rumble. "Any signs of pursuit?"

"No," Levi replied as Brandon guided the car out onto one of the feeder roads that would lead them back to the freeway. "Unfortunately, Matías did come out of the bathroom as I was just about to take Lucinda away."

"He saw you?" Hayley asked from the back seat. Levi couldn't see her face, but the tone of her voice revealed her obvious worry.

"Yes, he saw him!" Lucinda put in, then laughed. "Oh, he saw your boyfriend, little girl. And Matías is going to come after him, and then he's going to wish he was never born!"

"I wasn't born, so that's not possible," Levi said calmly. He shifted in his seat so he could reach back and put his hand on Lucinda's forehead. At once she slumped into the corner, her head lolling to one side.

Hayley's eyes widened. "What did you do?"

"Nothing to hurt her. I only made her sleep. It's for the best, anyway—she can rest while we drive, and with any luck, she'll have returned to something of herself by the time she wakes in Jerome. If not, I'll just knock her out again."

This explanation earned him a lifted eyebrow, but Hayley didn't say anything else, seemed willing to go with matters as they currently stood. Why wouldn't she? The alternative would have been a seat mate who thrashed and cursed and fought against the seatbelt that held her in. That was a good deal to contend with during a seven-hour journey.

Now they were on the freeway, the Camaro accelerating. Levi could feel himself relax slightly as the powerful car did its best to put more distance between them and the vengeful Escobars. Of course he wouldn't let down his guard until they were back in Arizona—and not even then, not really—but it did feel good to know that Pasadena was falling farther and farther behind with every minute that passed.

"What are you going to do with her once we do get to Jerome?" Brandon asked. "Are Angela and Connor going to put her up?"

"No, they thought it might be too chaotic at their house, because of the twins," Levi replied. "She's going to Rachel's place, to stay in what used to be Angela's room. Lucinda should be safe enough there."

Brandon nodded. "Makes sense. What if she doesn't snap out of it, though?"

"She will," Levi said, his voice firm. "Danica

recovered with no lasting harm, so there's no reason to think Lucinda won't do the same."

"Hmm."

That was Brandon's only response, but Levi could sense his doubt. Well, at this point, there wasn't much else they could do. They'd gotten Lucinda away, and that was the important thing.

Whatever happened next, all they could do was manage it as best they could.

10

It was past midnight by the time they pulled into Quartzsite once again to make another pit stop. Hayley had actually fallen asleep somewhere around Beaumont, lulled by the rumble of the Camaro's engine and her overwhelming weariness. Besides, there hadn't been much point in staying awake, not with Levi in the front seat and her brother Brandon playing the part of unknowing chaperone. They wouldn't have been able to talk about anything important anyway.

The fluorescent lights from the gas station blared out into the blackness of the desert night. This was the last gas station on the east side of town, before the highway headed out once again into no man's land. Lucinda stirred as Hayley unbuckled her seatbelt and climbed out of the back seat, but it seemed that Levi's sleep spell was holding, because the other witch never actually opened her eyes.

Brandon had already started pumping gas. Levi stood a few feet in front of the Camaro, his eyes appearing to scan the darkness, although Hayley didn't know what he might be looking for out there. They'd made it more than halfway, with no sign that the Escobars were even making an attempt to come after them.

The dry desert wind caught at Levi's fair hair, even as the harsh light from overhead traced the edge of his fine profile. Despite everything, Hayley's breath caught at the sight of him. It was hard to believe that she'd kissed such a godlike person, that he'd held her in his arms.

And hopefully he would do that again soon, once they were back in Jerome and Lucinda had been handed off to Rachel to be looked after. Levi had seemed confident that the Santiago witch would come back to herself eventually, but Hayley had to admit to herself that she hadn't given much evidence of regaining her sanity so far.

She pushed her worries aside, went into the gas station's convenience store and used the restroom there, which was cleaner than she'd expected it to be. Afterward, she paused to buy a packet of peanuts. It would be enough to tide her over; the sandwich she'd eaten on the trip out here had long since stopped doing anything to appease her hunger.

As she stepped out of the store, a blaze of crimson eyes came out of the darkness, swooping toward Levi and Brandon where they stood next to the car, talking quietly. Black leathery wings beat against the air, every hideous scale and bump and ridge all too clear under the blaze of the fluorescent lights.

The little bag of peanuts slipped from her hands. "Levi!" she screamed.

He started, looked at her, and then whirled toward the demons, as though finally sensing their presence. One hand went out, summoning a gale that knocked all three of the hideous creatures back at least a hundred feet, out of the circle of lights surrounding the gas pumps.

"Get in the car!" he called out, although Hayley wasn't sure whether he was talking to her or to Brandon. Her brother didn't seem inclined to argue, though—he hurriedly slipped the fuel nozzle back in its cradle and all but threw himself into the driver's seat.

As for her, well, she knew Levi needed her help. She ran over to him, laid her hand on his arm so he could draw from her gift.

How exactly he intended to drive off the demons, though, she didn't know. He couldn't use fire as he had back at Red Rock Crossing, not with these gas pumps all around. The same thing for lightning. Yes, the winds he'd called had driven them back, but she could already see them creeping into the illuminated area, slithering across the blacktop like something out of the nightmares she'd had as a child, when she'd been sure some horrible scaly monster lurked under her bed, just waiting to grab her ankle the second she set foot in the room. Her flesh crawled, but she forced herself to stay put.

"What are you going to do?"

Levi raised his hands again. "My options are limited—I'm sure that's why they waited to attack until we were here. Even so, with your power helping to fuel me—"

He stopped there, fingers flexing and unflexing. Hayley could see the way his jaw clenched, as though he was trying to reach down deep within himself, to summon something that would ensure their attackers were rendered helpless for however long it took Brandon to put the pedal to the metal and get them away.

A wild wind caught at Hayley's loose hair, snapping it like pale snakes around her face. That wind seemed to take on shape and substance, to form itself into a dark tornado at least twenty feet high. She staggered, fingers digging into Levi's bicep so she wouldn't lose her footing completely.

The tornado swirled away from them, headed

directly to the spot where the demons crawled across the asphalt. It caught them, yanked them up from the ground as if they weighed nothing. Hideous screeches emerged from within those whirling winds, and clawed hands reached out to scrabble at the cyclone that held them captive, but they seemed unable to break free.

"Come on," Levi said, dragging Hayley over to the car. He pushed her inside, but slid her hand down from his arm so her fingers were twined with his, never breaking contact. As soon as they were both seated, he used his free hand to slam the door shut. "Go, Brandon!"

Her brother didn't need any more encouragement than that. He floored the accelerator, and the Camaro screeched away from the gas pumps, going at least thirty in reverse. He hit the brakes for a split-second, wrenched the steering wheel, and spun them around so they were headed directly for the freeway on-ramp.

A semi was approaching the access road from the opposite off-ramp, and Brandon hit the gas again, making a left turn so close to the truck's grille that Hayley was sure they must have blistered some of the chrome. Then they were screaming down the on-ramp, and hit the east-bound I-10 going what felt like a hundred miles an hour. If anyone else had been driving, she might have been freaked out. Now she could only be glad that it was her brother behind the wheel, maneuvering them to safety.

"Can they—?" Brandon began, and Levi shook his head.

"I don't know how easily they can catch us. Obviously, they were able to locate us at the gas station. And their masters must have told them where we're headed, because this was the most obvious, and fastest, route for us to take. But I don't know how long the tornado will hold, now that we're gone and I'm no longer there to maintain it. Still, it should give us something of a head start—if they even survive at all."

Hayley maintained her death grip on Levi's hand. No way was she going to let go, not until he told her it was safe…and maybe not even then. "Should we…I don't know…take an alternate route so it's harder for them to find us?"

Brandon nodded. "She might have a point."

"I'd say yes, except that any alternates would take us through far more desolate territory than we already have to cover. There is a little safety in being in populated areas. Driving through Phoenix might help to shield us somewhat."

"Phoenix is still a long ways off," Hayley pointed out. "I saw the sign as we pulled off the freeway. We have more than a hundred miles to go."

"There may not be much between here and

there," Levi said, "but at least there are gas stations at somewhat regular intervals, small settlements. If we cut off at Highway 60, then I know we'll be going through areas where there might not be anyone on the road at all. At least on the interstate, we can be sure that we'll have other drivers around."

Well, she couldn't really argue with that statement. She didn't know Highway 60 very well, except that it cut off from I-10 and went northeast, and eventually came out somewhere around Wickenburg, where there was also a small branch of the McAllister clan. Probably not enough of them to help if it turned out the demons had somehow managed to follow the Camaro all that way, though.

Possibly sensing her hesitation, Levi continued, "We've already held them back once tonight. We'll do it again, if we must. However, I'm hoping that they were damaged enough by the tornado that they don't have the strength to continue their pursuit."

"Would it hurt them?" Brandon asked. He was hunched slightly over the steering wheel, fingers still wrapped around it in a death grip. His eyes never left the road. "I mean, they're demons."

"Yes, but they still have corporeal bodies. They're not made of mist and smoke. They can be hurt, they can be killed." Very gently, Levi untangled his fingers from Hayley's. They'd already gone about ten miles; maybe he thought that was far enough. "This is not their world. They are very strong, but even if they're only wounded, they'll have to make their way back to their master, so his magic can revive them."

When Brandon spoke again, his voice had a hint of accusation in it. "You seem to know a lot about demons."

In the soft glow of the dashboard lights, Hayley could see Levi's shoulders lift. "That's because I also come from outside this world. I can't say I understand everything about how they work, but—"

"Wait a second," Brandon cut in. "What do you mean, you're from outside this world?"

Levi's face almost preternaturally calm, as though he'd known this moment was coming and had already prepared for it. "I was summoned here by Zoe Sandoval, the *prima*-in-waiting of the de la Paz clan. That little venture didn't go quite as planned, and that's why I ended up living with the McAllisters."

For the first time, Brandon shifted in his seat so he could cast an accusatory glance over at his sister in the back. "Did you know about this?"

"Yes," she replied. No point in trying to cover it up. Actually, she was glad that the truth had come out—she didn't like lying to Brandon, but at the same time, the story of his origin had been Levi's secret to tell.

"You might have mentioned it at dinner last night."

Oh, hell. Hayley sat up as straight as the uncomfortable seat back and her seatbelt would allow, and replied, "I didn't think it was my place to say anything."

Her brother went silent for a moment, fingers drumming on the steering wheel. In the passenger seat, Levi wisely remained quiet, as though he knew this was something that needed to be worked out between the two siblings, and for him to interrupt now would only cause more problems.

At last Brandon said, "You look human."

"I am human."

"I thought you just said—"

"I was brought here by magic, true. But this body I inhabit—that's just as human as yours. A DNA analysis wouldn't find anything out of the ordinary."

This reply seemed to stymie Brandon, because he lapsed into another silence. Hayley forced herself to keep quiet as well, because she could tell her brother was trying to work through the problem, trying to figure out if he had grounds for any other protests. A sign for someplace called Centennial flashed past.

"Does everyone else know?"

"Yes," Levi said. "I've lived with the McAllisters for a year and a half now. They were told when I came to live in my apartment, a place that used to be Evan McAllister's. It seemed only fair."

"But no one bothered to say anything to me. Why—because they still look on us Payson McAllisters as outsiders?"

Now her brother sounded angry, and Hayley couldn't help but tense. Brandon didn't often lose his cool, but when he did—watch out.

"I don't think that was it at all," Levi replied. His tone was still calm, but again, he didn't usually sound anything but unruffled. "More that they thought it was up to me to tell you, and frankly, we didn't have enough interactions that it seemed necessary for me to take you into my confidence."

"Yeah, well, once you started playing kissy-face with my sister, it might have been time to tell me the truth."

"Brandon!" Hayley burst out, so loudly that beside her, Lucinda stirred for a second or two before once again lapsing into her spell-inflicted sleep.

"No, he's right," Levi said. "I should have been honest. I've done my best to study your behavior and interactions during the time I've been here, but every once in a while, some nuance of human behavior gets past me."

"I thought you said you were human," Brandon said accusingly, still with that edge to his voice.

"Physically, I am. But human psychology is very complex, and I've only been here for eighteen months, after all."

Hayley felt compelled to speak up. "I really don't think this is something we need to be worrying about right now. Or did you forget that we might have demons chasing us?"

"I didn't forget," her brother replied. "But I haven't seen a trace of them. Have you?"

This last question was directed at Levi, the ironic inflection seeming to indicate that he didn't think much of Levi's demon-detecting abilities. While Hayley would have liked to defend him, she had to admit he didn't appear to be very good at noticing that they were about to be attacked by demons. Both at Red Rock Crossing and at the gas station in Quartzsite, he'd only been able to react once the otherworldly creatures were almost upon him. Still better than nothing, because at least he seemed more than capable of driving them off, if not destroying them utterly, but it would have been even better if he somehow had the talent to be aware that they were approaching.

"Since they haven't attacked, I'd have to say

that they seem to have been defeated for now." Levi turned his head so he could stare out at the dark landscape flashing by. Far up ahead was a pale orange-ish glow, one that seemed to indicate they were approaching the western edge of Phoenix's sprawling suburbs. Seeing it, Hayley couldn't help but be a little relieved. Yes, the demons had attacked at a lighted gas station, but wouldn't they have to be a little more careful once they were someplace where they would be surrounded by people, even in the middle of the night?

She didn't know. There was so much she didn't know.

Problem was, she wasn't sure she wanted to find out, either.

Brandon didn't seem inclined to continue the conversation, but kept his gaze fixed on the road as the hour grew later and the miles they'd traveled increased. They drove through Buckeye and Goodyear, hung at left at the 101 Loop so they wouldn't have to go all the way into downtown Phoenix. More suburbs—Peoria and Glendale and Arrowhead Ranch. Then at last they were northbound on I-17, and Hayley felt herself relax slightly. Not because they still didn't have a lot of open country to drive through, but at least she recognized the freeway now.

It was around two-thirty when Brandon got

off the interstate in Camp Verde. This was completely familiar territory; if they'd turned right, they would have been heading east, toward Payson and the ponderosa forests that surrounded her home. But instead the Camaro made a left, going west toward Cottonwood and then Jerome. By that point, Hayley's eyelids felt as if they were made of lead, but she did what she could to keep them open. She'd gotten a few hours of sleep earlier, and that should be enough to tide her over until she could crawl into a real bed.

When they made the first turn on the road leading up to Jerome, she let out a breath. Yes, she knew the wards wouldn't really do anything to hold back demons. But they hadn't attacked so far, and surely that meant they must have given up, that the tornado Levi had summoned to fight them had wounded them badly, or maybe killed them outright. Anyway, even if the demons had been waiting until this moment to attack, they would have badly miscalculated, because at least here would be dozens of McAllister witches and warlocks to join in the fight.

However, that didn't happen. They crawled along through Jerome's dark streets, Brandon not driving much more than the posted twenty-five miles an hour because the road was so narrow and twisty. After they went around the curve that would have led off into Jerome's state park, Levi pulled out his phone and typed out a quick message, although Hayley couldn't see what it was.

"Who're you texting?" she asked.

"Rachel. She knew we would be coming in late, but I told her to sleep, that I'd contact her when we were five minutes away."

Right. Levi had said that Angela's aunt would take Lucinda in. That little detail had completely slipped Hayley's mind, thanks to her worrying about the demons. She glanced over at the sleeping witch, who still seemed to be pretty much out of it. "Are you going to wake her up?"

"When we get there," Levi replied. "I don't know how much of a fight she's going to put up, so I thought it better to let her sleep until the very last minute."

Considering the way Lucinda had struggled and squirmed and claimed that "her boyfriend" was going to get them, Hayley couldn't argue with that strategy. She hoped that Levi would be proved right, and that the hours of sleep might have helped to start detoxing her a little from Matías' influence. Still, better safe than sorry.

Rachel's apartment occupied the two stories above her store, which was only one shop down from the building where both Levi's and Brandon's flats were located. However, instead of going around back to park, Brandon pulled up directly in front of Rachel's store. At this time of night, they didn't have to worry about competing with tourists for parking spaces.

And there was Rachel, hurrying out the front door, wavy reddish hair falling over her shoulders, a floral shawl pulled over the nightgown she wore. Behind her was a large, burly bear of a man. Her husband? Hayley thought that must be who he was, even though neither Levi nor Brandon had mentioned him. His size reassured her; if Lucinda really flipped out, it could only help to have someone who looked like the warlock equivalent of a linebacker around to help wrestle her upstairs.

Hayley undid her seatbelt and waited for Levi to get out so she could extricate herself from the back seat. It might have been fine for short hops, but spending nearly fifteen hours bent like a pretzel in the back of a Camaro had done some nasty things to her spine.

Rachel gave her a smile, clearly recognizing her even though they hadn't really met before now. "And Lucinda's still back there?"

"Yes," Levi said. "I'll get her out."

He went around to the driver's side of the car, opened the door, and pushed the front seat as far forward as he could. Then he bent and slid his arms under Lucinda's still-limp form, and carefully pulled her out. Her long dark hair spilled like black silk over him as he carried her over to the sidewalk.

"I can carry her upstairs," said the big warlock, the one who must have been Rachel's husband. "Maybe it's better not to wake her until we get her in bed."

"An even better idea," Levi replied. "I'll go up with you, and release the spell once she's settled." He seemed to hesitate then, while his eyes sought Hayley's. "Thank you for your help, Hayley," he said quietly. "We can talk in the morning."

That was it? She wanted to protest, then realized that it probably wouldn't be a very good idea for all of them to squeeze into the room where Lucinda would be staying. That would definitely be enough to make her freak out. "All right," she said, all too aware of Rachel's curious gaze, as though she guessed something was going on, even if she didn't have all the details. It killed her to have to walk away without getting even a good night kiss on the cheek, but this wasn't the time to act entitled and needy. "I'll text you when I get up." She transferred her attention to her brother. "Come on, Brandon—it's past the witching hour. Time to go to bed."

"I have to move the car first."

Right. Well, there was no need for her to go with him; all she had to do was walk next door and let herself in the front entrance of their building. "Okay. Then I'll see you upstairs."

Hayley gave a half-hearted wave at the assembly, saw Levi hand Lucinda over to Rachel's husband. Then she went on down to her building and slipped in the front door, and began to resolutely walk up the two flights of stairs to the flat. Goddess, what a long day.

And she had no idea what the next one would bring.

11

———

EVEN AT NEARLY THREE-THIRTY IN THE morning, the room was a cheerful space, its walls painted a warm turquoise color, a coverlet in shades of turquoise and terra-cotta and cream on the bed. Levi watched as Tobias took Lucinda over to that bed and laid her down carefully, pulling the sheets and blankets over her. Since she still only wore a T-shirt and panties, it wasn't as though they needed to worry about getting her dressed for sleep.

Ah, sleep. Levi was tempted to allow the spell to remain in effect until the morning, but the Santiago witch had already been under for more than seven hours. It wouldn't be good to have that unnatural sleep completely destroy her body's regular rhythms, although he feared a restless night lay ahead for Rachel and Tobias. But they'd offered to take Lucinda, even knowing that it would require some time for her to come back to herself.

"I'm going to lift the spell now," Levi said. "She may become violent—she was when we took her. I'm hoping she's past that now, though."

"It's all right," Tobias replied. He'd stayed near the bed, as though he knew that having to restrain the young woman was a distinct possibility.

Levi reached out to touch Lucinda's mind, to carefully remove the heavy darkness he'd draped over her consciousness. He'd called it a spell, because that was easy shorthand, but in truth her forced sleep had been due only to the pressure of his will on hers. Time to take away that pressure, to let her swim back up into the light.

For a few seconds, she didn't move. Then her eyelids fluttered open, and she blinked at her unfamiliar surroundings, her eyes wide and dark and frightened.

"What—?" The word came out in a harsh rasp, and she swallowed. "Where am I? What am I doing here?"

Rachel stepped forward. She did present a slightly more reassuring image than Tobias did. "I'm Rachel McAllister. This is my husband Tobias, and this is Levi."

As Rachel gestured toward Levi, Lucinda's eyes

narrowed. "You—you were the one who took me!"

"Yes," he said quietly. "The Escobars were holding you hostage. You don't remember?"

"I—" The angry glint left Lucinda's dark eyes, which were really quite extraordinary, large and ringed with heavy black lashes to match her hair. "I don't know. I was with Matías…wasn't I?"

"In a manner of speaking," Levi replied, but he stopped himself there. The poor woman would learn the truth soon enough, once the fog of the dark warlock's influence had left her mind. Better to leave things vague for now, so she could come to realization in her own time.

"You're safe now," Rachel said quickly, as if she wanted to make sure to insert herself in the conversation before Levi could mention anything that might agitate their guest. "It's probably best if you sleep some more."

"Sleep," Lucinda repeated, and then gave a weak nod. "I do feel very tired."

"Well, it's late," Rachel said, her tone brisk. "So go to sleep, Lucinda, and then I'll make us all breakfast in the morning."

"Best breakfast in the Verde Valley," Tobias put in, and Lucinda managed a wan smile.

"That sounds good." Her eyes shut, and a certain tension seemed to go out of her body. Levi had worried that she wouldn't be inclined to sleep any longer, but it seemed she still craved real slumber, the kind that would help restore her to herself.

Rachel nodded, apparently satisfied that her new charge would sleep for a while now. A tilt of her head toward the door seemed to indicate that she thought they should all leave Lucinda alone. Levi didn't argue, but only went out into the hallway, and waited there as Tobias and Rachel also emerged, Rachel pulling the door nearly closed, but not quite.

"Thank you for taking her in," Levi said, making sure that he kept his voice pitched low. Yes, it seemed as though it would take more than a murmured conversation to keep Lucinda awake, but he thought he might as well be careful.

"We're happy to," Rachel replied. She glanced over at her husband. "Tobias, I'll see Levi out. You might as well get back to bed."

These words were offered as a suggestion, but the firmness of her tone seemed to indicate that she wouldn't brook any arguments. Tobias shrugged. "'Night, Levi."

"Good night," he replied, then watched as Tobias headed down the hallway to what must have been the bedroom he shared with Rachel.

She tilted her head toward the staircase, and the two of them went down to the next level of the apartment, where the kitchen, living room, and dining room were located. Clearly, Rachel McAllister was not the sort to subscribe to a minimalist style in decorating, because it seemed as if every square inch of surface area was covered in crystals of various shapes, sizes and colors, or plants in brightly colored ceramic pots, or figurines of a bewildering variety of gods and goddesses. Levi had been here before, of course, but every time he entered her apartment, he wondered how she could function in all this clutter.

At the head of the stairs that led down to the ground floor and to Rachel's shop, she paused and tilted an eyebrow at him. "Do you want to tell me what's going on with you and Hayley?"

Levi stared down at her, wishing that she wasn't quite so adept at picking up on subtle cues, subtexts he thought must be hidden. Ever since he'd come to Jerome, Rachel McAllister had taken it on herself to guide him along in this new life, and he would be always grateful for her assistance. Now, though, he had to think it might have been easier if she didn't feel entitled to explanations about his personal life, like a sort of honorary aunt.

"There isn't much to tell," he said. "We've become friendly."

That non-response earned him another lifted eyebrow, accompanied by a pair of hands firmly planted on her hips. "'Friendly'? I'm not sure if that's exactly the impression I was getting. And Brandon definitely didn't seem too thrilled with you. For three people who just got back from carrying out a very dangerous rescue—a successful one, that is—none of you looked very happy."

"I hadn't said anything to Brandon about my origins," Levi told her. "It…came out during the drive home. Obviously, he's going to need a little while to adjust to the idea."

"Especially because you're interested in his sister?"

"Yes, I suppose so." That response seemed neutral enough. "Interested" only implied a certain low level of attraction. It didn't necessarily mean that anything had happened between them. And, Levi reminded himself, not a lot had. A few kisses. That was all.

"Hmm." Rachel was silent for a moment, then shook her head. "I've hoped that you would meet someone, that you wouldn't have to spend your time in this world alone. But with everything that seems to be happening right now, are you sure this is the right time?"

"Some of it didn't begin to happen until Hayley came to town," he pointed out. "I don't think that was a coincidence. Somehow, the Escobars learned of her talent, wanted to seize it for their own use. That makes me think it's best for me to spend as much time with Hayley as possible. Is there anyone else here in Jerome who could do a better job of protecting her?"

"No," Rachel replied, although the way she hesitated before answering him seemed to indicate she wasn't happy about making that admission. "That is, Connor and Angela working together might be able to do what you can, but we need them focusing on the whole clan, not just one person. So I can see why it's best for you to be with Hayley. Only…you need to be careful, Levi."

"I am," he said. "I wouldn't do anything to put Hayley at risk."

That response elicited a chuckle. Rachel put a hand on his arm, a quick reassuring touch before she withdrew it again. "I wasn't talking about Hayley, Levi. You have a giving heart. Just…make sure you're making the right choice before you hand it over completely. I don't want you to get hurt."

"I won't," he assured her. While he understood Rachel's concern, he knew he didn't have to worry about his feelings for Hayley being reciprocated. She cared for him.

No, the real concern was whether the Escobars would even allow them a chance to explore their feelings for one another, or whether all that would have to wait until this nasty conflict had been settled.

He hoped not. Because at the moment, Levi couldn't begin to see how all this might end.

A clatter from the direction of the kitchen woke her. Hayley rolled over and opened one eye, noted that bright sunlight seemed to be peeking in from behind the curtains, and reached out with her left hand to pick up her phone from the table next to the bed. A push of the "home" button, and the screen came to life, telling her that it was nine-thirty in the morning.

Better than she'd hoped, but still nothing close to eight hours of sleep. Or even six, considering that she'd finally closed her eyes around four. Oh, well. She could function on the sleep she'd gotten, as long as she didn't make it a regular habit.

After setting her phone back down on the bedside table, she pushed herself out of bed, found a pair of yoga pants in a dresser drawer, and pulled them on. Since she'd passed out wearing her T-shirt, now she was basically dressed, at least enough so she could head out toward the kitchen. The warm, thick smell of coffee had begun to creep under the door, telling her what that noise in the kitchen had been.

Or at least some of it. Hayley had a feeling that making coffee usually didn't require quite so much of a racket. Brandon had been deliberately noisy on purpose. He wanted to wake her up.

So they could have it out, say the things they'd held back the night before?

Fine.

She ran her fingers through her hair to get out the worst of the tangles, then opened the door and went down the hallway toward the living room/dining area/kitchen space. Yes, there was her brother, just lifting the carafe from the coffeemaker. His eyes flickered toward her, deliberately incurious. "You want some coffee?"

"Sure."

Hayley padded over on her bare feet, wishing she'd paused to put on a pair of flip-flops. The tile in here was cold, even though the day outside promised to be warm and sunny again. She stood there silently as Brandon got out another mug and poured some coffee, then handed it to her.

"Thanks. Milk?"

"In the fridge."

Still holding her mug of coffee, she opened the refrigerator door and got out the container of milk, then doctored it to her preferred shade of dark beige. The whole time, Brandon just stood there, blowing on his own coffee. Since he drank it black, there wasn't much else he could do except wait for it to cool down.

She took a careful sip, just in case the milk

hadn't tempered enough of the heat to make the coffee drinkable. However, it wasn't too hot, and so she sipped at it again. That was better. The warm liquid flowed down her throat, hit her stomach, and began working its magic. Maybe by the time she was done with the entire mug, she'd start to feel like a human being again.

Or maybe not. It sort of depended on how much her brother was spoiling for a fight. He really didn't have much of a temper, but she could tell this whole thing with Levi had shaken him.

Since Brandon didn't seem inclined to speak, only stood there and kept blowing on his coffee, she decided she might as well get it over with. "Whatever you want to say, just say it."

He raised an eyebrow. Standing there in a T-shirt and sweat pants, his hair still sticking out in all directions, he didn't look particularly fearsome. Even so, Hayley couldn't help but hold her breath, just a little bit. She hated confrontations.

Apparently, Brandon didn't seem inclined to start one now. "What am I supposed to say?"

"Oh, come on. You were practically breathing fire last night when you found out about Levi."

This time, her brother did actually drink some of his coffee, although she could see the way his jaw and throat muscles tightened, as though it was still far too hot, and he'd only drunk it in an attempt to keep from answering her right away. "I think 'breathing fire' is kind of an exaggeration."

"Whatever. You weren't happy."

He set down his mug on the tiled counter and crossed his arms. "Of course I wasn't happy. I mean, I guess I was okay with you and Levi being…whatever…but yeah, it kind of came as a shock to hear he isn't even human."

"He *is* human," Hayley retorted. "Weren't you listening?"

"All right, physically human. But his soul, his spirit…whatever you want to call it…that came from someplace else. What can someone like that know about human emotions?"

She supposed she should be glad that Brandon had said "someone" instead of "something." At least it was a start. "And there are people who are supposedly 'human' who might as well be monsters—like the Escobars, for instance. Levi's origins might be a little unusual, but he's a good person. He's learned a lot in the time he's spent here. Tell me—if he hadn't actually told you that he'd come from someplace else, would you have ever guessed?"

Brandon frowned and ran a hand through his already messy hair. "I don't know. Maybe not. We didn't interact much—said 'hi' if we bumped into each other on the landing, that sort of thing. It's not as if we had any heart-to-heart talks."

"No, but if he couldn't pass at all as one of us, you still would have noticed something, even with as little as you seem to see each other."

"Maybe. But that's not the point, is it? The point is that even if he can 'pass,' he's still not human. Not really. Which means he's not the sort of person I'm all that thrilled to have macking on my sister, you know?"

"We're not 'macking,'" Hayley shot back. *Well, at least not yet,* she added mentally. She certainly wasn't going to rule out the possibility of things going further with Levi, although she knew she'd have to be discreet. Yes, she was an adult and so could do as she wished, but she could only imagine the shitstorm if she didn't get Brandon on her side, if he decided to take his protective big brother routine too far and actually called their parents to let them know what was going on with his little sister and the guy next door…who just happened to be not entirely human. "Anyway, you shouldn't be so narrow-minded. There's nothing wrong with Levi."

"Maybe not on the surface. But have you really stopped to think this through? Right now, he just looks like a regular guy—"

An insanely hot guy, she thought, but she knew better than to interrupt with that particular observation. Brandon was obviously trying his best to keep things civil, but she doubted he wanted a verbal reminder of how attracted she was to Levi.

"—but what about the long run? Will he age? Will he always stay looking human? You just don't know."

True, she didn't. This was all uncharted territory. But really, how many guarantees were there in any relationship? Illness happened. Physical changes occurred. People fell out of love for reasons that didn't have anything to do with appearance, though. Hayley wondered, however, if she even knew how she would react if Levi changed, if underneath that handsome face were hidden the features of—well, of one of the demons who'd attacked them, or maybe something even worse. She wanted to think it wouldn't matter, that it was Levi's strong and generous spirit that really attracted her, but she just didn't know. She doubted she would have reacted the same way when she'd first seen him if he hadn't been movie-star gorgeous.

"No, I don't," she said. "And it's something I have to think about, maybe talk over with Levi. I don't really know where all this is going...we've only known each other for a few days. The only thing I do know is that I like him...a lot. He's different from anyone I've ever met."

"No shit."

Hayley forced herself to stare back at her

brother, to compel him to meet her eyes. It was difficult; she wasn't used to this sort of forced intimacy. But she knew she had to do what she could to make him understand. "Maybe. But it's his very difference that allowed him to save Lucinda Santiago last night. To drive off those demons. No one else in this clan could have done that."

"I'm not disputing his courage, or his magical skills."

"Then what are you disputing?"

Brandon went silent. He reached for his mug of coffee, took a large swallow. Then he said, sounding very tired, "I'm not sure I know." Another swallow of coffee, and he put the mug back down on the counter. "Anyway, I need to get in the shower. I called work and said I'd be coming in late, but I still have to get down there before the morning's totally gone."

"Okay." While part of her might question Brandon going to work after the night they'd all just put in, on some level, she understood. Tinkering with engines was his Zen. He clearly had a lot he needed to work through, and trying to make him stay home, just so she could continue to plead her case, didn't sound like a good idea. This wasn't going to get settled right away, and she would have to deal with that. At least he wasn't threatening to rat her out to their parents. She could argue all she wanted that she was an independent adult, and in the civilian world she was, but things didn't work quite that way in the witch clans. Parents still had a good deal of say when it came to the lives of their unmarried children, and the last thing she wanted was them trying to meddle in what was already a delicate enough situation.

Brandon nodded, and drank the rest of his coffee before he disappeared down the hallway. Hayley hesitated for a moment, then went back to her bedroom and retrieved her phone. No messages from Levi, but then, she'd said she would reach out to him. Probably he hadn't wanted to take the risk of waking her up.

And if he was still asleep? Well, she had to hope that he'd been here long enough to learn how to turn on the "do not disturb" function on his phone. She went to the messaging app and typed in, *Late breakfast sound good?*

Maybe that was jumping the gun. After all, she was nowhere close to walking out the door. But she'd washed her hair the day before, which meant she could skip it now. If she moved fast, she could be ready in less than half an hour.

Her phone pinged. She picked it up, felt a rush of relief as she saw Levi's reply. *Yes. The Mine Café serves breakfast until noon. Do you want me to come over?*

I still need a half hour, she typed back. *Is that OK?*

Of course. Then just come and knock when you're ready.

Will do.

Hayley set down the phone, joyful anticipation filling her. So what if she was running on less than six hours of sleep, or that she didn't know whether the Escobars weren't already on the warpath, just waiting for their best chance to get revenge?

She was going to see Levi again very soon, and right then, that was the only thing that mattered.

12

HAYLEY CERTAINLY DIDN'T LOOK AS THOUGH she'd just spent half the night evading demons and traveling down dark highways. No, her fair skin was positively luminous, and Levi liked the way she'd drawn her hair back into a low, loose ponytail, with a few wisps falling around her face. The style called more attention to her fine, high cheekbones, the delicate lines of her jaw and chin.

They sat in the Mine Café, which at that hour of the morning wasn't particularly crowded. The restaurant was built slightly below street level, so the window in the room where they sat afforded them a view of the wheels of parked cars, and the feet of passersby, and not much else.

Not that Levi minded. Right then, all he wanted was to look at Hayley.

She'd ordered iced tea, saying that she'd

already had coffee with Brandon. Levi wondered how that had gone. Had they spoken of him? Argued? He thought that was a distinct possibility, considering how her brother had behaved the night before. Levi didn't hold any of that against the other man, because he knew Brandon was only being protective. Still, he didn't like to think that he might have been a cause of discord for Hayley and her brother. Levi wasn't quite sure how close they were, and he hated to think that she might walk away from her nascent relationship with him if Brandon made it clear that he would continue to be unhappy about the situation.

"Have you heard anything about Lucinda?" Hayley asked after the waitress brought their drinks and then retired, saying their food would be out shortly.

"Yes, I called Rachel earlier this morning. Lucinda is awake, and seems to be a little more herself. That is, she isn't acting out, isn't hostile. She seems confused more than anything else, doesn't understand how she got here to Jerome." Which, he thought, could only be a blessing. With any luck, the Santiago witch would forget all about the time she'd spent as Matías Escobar's hostage…and unwilling lover.

"That's good." Hayley swirled the straw through her iced tea, pushing the slice of lemon around. "It has to be so strange for her, to wake up someplace she's never been before."

"Yes, but hopefully she'll get her bearings soon enough, will understand that she's safe. It's good that she's staying with Rachel, since Rachel has always been one to look out for others."

"Did she look out for you, too?"

"Yes. Of course I didn't really know anyone when I came here, but she made sure that I felt as at home as I could." Looking back, he realized how much work Rachel had really done—introducing him to the other McAllisters, inviting him over for dinner practically every night for the first few months until he could muddle along on his own, or at least interact with the staff at the local restaurants without giving away what a stranger he really was. He had to hope Lucinda wouldn't require quite that much coddling, would be able to find herself at home here, once she was able to shake off the fog of Matías Escobar's dark magic.

Hayley nodded. "It sounds like Lucinda's in good hands, then."

"The best, I think."

The waitress returned with their food, and asked if they needed anything else. Both Levi and Hayley demurred, which meant they were left alone again soon enough.

She picked up a piece of sourdough toast and

broke off one corner. "I don't think Brandon is very happy with me."

"No, I suppose not."

A lift of an eyebrow as Hayley popped the bit of toast in her mouth and chewed thoughtfully. "You don't seem too worried about it."

"I—" Levi stopped himself there, because he had to pause and consider why he wasn't worried. After all, if asked, he would have said that the last thing he wanted was to be a source of friction between Hayley and her brother. "I suppose it's a lot for him to take in. I can't blame him for being upset. Did he forbid you to see me?"

"No, of course not." She picked up her fork and gathered up a mouthful of omelette. "He's not stupid. And he knows he can't really tell me to do anything. The thing is, we've always gotten along pretty well, but it's not like we're super-close, either. I know having to even think about my love life is uncomfortable for him. In this case, though, he feels like he has to, just because…." The words trailed off there, and a faint flush tinged her cheeks.

"Because of who I am."

"Exactly."

Levi thought he knew how she would answer, but he guessed it was better to ask, just to be sure. For one thing, he had very little experience with women. Yes, Hayley had kissed him, seemed interested in him, but it was quite possible she didn't intend for matters to progress any further than that. "And it doesn't bother you?"

"Didn't we already have this discussion, Levi?"

"Yes. But I feel as if I have to ask again, especially now that you've seen how your brother has reacted to the situation. It may be that he'll never understand. Can you live with that? What if your parents feel the same way?"

"Then I'd say they were being pig-headed and silly, just like Brandon." She set down her fork, and reached across the table and laid a hand on his. Her fingers were light and delicate, and yet he could still feel the way her power seemed to flow through her fingertips and into him, all heat and energy and strength.

Or perhaps that was simply the way his body reacted to her.

"You're not having second thoughts, are you?" she asked.

"No. I'm sure there are many who would say that it makes no sense for us to reach out to one another now, because of the situation with the Escobars, but I don't believe there's any point in postponing happiness simply because dark forces are at work in the world."

"Some might say that's exactly why we need to reach out. The best way to fight darkness is with light, isn't it?"

Gazing into her face, Levi knew it didn't matter that he'd only met Hayley McAllister a few days earlier. That light shone from her—not only in her outer beauty, but from her inner strength as well. And he knew she was the match to his soul...wherever that soul might have come from.

"Yes, it is," he said softly. Right then, he wished with all his heart that they didn't have this table separating them, that they could be someplace alone where he could take her in his arms and kiss her again. That time would come...he hoped. For now, though, he knew they needed to eat their meals, to act as if everything was normal. Like the clan's weather-workers, who could sense when a storm was approaching, even if the skies overhead were serene and blue, he knew this calm now was not something that would last. The Escobars might be licking their wounds for the moment, but Levi guessed they would not allow this insult to pass by without some kind of retaliation. As to what form that retaliation might take, well, he couldn't begin to guess. All they could do was brace themselves as best they could.

Seeming to sense something of what was going through his mind, Hayley asked, "So what do we do now? Just wait and see?"

"Are you asking about the two of us, or the clan in general?"

She smiled. "Well, it sounds as though you

and I are pretty much on the same page. I guess I was wondering what Connor and Angela have planned next."

"As to that, I don't know. I haven't heard from them yet today. It's possible they expected me to sleep later than I did. It's also possible that they've gone to visit Lucinda, to reassure her about being here in Jerome." That seemed like the sort of thing the *prima* and *primus* might do. Yes, he was sure that Rachel had told Lucinda she had a home here in Jerome for as long as proved necessary, but such reassurances would probably carry more weight if they came from the leaders of the clan. "And I'm certain they've spoken with Luz Trujillo as well, just to warn her."

"Warn her about what? The de la Pazes didn't have anything to do with kidnapping Lucinda."

"True, but they're still on the front lines, so to speak. We're isolated here in Jerome, far away from the borders of Santiago territory."

"That didn't seem to stop the demons who attacked us in Sedona."

Hayley did have a point there. Levi wondered, though, if the Escobars would try that route again, or whether they had begun to realize that demons were not quite such a formidable adversary when faced with the combination of his inborn gifts and Hayley's magic-enhancing abilities. Then again, it wasn't as though the Escobars viewed their demons as anything but expendable. It was probably worth it for those two practitioners of dark magic to keep flinging their otherworldly servants at their foes, just in case they were able to find a chink in their armor.

"No, demons are not nearly as bound by geography as mortal witches and warlocks. But they also know we're waiting for them."

No reply at first. She pushed her eggs around on her plate, ate another few mouthfuls. After she washed them down with some more iced tea, she asked, "Why is it that the Escobars can even summon demons at all? Until this whole mess blew up, I'd never even heard of anyone doing such a thing."

"Because the McAllisters follow the right-hand path, the path of the light."

"I'd never heard of the Wilcoxes trying anything like it, either, though…and I was brought up believing they were far from angels. Now I know that's not exactly the truth, but…." She stopped there and gave a small lift of her shoulders.

Levi wouldn't put such a thing past Damon Wilcox, but it was true—no one in the Wilcox clan claimed to know anything about that particular kind of dark magic. Damon had dabbled in areas of study that had been forbidden for centuries, but in the end, those explorations had only rebounded on him, making him a victim of the very powers he'd sought to control. That didn't seem to be the case with the Escobars.

"It could simply be another of their talents. Not one that most clans would seek to cultivate, but then, we don't know much about where they came from, whether Joaquin Escobar was an outcast among his own people because of the black magic he wielded, or whether he was a *primus* of a sort, and only came here when he learned of what had happened to his son."

Hayley appeared to consider that reply, then nodded slowly. "Do you think it's possible that Matías and his father were communicating the whole time? I mean, I've heard how Matías was basically raised by the Santiagos, but the timing seems a little suspect…like Joaquin only came north after he figured out what had happened to his son, so he could take his revenge on the Santiagos."

A theory Levi hadn't heard before, but one that made sense. Perhaps Joaquin had known all along where his runaway wife had fled with her children. Olivia, Matías' younger sister, would have been of no use to her father, since her powers were basically nonexistent. But it was entirely possible that Joaquin had allowed the boy to grow up among the Santiagos because he knew of the gift his son bore, since it was his own. A dark cuckoo, just waiting to take over the nest....

"I can see that," Levi said. "I know that Matías called demons to do his dirty work for him when it came to weakening and ultimately murdering Maya de la Paz. Or at least, that seems to be what Luz Trujillo believes happened, since she actually observed the place where Matías first used blood magic to call something dark to this world, and she also sensed the dregs of that magic, even though Matías and his accomplices had done their best to cover up what they had done."

Hayley pressed her fingers to her temple, as though her head suddenly ached—or perhaps she was only having a difficult time trying to process everything he'd just said. "I guess I just don't understand that kind of hate."

"I'm not sure it's hate," Levi told her. "I think all of this is driven by a terrible lust for power. If a man isn't content with what's in here"—he placed a hand to his chest, over his heart — "then he'll look for ways to fill that emptiness. Power over others is an intoxicating drug. It can help cover up the missing pieces in someone's soul."

Her blue eyes stared at him, wide and wondering. "How can you know that? You're the least power-hungry person I've ever met."

He offered her a sad smile, wishing he could give her more encouraging words than the ones he was about to say. "I haven't been here even two years, but in that time I've studied humanity. I had to, in order to understand what I was trying to be. I've read books, watched your television and your movies. It's not that difficult to see, once you know what you're looking for. And I have to confess that I was puzzled by these Escobars, who seemed so different from all the witches and warlocks I'd met. It's possible that Damon Wilcox was the closest in the Arizona clans to being their soul brother, and yet, all the things he did were in pursuit of ending the terrible curse that hung over the Wilcox clan. Getting rid of that curse would have helped him, of course, but I believe he was thinking of future generations more than he was thinking of himself, of the power he might wield. I can't say the same for Joaquin Escobar."

Hayley didn't reply right away. She took another bite of toast, then nibbled some of her eggs, although Levi got the impression she was only eating because she should, and not because she had any particular appetite. Finally she asked, "If that's really what's driving them…how do we defeat them?"

She looked small and forlorn, and he wished he could take her in his arms and offer what comfort he could. At the same time, he didn't want to lie to her, utter words of encouragement he didn't believe. All he could say was, "I don't know, Hayley. I just don't know."

≈

There wasn't any word from Angela or Connor, and nothing from Brandon, and so after breakfast, Levi suggested that they go up to one of the day hike areas on Mingus Mountain. It should be safe enough, since it was close to town and well within McAllister territory. That sounded like a good idea to Hayley; charming as Jerome might be, at the moment, the little town was only making her feel claustrophobic. Getting out into the forest and doing some communing with nature might help to clear her brain.

The spot they headed to wasn't actually that far outside town, maybe a fifteen-minute drive up the switchbacks cut into the mountainside, the foliage that lined the narrow highway gradually shifting from agave and yucca and cactus to ponderosa pine and sycamore and oak. Levi parked his truck in one of the designated spots, and they both got out.

Hayley couldn't help experiencing a small flutter in her stomach as she looked around. Oh, yes, it was beautiful up here, reminding her of the forests that surrounded the town where she was born, but at the same time, she remembered how the demons had attacked in Sedona, in a spot even more beautiful than this. True, these were all McAllister lands, and therefore should have been somewhat safe, but she didn't know if she could count on that.

Even if the Escobars held off, decided to wait to attack until they had a better chance of success —well, she was up here alone with Levi. Since it was a Friday morning, the chances of encountering anyone day-tripping from Phoenix were a lot lower than they would be on the weekend itself, and it was too early in the year for kids to be out of school. Theirs was the only vehicle in the parking lot. They might have been alone in the world. Was that a good thing? She wasn't sure, somehow felt as nervous as she had the first time she'd met him, even though they'd already gotten past the awkwardness of a first kiss.

It was a good thing that she'd worn her Keen trail shoes and jeans and a T-shirt, since she hadn't been sure where the day would take her. She'd only been here a few days, but she could already tell that people in Jerome tended to be fairly casual in their attire. Anyway, her clothing didn't keep her from following Levi as he led her away from the parking area and into the forest.

At once sounds seemed muted, the faint hum from passing cars as they took the mountain route over the hill to Prescott very far away. Hayley could hear the wind soughing in the pines, and some birdsong, but even those noises sounded more distant than they should. The air smelled of warm sap and pine needles, clean and fresh, and she felt herself begin to relax. Was that a mistake? Possibly, but she couldn't go around on edge all the time—she'd be too worn out to react if something bad really did happen. Even more, she just didn't want to live like that.

The trail was fairly steep, but she'd spent most of her life hiking and climbing around Payson, so it wasn't enough to throw her off her stride. What was far more likely to distract her was the sight of Levi's backside in his faded jeans, which clung to him just enough to show the outline of his ass and his well-muscled thighs, but weren't too tight.

No, they were just right.

Hayley told herself that she needed to pay attention to the trail, but that was easier said than done. Luckily, though, they reached the clearing that apparently had been Levi's destination without incident, and he gestured toward a fallen log.

"Do you want to sit for a while?"

"Sure."

She chose a seat close to one end of the log, since that spot didn't have any nubs of long-gone branches sticking out or obvious pools of syrupy sap, which she knew was an absolute beast to get out of clothes. Levi sat down next to her—not too close, but still close enough that she was acutely aware of him, the way the wind fanned his fair hair back from his brow, the hint of golden stubble on his cheek, the thin leather cord decorated with old silver and tiger's eye beads around his throat.

Was he also thinking of her, cataloguing all the little details, like the silver hoops in her ears and the leather barrette she'd used to pull her hair back? She couldn't know for sure, because it wasn't as though he was staring at her. In fact, his gaze seemed to be locked on a little cluster of white and pale purple flowers at the base of an oak tree, and not on her at all. Still, he could still be catching glimpses of her out of the corner of his eye, trying to look when he thought she wouldn't notice.

Finally, she said, "It's beautiful up here. Thank you."

This time he did turn toward her, his expression faintly puzzled. "'Thank you'?"

"For bringing me here. It's exactly what I needed. Just a place to…breathe."

"To breathe. Yes, I can understand that. It's why I would come up here a lot, especially in the early days. I couldn't drive yet, but I had a mountain bike that Kirby McAllister gave me."

This comment made her lift an eyebrow. "You

biked all the way up here? That hill is so steep!"

"Maybe, but I liked the challenge. I had a few close calls with cars that weren't very happy to be sharing the road with me. For all I know, that's why Tobias ended up teaching me to drive. I doubted anyone would have wanted the responsibility of telling Zoe Sandoval that I'd been hit by a tourist who was in too much of a hurry to get to Prescott."

Levi spoke blithely enough, but his words still made a shiver go through Hayley. The last thing she wanted to think about was a car sideswiping him while he was riding up the mountain. He'd said he was human, which meant he was mortal. He wasn't some godlike being who could withstand that kind of physical trauma. She'd never asked him if he could be hurt or killed, but surely if his body was genetically the same as a human man's, then it could suffer the same kind of injuries.

Although she hadn't responded, he must have sensed her distress, because he reached over and took her hand in his, held it firmly. "It didn't happen. I was always fine. I still ride up here on occasion, but I thought the truck would be more practical for the two of us."

"Are you saying I weigh too much?" she teased him, but he shook his head, looking sober.

"I wouldn't presume to guess at your weight,

but you appear quite slender to me."

About all she could do then was laugh. "Well, thank you for the compliment."

"I wouldn't say it was a compliment. It was only the truth."

They both fell silent then. Hayley looked into his clear blue eyes, and she could tell he was looking straight back at her. It should have been awkward, and somehow wasn't. No, right then she thought she would be happy to eternally fall into the oceans of those eyes, to always have him holding her hand.

She wasn't sure which one of them moved first…not that it really mattered. What mattered was that they each shifted on the log so they would be closer together, so it would be the most natural thing in the world for their lips to touch, for their mouths to open so they could taste one another.

A warm thrill flooded through her body. Levi let go of her hand so his arms could wrap around her, so he could hold her close. She felt the muscles of those arms, felt the reassuring beat of his heart against her breast. Human…oh, yes. And so very real, so very perfect.

How long did that kiss last? She didn't know. How could she know, as they sat in this sunny clearing, with the trees bending and rustling in the breeze, in this timeless place where the world seemed to have stopped and held only the two of them? Finally, though, Levi lifted his lips from hers, although he still held her close.

"No second thoughts?" he asked, his voice barely above a murmur.

Hayley thought of all the arguments Brandon had given her, all the reasons that pursuing a relationship with Levi might not be the wisest thing to do. But her brother couldn't know how she was feeling now, how she knew with every atom of her being that Levi was the one for her. In that moment, she couldn't imagine even trying to be with someone else—no, the mere thought was repugnant. It didn't matter where Levi had come from. All that mattered was who he was, here and now.

"None," she replied. Her tone was firm. She needed him to know that there would never be any second thoughts. "You—you're everything I ever wanted."

He let out a breath that was almost a sigh, and reached up to touch her cheek. The brush of his fingers against her skin was so tender, almost reverent, that she could feel tears start to her eyes. She'd never had anyone touch her like that, look at her in such a way.

"I love you, you know," he said, and her breath caught.

"I love you, too," she whispered. She wanted

to ask, *So what do we do now?,* but she wasn't given the chance, because he was kissing her again, kissing her with such a breathless intensity that she had to fight to keep her balance so she wouldn't go sliding right off that damn log. What a place for declarations of love.

No, she thought, once Levi let go of her again, and she tried to steady herself so the world wouldn't keep spinning around her. The sun shone down on them, and the trees whispered in their own rustling language, and far, far away, a diving hawk let out a keening cry. No, this place was perfect. It was as beautiful as Levi—both his face, and his sweet, sweet soul.

He began to reach out to touch her hair, which had started to slide out of the barrette that confined it. However, he stopped, looking startled, and pulled his phone, which was buzzing fiercely, from his pocket. His brows drew together as he stared down at the screen, and then he stood. "We have to go."

"What's the matter?" From his expression, Hayley knew it couldn't be anything good. "What's happened?"

"The text was from Connor. Someone crashed their car into Rachel's store." Levi took Hayley by the hand and began to hurry down the path that led to the parking area. "He says it looks like it was deliberate."

13

MAIN STREET WAS UTTER CHAOS, WITH
emergency vehicles choking the narrow section of
highway and crowds of tourists gathered around
to gawk at the destruction. Levi knew there was
no way he would be able to get around the curve
of the road by the fire department and so to his
usual parking space behind his building, and
instead squeezed the truck to the left, to the
narrow street that led to an ancillary parking lot
near the Gold King Mine museum. Once he'd
parked, he and Hayley ran back down the way
they'd just come, arriving on the scene just as
paramedics from Cottonwood were loading
Rachel into the back of an ambulance.

"What happened?" Levi asked of Angela, who
stood next to Connor in front of the shattered

display window of her aunt's store. "Is Rachel all right?"

"They want to take her in for X-rays, maybe an MRI," Angela replied. Tears glittered in her eyes, and Levi could see the way she forced herself to swallow, as though fighting to get past a knot in her throat. "The paramedics couldn't say much more than that."

A rustling in the crowd, and someone saying, "Let me through! Let me through!"

Tobias, pushing his way through the onlookers, only to stop as he realized the paramedics had already shut the ambulance doors and were pulling slowly away from the curb, and he wouldn't be able to reach his wife in time. At once Connor went over to him. "It's okay, Tobias. She's alive. Angela and I are going to follow the ambulance down to the hospital. You can ride with us."

"What about the person who drove into the store?" Hayley asked, and Angela turned slightly toward her, a frown pulling at her dark brows.

"He's gone. He—" Her voice caught, and she shook her head, as if reprimanding herself for that momentary weakness. "From what people have said, the person was driving a silver sporty-looking car, but no one seems able to identify what it was. They came down around the curve and plowed right into the front window. I guess R-Rachel"— Angela had to pause again and take a breath—"it sounds as though Rachel was right there, putting some stock in the display area. The car knocked her down, but then it just backed away and went speeding down the hill before anyone could stop it."

"No one saw who was driving?"

"I don't think so. A couple of people said the windows were tinted."

"Angela." Connor approached, Tobias right behind him. "We need to get down to the hospital."

"I know. But…." She cast a helpless glance at the shattered window, the smashed pottery and crumpled books in the storefront. "What are we supposed to do about all this?"

"We'll take care of it," Levi said. "Don't worry—I'm sure there are plenty of people who will be willing to pitch in."

"All right." Then one hand went to her mouth. "Oh, hell—Rachel was watching Lucinda. What are we supposed to do about that?"

"Levi and I will take care of her," Hayley said at once, and Levi felt another rush of love for her, that she would jump in and offer to help, even though she was a newcomer here, and still finding her own way. "At least she's seen us before, so we won't be total strangers."

"Thank you," Angela replied, sounding so relieved that Hayley smiled in response, clearly glad that her offer had been accepted without argument. "I'll call as soon as we know anything."

And then she and Connor and Tobias were hurrying away, up the hill to the house so they could get their car. Deprived of further spectacle, the tourists who'd been watching the commotion began to disperse, leaving Levi and Hayley…and a gathering crowd of McAllisters, who'd apparently just gotten the news.

In the front of the group were Kirby, Angela's cousin and friend, and Kirby's boyfriend Jordan. "What can we do?" Kirby asked.

"Start cleaning up as best you can," Levi said. "We'll need to board up the window until it can be replaced. I suppose throw out anything that was damaged?"

"Better save it," Hayley put in, surprising him. "Rachel might need to make a claim with her insurance company, and it'll be easier if she has the broken stuff on hand so she can match inventory numbers or whatever."

"Of course." He hadn't even thought about insurance, or the mechanics of making a claim. Then again, he'd never had to do such a thing. He'd learned much during his time here, but it was obvious that gaps still existed in his knowledge. The lack bothered him, even though Hayley had made it clear that she didn't mind his unusual origins, or the limitations he suffered because of them.

"Not a problem." Kirby glanced around at the group of family members who'd gathered, everyone from Bryce, one of the clan's elders, to young Lisa McAllister, who couldn't even drive yet. "We'll make sure we put everything in a box."

"And I'll get some boards," Bryce said. "Got a bunch in my garage."

Hayley came closer to Levi and murmured, "We should really check on Lucinda."

She was right. Had Rachel locked the door to the apartment, or was there a possibility of the Santiago witch emerging at any moment to see the damage done to the place that was supposed to be her sanctuary?

"Hayley and I need to go upstairs for a bit," Levi told the group. "Take care of the mess however you think is best."

Bryce raised a gray-frosted eyebrow at that—he was probably used to being the one to give orders—but then shrugged and said something to Kirby, who nodded. The elder headed off, presumably to fetch the boards for the window.

Satisfied that the wreckage would be handled, Levi went inside the store, doing his best to avoid crunching on too much broken glass. Hayley followed, also stepping gingerly. Rachel's apartment—well, it was now also Tobias' place, although he still had the studio space and apartment he'd lived in before the two of them got married—was accessed by a staircase at the back of the shop, hidden behind a door. That door did turn out to be locked, but that was no real impediment. Levi put his hand on the knob, and it turned at once. They went up to the first floor of the apartment, but it was empty.

"Maybe she slept through it all?" Hayley asked.

That would be a blessing. "Possibly. But she must still be up in her room, even if she is awake."

They headed to the third floor, where the apartment's bedrooms were located. Levi went immediately to the one where Lucinda had been installed, and knocked softly on the door. "Lucinda? Are you all right?"

No answer at first, and Hayley gave him a worried glance, although she remained silent, her hands jammed in the pockets of her jeans, as though she didn't know quite else what to do with them.

Then the door opened, and Lucinda gazed out at them, her expression puzzled. She did seem much calmer than she had been the night before. All Levi could see in her face was confusion, but not the snarling anger that had led her to fight back against him. Also, her hair had been neatly brushed, and she was wearing real clothes—jeans and a short-sleeved top with some pretty flowers embroidered around the neckline.

"I'm fine," she said, her arched brows pulling together. "You—you were there last night, weren't you?"

"Yes," Levi replied. He glanced over at Hayley, who offered Lucinda a hesitant smile. "Hayley and I were both there. I'm Levi."

"Right. Rachel mentioned you...I think." She put a hand to her forehead. Her fingers still had faint traces of chipped dark red polish on them. Levi wondered if she'd been wearing that polish when Joaquin Escobar invaded her life and changed things forever. Certainly she wouldn't have had much opportunity to remove it after that. "Sorry," Lucinda went on. "Things are all kind of muddled together still. Rachel said I'll get less foggy as time goes on, but right now...."

"It's all right," Levi assured her. "But we needed to talk to you about Rachel."

Lucinda's dark eyes immediately flared with alarm. Maybe she had heard the commotion after all, or possibly she'd picked up a hint of psychic residue from Rachel's shock and pain. "What's the matter?"

"There's been an accident," Hayley said. "Some bastard drove his car into the front window of the store, then took off before anyone could stop him. Rachel was hit—they're taking her to the hospital now."

"We think she'll be all right, though," Levi put in hastily, because he could tell from the sudden grayish pallor of Lucinda's warm-toned skin that she'd immediately assumed the worst. "They want to run some tests, just to make sure."

"I want to see it," Lucinda said. "Where the accident happened."

Levi glanced over at Hayley, who gave a very small lift of her shoulders. Because he hadn't had a real chance to talk to Rachel yet, he didn't know for sure how much freedom Lucinda had been given to roam around the apartment—or the store, for that matter. But since word had presumably gotten out about her presence here, there didn't seem to be much point in hiding her away. Besides, the only people downstairs in the shop would be other McAllisters. He didn't have to worry about Lucinda saying or doing something that might attract the attention of any civilians in the immediate vicinity.

"It's something of a mess," he told her. "But if you really want to—"

"I do," she said.

Now it was Levi's turn to shrug. "All right. Better put some shoes on, though," he added, noticing for the first time that she was barefoot. "There's a lot of broken glass."

Her full mouth tightened slightly, but she only nodded, and walked away from the door so she could pick up a pair of flip-flops that had been resting on the floor next to the bed and put them on. Still not the best foot coverings he could think of, but of course the flip-flops were better than nothing.

The three of them headed downstairs, Levi in the lead, with Hayley bringing up the rear. Even in the midst of all this chaos, he could still recall the sensation of her lips pressed against his, the sweet scent in her shimmering golden hair. They should have been able to return to town and walk hand in hand down Main Street, look in the shops, possibly go to one of the wine tasting rooms once the afternoon was a little older. Instead, Rachel was in the hospital, and the other members of the clan were trying to help pick up the pieces.

They'd already done a good job. Kirby and Jordan and several others had carefully gathered up the damaged items and put them in several plastic bins. Where those had come from, Levi wasn't sure, but he supposed a general call had gone out among the McAllisters for any items that could help with the clean-up. Bryce and David Moss, the husband of Allegra, another clan elder, were in the process of boarding up the window. Already the interior of the shop was getting darker

—Rachel had always relied on natural light during the daytime hours—and so Levi paused and went over to the little alcove where the switches for the overhead fixtures were located, and turned them on.

Warm light shone down on them; Rachel hated fluorescents. While the lighting was friendly enough, it couldn't conceal the damage that had been done to the quaint storefront.

Lucinda moved forward, toward the window. Levi almost put out a hand to stop her, because he knew that Bryce wouldn't appreciate being interrupted while he was in the middle of boarding up the damage. However, the Santiago witch stopped a few feet away from the window itself, one hand going out to grasp the edge of a table filled with crystals and pottery. Luckily, it was just far enough away from the point of impact that it appeared to have escaped unscathed.

"The Escobars did this," she said, her voice not much more than a whisper.

"What?" Hayley demanded. Her blue eyes were wide with shock. "How can you know that?"

"I just know." She smiled slightly, but it was a sad smile. "It's not that I have some special power that can sense dark magic. I wish I did—if I'd been stronger, then maybe I would have been the *prima*-in-waiting." The smile faded, her eyes dark and tragic. "But if that was the case, I would have ended up as Joaquin Escobar's plaything. Then again...father...son...how much difference does it really make?" Her hands knotted into fists where they hung at her sides.

If Levi had known her better, he might have tried to go to her and put a reassuring hand on her arm, provide a simple touch to let her know that not all men were like the Escobars. But because he and Lucinda were nearly strangers, he remained where he was, even as Hayley stood close by, her eyes filled with the same sympathy, one she obviously wasn't sure how to express.

Then Lucinda pushed her hair back from her shoulders and shook her head. "Not much of a difference, from where I stand. Anyway, I'm sure they did this because they were looking for revenge. You stole me from them. Some might argue I'm not all that valuable, but that's not really the point. You invaded their territory. So they invaded yours, and they hurt someone who was close to your *prima*. Simple math on their part, really. If they'd tried to strike at the *prima* herself, or her husband, or their children...that would have caused too much of a reaction. But Rachel? Now you're distracted. You're worried and upset... but you're not quite out for blood."

"I'm not sure about that," Levi replied. Lucinda's words had shaken him, but if it was the Escobars' plan to make sure the McAllister clan was knocked off-balance by this latest act of violence, then he had to make sure he remained calm and in control. "I saw Bryce's face as he was boarding up the window. He looked rather like he wished he was hitting something other than nails with his hammer."

"Maybe. But you're not planning a council of war. Your *prima* and *primus* aren't here…leaving your town undefended."

A chill went over Levi then, even though the shop felt quite warm, most of its air conditioning pulled out through the shattered glass of the display window. He hadn't even stopped to consider such a thing, but he was forced to admit that if it had been the Escobars' intention to make sure the McAllisters' leaders were safely away from Jerome, they'd done a good job of executing their plan.

"There are still enough witches and warlocks here to protect the town, if it comes to that," Levi said.

Lucinda raised an eyebrow, but her expression wasn't mocking…more sad than anything else, as if she pitied him for his over-confidence. But then, she couldn't know that he wasn't quite an ordinary garden-variety warlock, that his powers were certainly a match for the Escobar father and son.

The two of them working together…along

with any demons they might summon…well, that was a different question, one Levi wasn't sure he wanted to answer. His powers were strong by any method of measurement, but he didn't know if they were quite that strong.

Hayley stepped forward then. "Exactly. I don't think the Escobars know what they're up against in Levi here. He's already beaten their demons twice."

This revelation did seem to surprise Lucinda. She glanced from Hayley over to Levi but didn't say anything, her entire stance showing that she expected some kind of clarification.

"It's true," Levi admitted with some reluctance. "But only a few at a time. I have no idea how many they can summon, if they truly put their minds to it."

Lucinda appeared somewhat discomfited by his comment. One hand went up to nervously tuck a heavy lock of black hair behind her ear. "I don't have any idea. They didn't work their powers around me. Well, those powers, anyway. Obviously, Matías was back to his old mind-control tricks, or he wouldn't…." She stopped there, a slight shiver running through her slender form.

Not wishing for her to dwell on those horrors, Levi said quickly, "Even if we don't know how many demons they can summon at once, at least we have some experience fighting them…which means we're not completely unprepared. I will talk to the elders. And—" He stopped there, not sure what to say next. For while he knew it was important to let the clan elders know exactly what they were facing, he wasn't sure if Hayley and Lucinda needed to be present for that meeting. In fact, it was probably better if they didn't come along, simply because Lucinda obviously couldn't provide much more information than she already had, and he wasn't sure whether Bryce and Allegra and Tricia would feel comfortable speaking freely in front of the Santiago witch, considering she'd been so recently freed from Matías Escobar's influence.

Some of his hesitation must have communicated itself to Hayley, because she said, "How about I take Lucinda up to my place for now, and you can go talk to the elders? It seems the most logical thing to do, considering how the store is wrecked and everything."

Levi wished he could kiss her all over again. She'd carefully attributed the reason for taking Lucinda over to the flat to the destruction of the store, and not the need to make sure that the other witch wasn't left alone for any length of time. "That sounds like a great idea. Do you mind, Lucinda?"

A lift of her shoulders. "No. I don't really want

to stay here…at least, not until Rachel is able to come back."

Which meant that they'd have to make arrangements for alternate lodgings for Lucinda. Levi pushed that worry away for now. They'd work out something. In the meantime, though, he needed to speak to the elders.

Together, they might be able to drive off the Escobars' next evil incursion.

Perhaps.

14

Bryce had already taken off by the time the three of them emerged from the store. Hayley watched as Levi asked Kirby where the elder had gone, with Kirby pointing up the hill, presumably toward the street where it seemed like most of the prominent members of the clan had their fancy restored Victorian houses. Levi touched Hayley's hand, bent down to murmur, "I'll be as quick as I can, but it may still be some time before I can get back."

She summoned a smile. "It's all right—Lucinda and I can have some girl time while you're gone."

How exactly she was supposed to manage that, when she barely knew the Santiago witch, Hayley had no idea. Also, after everything she'd been through, Lucinda didn't really seem like someone who would be in the mood for mixing up skinny margaritas and discussing the relative merits of Channing Tatum versus Tom Hardy. But Hayley supposed she'd figure out something. Better to have to play babysitter for a while than sit down with the elders and work on the impossible task of trying to figure out how to make a town full of pacifist witches and warlocks face down whatever supernatural army Joaquin Escobar planned to send against them.

Lucinda was quiet as she walked with Hayley down to the building where the flat was located. Even though she was silent, her eyes scanned the streets around them, looking at the tourists, nodding to herself as her witch sense detected the others of her kind mixed in with the civilians. There was also a certain amount of surprise and interest in her expression as she looked at the restored buildings, the steep hillsides above them.

Well, Jerome was certainly nothing like Pasadena.

As Hayley opened the door to the flat, she said, "This is actually my brother's place. I'm kind of crashing here—my parents started to get a little freaked about everything that's been going on, and they thought I'd be safer in Jerome."

The corner of Lucinda's mouth quirked slightly. "Joke's on them, I guess."

Hayley couldn't really argue with that

comment. And as insane and horrible as the last half hour had been, she was also glad to see that Lucinda appeared to be a little more connected, not quite as out of it, as though having come face to face with even more trauma had helped to knock some of Matías Escobar's fog right out of her brain.

"Do you want a glass of water?" Hayley asked. Having seen the inside of her brother's refrigerator, she knew there wasn't much more she could offer besides water, except maybe a bottle of Lumberyard pale ale. But as much as the notion of having a beer sounded pretty good right about then, she wasn't sure alcohol was such a good idea, considering Lucinda's still somewhat fragile state.

"Sure." She looked around at the living room, but her expression was so neutral that Hayley couldn't really guess what she was thinking. At least the furniture was in a more pleasing arrangement now, and the odds and ends she'd bought while shopping with Levi had been put in their proper places, but the flat still wasn't exactly what you could call elegant. From what she'd heard, the Santiago *prima*'s house in Pasadena was pretty ritzy. But, since that house was currently occupied by the Escobars, it made this humble little flat a haven in comparison.

Hayley busied herself with getting a couple of glasses from the cupboard, then dispensed some

ice and water from the refrigerator door. Thank
God that the place had up-to-date appliances.
Lukewarm water out of the tap probably wouldn't
have cut it.

She went into the living room and handed
Lucinda one of the glasses. "Here you go."

"Do you know her well?" the other witch
asked abruptly.

Hayley didn't have to ask who she was talking
about. "Not really. I actually only met Rachel for
the first time last night, when we dropped
you off."

Lucinda frowned. "But aren't you a
McAllister?"

"Yes, but I'm from the branch of the family in
Payson. That's about a hundred miles from here.
Like I said, I came here to stay with my brother
because it seemed safer at the time. I've only been
here a couple of days. Not very long."

"Long enough, though."

Hayley tilted her head and gave Lucinda a
questioning look. "What do you mean?"

"I saw you with Levi. You seemed…close. So I
guess the McAllisters are like most witch families
and don't care too much about cousins being
together, as long as they're distant enough?"

Obviously, Lucinda had been paying closer
attention than Hayley had thought. She would
have liked to tell the truth, to say that while Levi

had taken the last name of McAllister, he wasn't genetically related to the clan at all. But doing so would require divulging his secrets, and she knew she wouldn't do that. In time, he probably would want to tell Lucinda the truth. It was his place to do so, however…not hers. "Yes, that's pretty much how it works. We marry civilians, too. Don't the Santiagos do the same thing?"

"Mostly. But our clan is big—we have people everywhere from San Diego all the way up past Santa Barbara. And we've been in California for a long, long time. It's not quite the same thing."

Hayley didn't know if Lucinda was trying to be condescending, or whether she just didn't realize how her words had come across. Yes, so the Santiagos had a huge clan, and it was therefore a lot easier to be with someone who was technically a cousin but who might not share any more genetic material with you than a stranger down the street. Probably best to ignore the comment for now. She did seem remarkably recovered for a woman who'd been under a dark warlock's mind control for the past few weeks, but that didn't mean she was all the way back to herself.

"I guess," Hayley said, her tone noncommittal. "But yes, Levi and I…made a connection, I suppose. He lives in the apartment across the landing, so I guess it's not that strange that we'd bump into each other. My brother Brandon works long hours, and so at first I think Levi was just trying to make sure I wasn't left alone in a new place."

As if to give the lie to her words, since it was only a little after two in the afternoon, the door-knob turned and Brandon walked in. He stopped dead a foot or so inside the door, his gaze locked on Lucinda. "Um, sorry. I didn't know you had company."

"It's okay," Hayley replied. Should she get up from the sofa? No, that would make the situation even more awkward. "Lucinda and I were just chatting. But what are you doing home in the middle of the afternoon?"

He fished his iPhone out of his pocket and sort of waved it at her. "I got a text alert about Rachel. Tricia set up the alerts right after that whole Escobar mess down in Scottsdale."

Lucinda flinched at the mention of the Esco-bars, but otherwise she seemed content to stay silent, watching Brandon out of slightly narrowed eyes. Taking his measure? Hayley couldn't really be sure. Yes, her brother looked even scruffier than usual, his sandy hair tousled, a haze of dark beard on his chin since he hadn't bothered to shave that morning, the usual oil and grease stains on his T-shirt, but certainly no one could have ever detected an aura of evil around him.

"That's a good idea," Hayley said. "I didn't get one, though."

"Probably I didn't think to give Tricia your number. My bad." Once again, he looked over at Lucinda and then quickly glanced away. If Hayley didn't know better, she would have said that was a slight flush she spotted in his cheeks.

Was he interested in Lucinda? Hayley had to admit that the Santiago witch was very pretty, with those big dark eyes and lashes that looked fake but obviously weren't, considering she wasn't currently wearing a speck of makeup. And with her full mouth and that long fall of near-black hair, she was certainly not anything like the McAllister witches Brandon would have met over the past few months.

Maybe it wasn't that he wasn't interested in women. Maybe it was only that he hadn't encountered the kind of woman he'd be interested in.

Hmm....

"It's all right," Hayley told him. "I was with Levi, and he got the text. We were up hiking on one of the trails on Mingus, and came back down as soon as we heard." Now it was her turn to feel a flush touch her face, one that couldn't be blamed on the sun exposure she'd gotten earlier. Just thinking of the mountain trail made her remember that bright clearing, and the way Levi had kissed her as they sat on the fallen log. "Anyway," she went on hurriedly, "Rachel has already been taken to the hospital, and a bunch of the clan members are cleaning up the mess from the accident. About all we can do now is wait to hear from Connor and Angela—they went down to Cottonwood Regional to be with Tobias."

"I saw the boarded-up window at the store," Brandon said, his tone somewhat absent. Then he looked down at the stained T-shirt he wore and tugged at the hem. "I'd better get changed. I doubt I'll be going back down to the shop today."

"You work on cars?" Lucinda asked.

"Yes," he replied. "Mostly restorations, vintage muscle cars, that kind of stuff. We're going to be featured in an episode of *Dream Machines* next month."

"Oh, that's interesting," she replied, although Hayley could tell from the politely empty intonation in those words that Lucinda had absolutely no idea what *Dream Machines* even was.

Brandon apparently noticed as well, because he gave a hitch of his shoulders and said, "Anyway, I'll be back out in a few."

He went down the hallway and into his room, closing the door behind him. Lucinda seemed to watch for a few more seconds before she shifted on the couch and once again faced Hayley. "What's *Dream Machines*?"

"It's a TV show. You know, on cable. Every

week they feature a different car restoration. It's kind of a big deal to get chosen. Brandon and the rest of the guys at the shop are pretty excited about it."

"Ah." Lucinda went quiet for a moment, her fingers playing with the embroidered edge of her shirt in an unconscious imitation of Brandon's gesture from a moment earlier. "That seems like an odd occupation for a warlock."

"Well, his talent is working with mechanical things. Engines and wiring and all that stuff. He can fix pretty much anything." Belatedly, Hayley realized it was a breach of witch-kind etiquette to divulge someone else's talent without their permission, but she doubted her brother would mind too much. His wasn't the sort of gift that needed to be hidden away, and besides, it might help to enhance him in Lucinda's eyes.

"That's a good talent to have. He's lucky that he found someplace to work where he could put it to use." She let out a small sigh then, her gaze moving away from Hayley's so it could rest on one of the new pictures that hung in the living room, this one of a serene river with willows bending over it. "Mine was never much good. A small talent for predicting the weather. I knew I was a disappointment to my parents."

"I doubt that," Hayley said, her heart aching for the other witch. All right, Lucinda hadn't been strong enough to be *prima,* but everyone knew that the succession in witch clans didn't always run in a straight line.

"You didn't know them." Lucinda smiled then, a small, bitter smile. "My mother would never say anything, and because she was injured when I was very young, she didn't have the strength to show her disappointment, but my papa—he was a different story. I saw it in his eyes every time he looked at me. Maybe it would have been good for me to use my talents in the civilian world, as your brother has. I have no doubt I would have made a passable weather girl on a local television station. Not, of course, that my father would have ever allowed such a thing."

"I'm—I'm sorry about that," Hayley said in a small voice. No, she hadn't known the Santiagos, but it didn't seem as if anyone else had yet offered Lucinda any condolences over the loss of her parents. Possibly Connor and Angela would have, once they came to visit their refugee, but the accident that sent Rachel to the hospital had probably driven any thoughts of condolence calls straight out of their minds. "And about your cousin Marisol and her husband."

Lucinda rubbed her hands over the knees of the jeans she wore. Hayley wondered where she'd gotten the clothes. Maybe from Angela; the two of them looked as if they were roughly the same size.

"It's…well, it's not all right, but it's just what is right now. We witches have many powers, but raising the dead isn't among them." A shiver went through her. "At least, I have to hope it isn't. I still don't know everything about what Joaquin and Matías are capable of."

It was Hayley's turn to shiver. Demons were bad enough; the last thing she wanted to think about was whether the Escobars had learned the dark spells required to raise the dead. She tried to comfort herself with the notion that they certainly wouldn't want to raise the very people they'd murdered, as they wouldn't make very good servants. Unless, of course, Joaquin and Matías were able to force the formerly deceased Santiagos to their bidding, just as they had done with Lucinda and her cousin Marisol and everyone else who'd crossed their path.

"Anyway," Lucinda went on, "since the past can't be changed, about all I can do is pray that the Escobars meet their final justice. It won't bring back the dead, but at least if the two of them end up rotting in the ground, then I'll know they can't cause any more damage."

Strong words, but Hayley couldn't argue with the sentiment. It did seem as though the only way anyone would be able to rest easy was after father and son met their all-too-deserving fate. But who would mete out the justice they so richly deserved? Connor and Angela? Luz Trujillo, or possibly all three of them working together? It was both their place and their right, as clan leaders.

And yet…would they be able to prevail, when the time came? Or would they turn to Levi, as they already had once before?

Footsteps came down the hallway, and both women fell silent as Brandon entered the living room. He looked much more socially acceptable now, in a clean dark T-shirt and jeans that didn't look as if they'd just been dragged across a hundred miles of bad road, his hair combed, his face and hands washed. Next to Hayley, Lucinda sat up a little straighter, and pushed a lock of long dark hair back over her shoulder.

It seemed as though the interest just might be mutual, although Hayley told herself it was kind of silly to be thinking about such things at the moment. Lucinda had just been extricated from a damaging, abusive situation, and probably wouldn't be too interested in starting anything for a long time. And, as Hayley herself had just pointed out to Levi earlier that afternoon, this didn't seem the right moment for any of them to be looking at a new relationship, not with the threat that hung over all their heads.

But she and Levi had kissed anyway, which meant she was the last person who should be lecturing someone on being cautious in these dark times.

She couldn't tell if Brandon had overheard any of hers and Lucinda's conversation. His expression was neutral enough, but that, Hayley thought, probably stemmed more from a need to prevent himself from staring at Lucinda than because he'd heard something he knew he wasn't supposed to.

"Nothing new yet," he said, indicating the phone he held in one hand.

"Well, it's probably going to take a while to run all those tests," Hayley replied.

"Where's Levi?" her brother asked, as if noticing his neighbor's absence for the first time.

"He went to talk to the elders. Lucinda was worried that this might have been an attack by the Escobars."

Brandon's eyebrows lifted, and his gaze shifted to the Santiago witch. Something about the change in his posture told Hayley that he was glad of the chance to be able to speak to Lucinda directly. "What makes you think that?"

"It's the sort of thing they would do," she said, her tone hard. Hatred flashed in her dark eyes. "I doubt they were happy that I was taken. Not because they valued me so much, but more because doing such a thing right under their noses was a direct challenge. It was like spitting in their faces."

Well, Hayley couldn't really argue with that assessment. And although the whole experience had been frightening enough as it happened—she was glad she'd been there. It had felt good to strike a blow against the Escobars.

"I'm sure the elders will investigate what happened," Hayley said. "Even with Connor and Angela down at the hospital, they should be able to find something."

"I hope so," Brandon said, his tone grim. "Going after Rachel—that's just not right."

Lucinda's dark eyes held his. For that moment, they might have been the only two people in the room. "I am afraid the Escobars care little for what is right."

Levi had been at Tricia's house before, but not in an "official" capacity such as this. Yes, he'd become a confidant of sorts to Angela and Connor, but they didn't interact with the elders as often as some might think, instead preferring to allow that trio of two witches and one warlock to manage the day-to-day affairs of the McAllister clan.

Now he sat on a comfortable overstuffed chair, while the three elders took their seats on a large beige linen couch. Although Tricia had poured sparkling water with lemon for everyone, none of them seemed inclined to drink. Bryce's blue eyes were still crackling with angry fire, while Allegra's usual air of detached bewilderment seemed stronger than usual. Tricia herself appeared calm and collected, not one hair out of place in her red bob. Even so, Levi detected the smallest shake of her hand as she set down the last of the glasses of water, and realized the youngest elder wasn't quite as composed as she wanted everyone else to think.

"Angela called me a few minutes ago," she said. "Rachel is stable…for the moment. She has a concussion and two cracked ribs, and they still want to do an MRI, but it sounds as though she's going to be okay."

"Thank the Goddess," Allegra breathed, even as Bryce said, his tone as gruff as his eyebrows,

"That doesn't help us with trying to find out who did this. Does she remember anything about the accident?"

"I don't think Angela or Connor have asked her," Trish replied. "She's in a good deal of pain, and medicated. They probably want to wait until things have stabilized a bit."

"Well, we can't wait forever," Bryce said. "I've asked around, and asked others to ask around, and no one can say much about the car involved except that it was silver and sporty and had tinted windows."

Allegra frowned. "But surely any car that

crashed into a building like that would have sustained a great deal of damage. It wouldn't be that hard to find it, would it? You wouldn't think it could have gotten very far."

"Unless…." Levi began, and paused as the others suddenly focused on him.

"Unless what?" Bryce asked.

"Unless it wasn't a real car, but something conjured to bring destruction to our town. Lucinda Santiago said she thought the Escobars had sent it to bring harm to the McAllisters in retaliation for rescuing her."

A silence fell after that pronouncement. The two women exchanged worried glances, while Bryce crossed his arms, his scowl deepening the heavy lines around his eyes.

Tricia was the first to speak. "Does she have any evidence for this?"

"No. It was just a feeling. She's still a little disoriented, and that could have something to do with it. But I'm worried that she's right."

"I was right there, helping to board up the window, and I didn't sense anything," Bryce protested.

"But were you looking for it?" Levi asked.

Another pause. Then Bryce said, "No. No, I wasn't. That's not really my kind of thing, anyway. Allegra's better at picking up on vibes that aren't quite right."

"We'd better go check," she said, looking pleased at her fellow elder's sideways compliment. "If there's any residue from evil magic still lingering there, it won't last forever."

Levi hadn't considered that angle. Then again, there was so much about this situation that was novel…and not in a good way. "Let's take a look, then," he said, getting up from his chair.

The elders rose as well, and the group of them exited the house and went down the porch stairs and on to the street. As they walked, Levi couldn't help glancing around him, trying to see if anything was amiss. But everything seemed just as it should be, the bright May sunlight shining down on the fresh grass and budding roses in everyone's front yards, the various hues of the "painted lady" Victorian houses gleaming in the sun. Down the street, he saw two small dark-haired children throwing a ball at each other in someone's front yard, and an older witch he didn't know very well looking on, and realized those children must be Connor and Angela's twins, sent to a neighbor's house while their parents were at the hospital keeping watch over Rachel.

All in all, it was a very ordinary scene, one so ordinary, in fact, that it was hard to believe all the people who lived on this street were witches and warlocks, or that dark magic might have been worked on another of these streets only a few blocks away. The little group continued down to Main Street, back to the scene of the crime, as it were. A few passing tourists paused to stare at the boarded-up window and murmur to themselves, but they soon lost interest and continued to their destination, which appeared to be the T-shirt shop across the street next to Grapes.

Allegra went to the window and pressed one pale, slender hand against its frame. Her eyes shut, and she murmured something to herself, although Levi couldn't quite hear what she was saying. A spell of some sort, he supposed, which could have been anything from a formal ritual to words she'd strung together herself, to help with focusing her mind and her abilities. From what he'd seen, the McAllisters did tend to be rather freeform about such things, and didn't rely on spell books the way the de la Paz clan did. But no one could argue that they weren't strong, even if theirs was a different kind of strength from that of the other witch families.

A tremor went through her, and the dangling silver earrings she wore jingled softly. "Yes, there was dark magic here," Allegra said. "I can't tell where exactly it came from, or who sent it, because it's already begun to fade. But I definitely feel something that isn't right."

"We don't have to guess at who sent it," Bryce

growled. "Those damned Escobars had to have been behind this."

Tricia crossed her arms, a frown creasing the fine ivory skin between her brows. "Can you sense anything more than that, Allegra? What I mean is, did the Escobars somehow reach out to influence someone who was driving by anyway, or was this some new kind of demonic manifestation?"

Her question made Levi frown as well, because he hadn't even considered that angle. He'd assumed the Escobars must have figured out a way to control minds at great distances, or possibly sent one of the Santiagos here to do their dirty work, somehow masking that person's identity so he or she could get past the wards. Such things weren't outside the bounds of possibility, since Damon Wilcox had done the very same thing to get his brother Connor safely into Jerome without being detected.

No response from Allegra at first. She moved over slightly, and stooped so her fingers could trail along the bottom edge of the window, although she was careful to avoid any of the nails that held the boards in place. Some of her graying fair hair fell in her face, and Levi shifted his position just a little so he could shield her from being seen by anyone who might be casually driving by. Yes, Jerome had a reputation for being populated by eccentrics, but Allegra's behavior would have appeared unusually odd to any passersby.

At last she straightened, one hand going to the small of her back, as though it pained her slightly. Perhaps bending over like that for an extended time had been difficult for her; Levi didn't know her precise age, but he thought she was probably in her early sixties.

"I sense nothing human here," she said, her faded blue gaze moving briefly to Levi before it returned to Tricia and Bryce, who stood close together, both of them practically radiating tension. "Or rather, I can still feel something of Rachel, because this is her shop and she's spent so much time here. But anyone involved in a sudden, violent act—whether intentional or not—should have also left a bit of residue. I can't feel anything like that at all. So whatever it was—a vehicle driven by a demon, or a vehicle with no driver at all, something animated purely by the power of Joaquin Escobar's mind—it definitely didn't involve a human."

Those words were not what Levi wanted to hear. As frightening as the thought of a civilian being suborned by the Escobars might be…as terrible as it might have been to think of a Santiago witch or warlock sent hundreds of miles to do their bidding…it seemed somehow worse to consider that otherworldly powers had been involved here as well. Demons showing their true forms and attacking in lonely, unpopulated areas…that was one thing. A demon behind the wheel of a car, or a demon in the form of a car, seemed so much worse.

"How do we defend ourselves against something like that?" Tricia asked. Maybe the question had been meant rhetorically, but Levi still felt he should try to answer.

"I know something of these demons," he said. "Not everything, of course, but maybe enough to help make our wards much more powerful, alter them so the demons simply can't pass through the town limits and only set off an alarm. I'd need to know how you cast the spells, though."

Bryce obviously didn't care much for that request; his mouth thinned, and his arms crossed. "Those wards are the business of the clan elders."

"I think we're past caring about tradition, Bryce," Tricia said crisply. "If Levi can help, then of course we need to let him try."

Levi smiled at her in gratitude, glad that she didn't seem nearly as stubborn as the sole warlock among the trio of elders. Allegra nodded.

"Yes," she put in. "Desperate times, as they say. What do you need from us, Levi?"

He hesitated for a moment. It was one thing to ask to be let in on this one secret of the elders —they might regard him as something of an outsider, but at least they'd had some time to get used to him. However, he also knew the best chance of truly being to help was to have Hayley assist him, to lend her power to strengthening the wards. He couldn't help but think that Bryce would balk at such a request. Hayley might be a McAllister, but she'd only arrived in town a few days earlier. In the elder's eyes, she might very well seem like a stranger.

Still, Levi knew he had to ask. Otherwise, the endeavor might be doomed to failure from the start.

"I need you to take me to where all the wards are set," he replied. "I need you to say the words of the spell, or perform the ritual, or whatever else it is you do. And I need to bring Hayley McAllister with me, because her gift will greatly strengthen mine."

Silence. A couple of tourists walked past and sent them some curious glances, but because the elders and Levi hadn't been discussing anything sensitive at that precise moment, it was unlikely that the civilians had overheard anything.

Once the coast was clear, Bryce said, "Do you really think that's necessary?"

Interesting that none of them had asked what Hayley's particular gift was. Then again, while such matters weren't generally shared amongst the clan, it was quite different for that kind of topic to be discussed amongst the elders. Angela had probably let them know as a matter of courtesy.

"I think it's the only way," Levi replied. "She's already helped me twice when I had to drive off some of the Escobars' demon slaves. We stand a much better chance of having truly effective wards if she's helping me."

Another silence. At last Bryce gave a grudging nod. "All right. If we have to, we have to. Go fetch her, and meet us down at the bottom of the hill, at the bend in the road by the abandoned gas station. That's the location of the first and most important of the wards, so we might as well start there."

"I'll get her," Levi promised. Both Tricia and Allegra offered him encouraging smiles, quite a contrast to the scowl that hadn't quite erased itself from Bryce's features.

Well, Levi thought as he walked away, toward the building where presumably Hayley and Lucinda still occupied one of the apartments on the top floor, he had wanted to spend more time with Hayley.

He just hadn't imagined it being quite like this.

15

THE KNOCK AT THE DOOR WASN'T A COMPLETE surprise, since Hayley had hoped that Levi would come by once his meeting with the elders was done. However, because Brandon was still standing up and therefore the closest person to answer that knock, he was the one who opened the door. He didn't exactly give Levi a smile of greeting, but at least he had enough courtesy to say, "Hey, Levi. What's up?"

"The elders need Hayley," Levi replied.

At the sound of her name, Hayley startled slightly, then got up from the couch. Trying to ignore Lucinda's curious stare, she said, "Me? What for?"

"We're going to strengthen the wards, and I want you to help."

"Okay." Although Levi didn't seem particularly agitated, Hayley couldn't help but experience a flutter of worry in the pit of her stomach. She hadn't even met the elders yet; there hadn't been any reason for her to. But now they needed her assistance. Her gaze moved to Lucinda, who hadn't moved from her spot on the sofa, but who also now seemed a bit nervous as she realized she was about to be left alone with Brandon.

Levi must have noticed her unease, because he said, addressing Lucinda directly, "It shouldn't take very long...I hope. I don't know for sure, though."

"It's all right," Brandon put in unexpectedly. "We can go for a walk or something, see a little of Jerome. Would that be okay?"

A flush tinged Lucinda's high cheekbones. "Um...sure. It looks like an interesting town. And it would be good to get some fresh air."

Whether or not the Santiago witch was really up to strolling around Jerome, Hayley didn't know. At the moment, though, they didn't have much of a choice. It would have been awkward in the extreme to leave Lucinda and Brandon alone in the flat, so Hayley could see why her brother would have opted instead for some sightseeing, something completely innocuous where they'd be out and around other people. And, the attack on Rachel's store notwithstanding, they should be safe enough while surrounded by civilians. The

Escobars were out for blood, but even they wouldn't want to do something that might draw the attention of the authorities by injuring someone who wasn't part of the McAllister clan.

"Well, then," Hayley said, "we'll leave you guys to it."

She got up from the couch and went to meet Levi at the door. Should she have gone back to her bedroom to get her purse? No, that seemed like a waste of time. It wasn't like she would need it for anything. She could always use Levi's phone to text Brandon if she really needed to.

As Hayley went out, she gave Lucinda a little wave, one that was returned with some hesitation. Well, the other witch probably had thought she'd have more time to recover from her captivity, wouldn't have to socialize quite yet, but fate had intervened.

No, not fate, Hayley thought as she descended the stairs with Levi. *The Escobars.*

To her surprise, Levi didn't take her out to the street, but around back, to where his truck was parked. "We have to start at the bottom of the hill," he explained as he put the key in the ignition. "It would take too long to walk, so we're driving."

"Got it." She waited until he'd backed out of his parking space to ask, "And the elders are cool with me butting in?"

"I don't know if 'cool' is the right word," he replied. "It's more that they need my help, and they know what your gift can do to my talents, so it makes sense to have your assistance." He lifted one hand from the steering wheel and put it on hers, where it had been resting on the seat. It was good to feel his strong fingers against hers, even if she knew that was the only touch he'd be able to spare her for a while. "That wasn't a human driver who hit the front of Rachel's store. It was something else the Escobars summoned."

"Goddess," Hayley whispered. "And right in the middle of Jerome."

"Exactly. So we have to do what we can to shore up our defenses. Maybe Connor and Angela could have helped, but they're busy, obviously. Besides, this is the sort of thing the elders should be doing. They just need some extra firepower."

He sounded casual and confident, but Hayley sneaked a quick sideways look at him and saw the way his lips pressed together, noticed how tense the muscles of his throat were. Not that she could blame him, but still, it was disconcerting to realize he maybe wasn't as in control of his emotions as he would have liked to be.

Was he frightened? She knew she was, could feel the creeping dread constricting her chest and making her stomach roil. Even if she tried to tell herself that she was perfectly safe, she wasn't sure she believed those inner reassurances. The car that had crashed into the store and injured Rachel had appeared out of nowhere, in bright daylight. Who was to say another one wouldn't materialize right here on Highway 89A as it wound its way down toward Cottonwood, accelerating and forcing them off the road? It was a very long drop…most likely a deadly one, if the small crosses and other memorials that cropped up here and there along the roadside were any indication.

After all, Angela's own mother had died here more than twenty-five years ago now, on an icy February night….

Hayley told herself to stop manufacturing problems, that it was now a sunny May day without a cloud in sight, let alone any black ice on the roadway. Besides, the man driving the motorcycle that had crashed and taken Sonya McAllister with it had been a civilian. Hayley was confident that Levi could handle whatever they might encounter, even if it turned out to be a modern-day version of the car from that Stephen King book, only this one powered by the Escobars' own malevolence.

However, Levi wasn't forced into a confrontation with a reanimated Plymouth Fury, because they reached the bottom of the hill without incident. The elders were already there, all of them standing by a white Volvo station wagon. They made an odd trio—a man in his late fifties, with graying brown hair and piercing blue eyes, one woman around the man's age, maybe a little older, with dishwater gray-blonde hair and dangling earrings and a long patchwork skirt, the other woman quite a bit younger, with a chic red bob, in black capri pants and black flats and a crisp green tailored shirt.

Bryce, Allegra, and Tricia, Hayley reminded herself. They were the elders, so of course she knew their names, but this was the first time she'd been able to put faces to those names. All those faces looked grim enough, although Tricia did smile at Hayley as she got out of Levi's truck.

"Hello, Hayley," she said. "I'm Tricia, and this is Bryce and Allegra. Levi says you're going to help us out today?"

"I hope so," Hayley returned, giving an awkward little wave at the other two elders. Allegra nodded in encouragement, her eyes kind, but Bryce just stared at Hayley, his expression indicating that he preferred to reserve judgment until he saw some results.

With any luck, she'd show him soon enough that she wasn't here merely to keep Levi company.

He had just gotten out of the truck as well, and stuck his thumbs in his belt loops as he stood there and surveyed the surrounding landscape. It looked innocuous enough to Hayley—although abandoned gas stations always seemed slightly creepy to her—but she knew the wards that protected Jerome had to be here somewhere.

"Right here," Bryce said, leading Levi over to one of the derelict, rusting gas pumps. "Can you feel it?"

Levi put his hand on the pump, his expression distant, as though he listened to far-off music only he could hear. "Yes, I feel it."

"We come down and refresh it every quarter of the year," Allegra added in as she walked over to join them. "As we do with the rest of the wards. But even though we did that less than a month ago, at the equinox, clearly it wasn't enough."

"Can you show me?"

"Of course. Tricia?"

The red-haired elder, who'd bent inside the Volvo to check on something, straightened and headed over to join her compatriots. "Is the coast clear?"

Bryce nodded. "We have a few minutes before the next car gets to this spot."

"All right."

The three of them joined hands, making a small circle. Eyes shut, they recited in unison,

Forces of earth, air, fire, and water
  Forces of light, forces of dark

Light of the sun, dark of the moon
Join here and create a golden rope
Shining day and night
Protection for the clan, for all McAllister blood
Here and now and always.

They stopped there, and let go of each other, breaking the circle. "That's it," Bryce said. He looked vaguely embarrassed, as though he really didn't enjoy having anyone else participate in an activity that probably looked to an outsider like a bunch of mumbo-jumbo. It wasn't, though. Magic was real, no matter what civilians might think.

"I felt it," Levi said. "Stronger this time. But I think I can make it stronger still. Hayley?"

She stepped over to stand in front of him, and he held out his hands palms up so she could take them in hers. Crazy how even this touch, ritual in nature and with the clan elders looking on, could still send a shiver through her. Goddess, he amazed her, awoke something in the core of her being she hadn't even known existed until she met him.

"I'll say the words again," he murmured to her. "You might feel the spell building, but that's normal. Just don't let go."

"I won't," she promised. No, she would never let go of him—no matter what.

He spoke the words of the spell, enunciating them clearly. As each syllable left his lips, she could sense how her power was twining with his, creating a shimmering barrier of golden light that seemed to stretch all the way across the road—and really, up the hillside until it intersected with the next switchback, blocking every turn of the highway until it reached the spot where the road leveled out slightly and headed into Jerome proper.

"Goddess," whispered Allegra. "It's so strong. I've never felt anything like that before."

"Nor I," Bryce said, although his tone sounded grudging. Was he annoyed because he hadn't been able to cast a spell that strong on his own, or simply because it was Levi and Hayley working together who had managed such a thing?

"It should keep out pretty much anything Joaquin Escobar tries to throw against it," Levi said. The words weren't boastful, just a simple statement of fact. "Actually, it might be a little too strong in some ways. It could also keep out some people who simply are harboring bad feelings, who don't wish to be in this place. You might find tourism dropping off a bit—those who aren't spiritually attuned to being here will find themselves turning around and going back down the hill."

"I think we can handle that," Tricia said briskly. "It's certainly better than the alternative. Now, let's go on to the next one."

"Which is where?"

"Up 89A, at the spot a few miles outside town where the overlook is located. There's also one in the center of Jerome, right by the fire station, but we'll do that one last. If we block the road up by the overlook, then there isn't much chance of anything getting past that."

Unless they fly in, Hayley thought uneasily as she recalled the black, leathery wings of the demons Levi had defeated, first in Sedona, and then at the gas station in Quartzsite. But no, surely the wards would block any kind of an approach. Just because she'd visualized them as a golden barrier cutting across the highway didn't mean they weren't protecting the town in other ways.

The next rendezvous having been determined, the elders climbed into Tricia's Volvo, while Hayley and Levi got back in his truck. They drove slowly through town, waiting for the inevitable tourists who jaywalked at inconvenient moments. She even caught a quick glimpse of Lucinda and Brandon, who stood outside the Jerome Winery tasting room. Brandon appeared to be pointing inside, while Lucinda's entire posture seemed to signal reluctance. Was Brandon trying to convince her to go inside to get a drink? That seemed very out of character for him—he was definitely a beer drinker—but maybe he'd decided his companion needed to relax a little.

Either way, Hayley knew she wouldn't find out until she got home and had a chance to talk to him alone. Or not. She might have sensed a hesitant interest from both of the parties involved, but she had a feeling that trying to push too hard would only make the situation that much more awkward.

The overlook Tricia had mentioned was a wide spot in 89A as it wound down the mountainside on its way into Jerome, offering an absolutely spectacular view of the Verde Valley, framed in cliff walls on either side. From up here, Hayley could see the narrow green ribbon of the Verde River cutting through the rolling, golden landscape, and on past the river to Sedona's red rocks.

Problem was, because the overlook offered such an amazing prospect, they weren't the only people who'd decided to park there. Bryce was scowling as he got out of the passenger seat of Tricia's Volvo, and it was easy to see why—at one end of the overlook sat a black Ford Explorer, a middle-aged couple leaning against the front bumper and aiming their phone cameras at the astounding view, while at the other end was parked a Harley, its rider taking advantage of the space the overlook afforded to adjust his saddle-bags and grab a drink of water.

"How long do you want to wait?" Levi asked in an undertone as he approached the three elders, who'd gone up to the protective guardrail and were doing their best to gawk at a sight they'd seen their entire lives.

"As long as it takes," Bryce replied. He dug his phone out of the pocket of his Carhartt jeans and pretended to take a few pictures. "It's not like we have a choice."

Well, that was true enough. They'd blocked one entrance into Jerome, and that had to help, but until all the wards were given the same treatment, the Escobars could still send the next wave of their army of darkness into the town. All right, one rogue demon-driven car wasn't exactly the same as an army, but—

"What is that?" the woman leaning against the Explorer asked, in tones loud enough that the group from Jerome could hear her clearly. She wasn't looking down toward the Verde Valley anymore, but had swiveled slightly so she was staring up toward the face of Mingus Mountain, stretching another thousand feet or so above them. "Is it an eagle?"

Hayley turned, as did the rest of the elders. A shocked gasp escaped her lips before she could stop it. No, that definitely wasn't an eagle. Not with those huge wings like black leather scraped over bone, or those glowing red eyes, or those skeletal fingers tipped with claws like scythes.

Levi's hand descended on her wrist in a grip of steel. "Stay with me," he said. "No matter what."

Her heart was pounding like thunder in a monsoon storm, but she nodded. "I will. Don't worry."

Raising his voice, he shouted, "Down, everyone. *Now!*"

The elders did as he said, because of course they knew Levi had a far better idea of what they faced than they probably did. Their magic might have been strong, but it wasn't the sort of magic that could prevail in an open confrontation with a demon summoned straight from the pit of hell. And because they dropped to the asphalt, using the car to help shield themselves, the couple from the Explorer did the same thing—or rather, they took another look at the nightmare descending from the sky and jumped into their vehicle.

A shot rang out, echoing off the canyon walls. Hayley allowed herself a shocked glance over one shoulder, saw the biker had pulled a gleaming blue-steel pistol from somewhere on his person and was calmly aiming it at the demon. Since the creature jerked, one wing flapping in sudden frenzy, it seemed that the bullet had connected.

"That won't work!" Levi yelled at the man, who looked ready to fire another shot.

"I hit the bastard!"

"Hitting it and hurting it are two entirely different things!"

That exchange was all they had time for, however, because now the demon was almost upon them. The beat of its wings stirred up a strange, acrid smell, as though it had brought with it the very stink of hell. Was that actually where it had come from, though? The McAllister witch clan didn't really believe in heaven or hell, but they did understand there were worlds beyond this one. Maybe one of those worlds was similar enough to hell that it might as well be the under-world described in Christian theology.

Hayley realized now wasn't the time for philo-sophical examinations of their enemies' origins. Not with the biker getting off shot after shot, all of which seemed to connect but didn't do much to slow down the demon, and not with Levi raising his hands, clearly preparing for a more effective kind of assault. She clung to his arm, willing every ounce of her strange gift to flow from her fingertips and into him, so he might meet the demon with the kind of blow that would finally have some kind of an effect.

Fire roared out from his hands, so fierce and bright, it looked as though his palms had turned into miniature flamethrowers. The demon screeched, the sound tearing at Hayley's ears, seeming to rip at the very fabric of the world. Standing next to them, the biker said, "Holy fuck," but he held his ground, pausing only to get a fresh magazine from an inside pocket of the vest he wore before continuing to fire.

Unbelievably, though, the creature didn't fall out of the sky, despite the onslaught. Its ragged wings beat at the air, and it spat at them, the greenish spittle hitting the ground just a few inches away from where Levi and Hayley stood. The asphalt began to smoke, crumbling as though it had been hit by acid.

However, Levi didn't back away, which meant Hayley had to stand there next to him, her hand still wrapped around his bicep, although every instinct she possessed was screaming at her to run, to jump into the truck and get the hell out of there. No, Levi lifted his hands again, and this time lightning rained down on the demon, so intense that she could actually see the blowback from the electric shocks dancing over the surface of the creature's scaly skin, like a weird glowing mist. This time it did stagger backward a few feet, something about the way its wings pummeled the air looking a little weaker, not quite so forceful.

Levi redoubled his attack, more lightning pouring into the demon. Now its skin was what began to smoke, pieces of it even peeling back to reveal the livid flesh below. It let out another cry and spat again, but this time the acidic saliva didn't even reach the parking lot, instead dropping into the brush on the hillside below the overlook. It crackled and shivered as the poison worked on the dry grass and manzanita and agave there, but it didn't seem as though any of the vegetation was going to actually burst into flame.

"More," Levi whispered to Hayley, and she gulped in a breath, tried to imagine her talent as a living thing, a river of golden energy flowing into the man who stood beside her. The scene around her blurred, but she blinked, forcing herself to stay focused, to not let herself succumb to the growing weakness she felt in her knees, the shaking of her legs. She had to keep standing. She'd promised Levi she'd stay with him, no matter what.

And now it wasn't simply bolts of lightning, but what looked like a wall of electricity, crackling with deadly blue-white fire as it rushed toward the demon. It screamed, and screamed…and then a silence fell that was almost as shocking as the creature's cries. After blinking, dazed, at the spot where the demon had been, Hayley realized that the wall of electricity had passed right through it, leaving behind only a strange, sooty mass that hung in the air for a second or two more before it shivered apart into thousands of pieces carried away on the wind, like a cloud of gnats dispersing.

Levi coughed and bent over slightly, hands braced against his thighs as though he had just run a marathon and was now desperately trying to catch his breath.

"Are you all right?" Hayley asked, still clinging to his arm. Actually, she prayed that he wouldn't collapse, because she knew she barely had the strength to stand on her own, let alone prop him up as well.

"I will be," he replied, his voice raw, hoarse. He coughed again, then straightened, and seemed to notice how the biker was staring at him, dark eyes wide with shock.

"What the ever-loving hell was *that?*" the man demanded.

"It was nothing." Levi's eyes narrowed, glinting like a pair of blue lasers between the heavy dark gold lashes. "You saw nothing here, did you?"

"I—" The biker blinked. "Saw what?"

"Exactly."

Another blink, and then the man shrugged and headed over to his Harley. Levi nodded, apparently satisfied that his little mind-control trick had worked, and went to the Explorer. The engine had just roared to life, and Hayley saw how the driver's hands gripped the steering wheel.

With an odd little smile, Levi made a "roll down the window" motion with one hand. To her surprise, the driver did as requested. "I don't want any trouble—"

"No trouble," Levi said smoothly. "There wasn't any trouble here, was there?"

"Um…no. I guess not. I mean, I didn't see anything. Did you, Sherri?"

"What?" the woman asked, her expression blank. "Was there something to see?"

"You folks have a nice day," Levi told them, still wearing that strange smile.

The driver put one hand to the side of his forehead in a sort of mock salute, and then he backed out of the parking area and headed onto the highway proper. For a man who hadn't seen anything out of the ordinary, he sure looked like someone in a hurry.

Hayley stared up at Levi, not sure how she should react to what she'd just observed. Best to be direct, she supposed. "What the hell was that?"

His shoulders lifted. "We couldn't let them leave here and tell others about what they'd seen. It's a very minor enchantment, really. They'll remember that they were at the overlook, but the past five minutes…those are gone."

He sounded so matter-of-fact about what he'd done. While she understood that it was better for everyone involved if those civilians didn't recall a single thing about the demon attack they'd just witnessed, it was still freaky to think about how Levi had casually meddled with their memories.

As she stared up at him, trying to think of how she should reply, the three elders approached. Allegra looked a little shell-shocked and Tricia's brow was knitted, as though she was still trying to process what she'd just seen, but Bryce was actually smiling.

"That was impressive," he said. "Fried that bastard to a crisp! I've never seen anything like it before in my life."

Hayley wished she could say the same thing, but since this was now her third demon attack in the same number of days, that wasn't really possible. It did seem as though this one had been stronger than the others, more difficult to vanquish even though it was alone.

"Thanks," Levi replied. His expression sobered. "We need to get the wards in place, though. That demon—it was the most powerful yet. For a minute there, I wasn't sure whether I'd be able to defeat it or not. The last thing we need is another one getting through while we're standing here, patting ourselves on the back."

"Of course," Tricia said. "We usually set this one right there at the end of the parking area."

Levi looked over at Hayley. His eyes met hers, worried, almost pleading. Was he afraid she didn't have the strength left to set another ward, or was it more that he feared she somehow condemned him for erasing the memories of those civilians?

She knew she was weak, but she'd call up whatever reserves of strength she needed in order to get that ward in place. As for the rest…it wasn't so much that she was judging Levi for what he'd done, but more that it was difficult to come to terms with the powers that lay hidden within him. Just when she thought she'd seen it all, he used another strange and formidable talent. It didn't change how she felt about him, but she understood then that she'd have to allow herself to be more flexible, to realize that just because Levi looked human, he really wasn't. He was something more.

"I'm fine," she said. "Let's get this ward up and running."

A corner of his mouth lifted, his clear blue eyes shimmering with gratitude and relief. "Yes, let's do that."

16

THERE WERE NO DEMONIC INTERRUPTIONS
after that. Levi and Hayley set the ward at the
overlook, and then the intermediate one by the
fire station, where Perkins Valley Road came
wandering into town after cutting across miles of
open country. Not too many people arrived in
Jerome by that route, since it was all dirt road,
some of it not very well tended, but every once in
a while some adventurous soul would decide that
the best way to get to the former mining town was
by off-roading it for most of the drive. At any rate,
Levi was relieved when the work was done.

Well, at least as relieved as he could be,
considering what had occurred less than a half
hour before.

As Levi and Hayley were setting the final
wards, Bryce received a text from Connor at the

hospital. It turned out that Rachel hadn't suffered anything worse than a concussion and two broken ribs, and so, even though the doctors wanted to keep her overnight for observation, she should be allowed to come home the next day. Tobias would remain with her, but Angela and Connor were on their way back from Cottonwood.

Good. Although Levi had managed to fend off this latest attack, the strength of the demon both worried and confounded him. How had the Escobars managed to summon such a powerful being? The strictures of such lore usually stated that a witch or warlock should never summon anything more powerful than themselves, lest it wrest itself from their control, but either the Escobars were growing reckless in their desire to inflict hurt on the McAllister clan, or their combined talents truly were as strong as the demon they'd conjured. Neither explanation was particularly reassuring.

The elders thanked Levi—and Hayley, although those thanks were somewhat subdued, as if they hadn't quite realized how much help she'd provided—for everything he'd done to protect the clan, and, by extension, the town. "We'll let Connor and Angela know what happened," Tricia said in her brisk, no-nonsense way, as if she was discussing something trivial, like a minor fender-bender on Main Street. "I have a feeling they'll want to talk to you, but in the meantime, you might as well try to rest a bit. You've earned it."

Yes, Levi thought he had. Although this human body of his was fit and strong, and in general up to whatever physical challenges he might wish to throw at it, right then he felt as though every muscle ached.

Come to think of it, he was experiencing a very human urge to have a drink. He saw that as a good sign—he wanted to react to situations as a human might.

"I will," he said. "We both will."

He took Hayley by the hand and walked with her down the hill toward the apartment that had been his home for the past year and a half. She didn't shy away from his touch, so whatever had troubled her as she watched him erase the memories of those civilians, she apparently had come to terms with it.

As the two of them came up to the building's entrance, Lucinda and Brandon approached as well. The two of them were smiling and talking, and clearly had enjoyed the past hour a great deal more than Levi himself had. They looked a little startled to bump into Levi and Hayley, but Brandon seemed to recover himself, saying, "Oh, hi. I was just about to text you, Hayley. Lucinda and I are heading down to Cottonwood—she wants to see the shop."

Clearly, this news surprised Hayley, because her eyes widened for a moment before she replied, "Are you sure that's safe?"

"I thought Cottonwood was safe," Brandon said, even as Lucinda began to frown slightly.

"Well, considering there was just another demon attack, and Cottonwood isn't warded—"

"Are you serious?"

"Yes, she's serious," Levi responded. "However, I think Cottonwood should be all right, as long as you stay around other people."

Brandon appeared to relax slightly at that comment. "No worries there. The shop always has at least five other guys working there, and if we don't come straight back to Jerome afterward, the only place we'd go is Old Town Cottonwood. Totally public."

"It should be fine, then."

Lucinda spoke for the first time. "No one will mind that I go, will they?"

Hayley offered her a reassuring smile. "Of course not. It's good for you to be getting out and about. Also, we just heard that Rachel is okay and should be coming home tomorrow, so that's one less thing to worry about."

"Oh, that's great news." Lucinda smiled as well, although something about her expression seemed slightly hesitant. Possibly she was wondering whether she would be going back to stay at Rachel's apartment that night, even though she'd have to be there alone.

Good question. Hayley didn't know if anyone had thought that far ahead, but they'd have to make some kind of arrangements. Maybe she could go crash there, too, so Lucinda wouldn't be by herself? That was something they could ask Angela, she supposed, once she was back home, especially if it turned out that the *prima* and *primus* wanted to talk to Levi.

Brandon nodded. "Anyway, if you need us for anything, just text me. We might stay down there for dinner…it depends on how long we hang out at the shop."

"But be back before it gets too dark," Levi warned him, and Hayley watched as her brother's expression turned guarded. Clearly, he would rather not have been reminded of the shadow looming over the town.

"We will. No worries there. 'Bye, Hayley."

The two of them headed toward the back of the building, where Brandon's car was parked. Hayley watched them walk away, then gave a small lift of her shoulders. "Let's go in."

An excellent idea. Before today, Levi had never minded the multiple flights of stairs he had to climb to get to his flat, figuring they were good exercise if nothing else, but now he was reminded of how weary he was, of how every step began to feel like torture. The confrontation with that demon had drained him far more than he first thought, and he didn't like the sensation. At least he wasn't alone, however—from the way Hayley followed a few stairs behind him, he guessed she must be almost as tired.

Eventually, though, they reached the landing, and he went to the door to his flat and turned the knob. "I was thinking about some wine," he said, but in a neutral tone, since he didn't know for sure whether Hayley was also in need of some liquid relaxation, or whether she wanted to go lie down and be alone for a while.

A bright smile spread over her face, though, and she replied, "That sounds perfect. After that nightmare, I need a drink."

"Then come on in."

She followed him inside his flat and into the kitchen, where he got down a pair of wine glasses from the cupboard. The bottle of chardonnay they'd opened the day before but never finished was still sitting in the refrigerator, so Levi got that out and poured some for each of them.

"I also have the leftover cheese and crackers," he offered, but Hayley shook her head.

"No, thank you. That is, not right now, anyway. That encounter with the demon kind of killed my appetite."

"I understand." Or, he thought he did, even

though he was starting to feel hungry himself. The battle up at the overlook in the canyon had sapped more of his strength than he'd thought. For now, though, the wine should suffice.

Hayley sat down on the couch, and Levi took a seat next to her, although not too close. More than anything he wanted to reach out to her, hold her in his arms and taste her sweet lips again, but he wasn't sure if that was what she wanted right now. She still seemed a little shaky, a little diffident, as if she hadn't yet quite come to terms with what she'd witnessed during that battle and in its aftermath.

"Lucinda seems like she's doing okay," Hayley said after sipping at her chardonnay. A small frown creased her fine brows. "Actually, I'm surprised at how well she's doing. I didn't think she'd bounce back that quickly, especially after what I heard about how long it took Danica to recover from the same kind of ordeal."

"They are different people," Levi said. He realized the words might have come off as sounding harsh, and so he went on, "That is, Lucinda had already had some experience of Matías Escobar. She knew what to expect, as terrible as it might have been. Also, although he used his powers to draw her to him, he did not otherwise hurt her. When Danica was taken by him, she also had to witness him and his cohorts using her friend to power their evil spells. That was not the situation at the Santiago house in Pasadena. Marisol was under Joaquin Escobar's power and passive but pleasant. I'm not even sure how much interaction she and Lucinda had."

"It was still terrible." Hayley's eyes were haunted, dark with imagined horrors.

Had he blundered in making those statements? All he'd been trying to do was point out why Lucinda Santiago might not have been as damaged by her interactions with Matías Escobar as Danica Wilcox had been. "Of course it was terrible," he said quickly. "I didn't mean to imply that it wasn't. But her experience was still different. She's a different person, too—older than Danica was when she underwent her ordeal. She had already formed mechanisms for coping with what Matías had done to her, whereas Danica had no such experience."

"I suppose that makes sense." Hayley ran a finger around the base of her wine glass, her gaze turned away from him. "And really, I'm glad to see she's doing so well, and glad that she and Brandon have hit it off. I wasn't really expecting that."

"Your brother doesn't enjoy the company of women?" Levi hoped he had phrased the question delicately enough. He'd wondered several times over the past few months whether Brandon McAllister was like his cousin Kirby, who obviously preferred to be with men. Not because of anything Brandon did or said, but more because Levi had seen women in town attempt to be flirtatious with his next-door neighbor and not get very far. He was always polite, but distant at the same time.

"Oh, he does. I mean, he's had girlfriends in the past, but it always seemed as if he was more wrapped up in working on his cars." Hayley swirled the straw-colored wine in her glass a few times, then sipped at it. "I guess he just hadn't met the right person yet."

"And you witches and warlocks tend to know when you've met the right person."

"That's the theory." Her shoulders lifted, and she added, "It doesn't always work out that way. I didn't think it was going to for me." As she spoke, she looked up from her wine glass so her gaze could meet his. "But then I met you."

Her eyes were so very blue, deep and vast as the oceans he'd never seen. Levi didn't recall setting down his glass, but he must have, because he reached out with both hands to cup her face, to feel the petal softness of her skin against his fingertips. Her lips parted, and that was all the invitation he needed to kiss her again, to taste the crispness of the chardonnay on her mouth, and something beneath that, a savor both sweet and wild, one that was only her. He lifted one hand from her cheek so he could take the wine glass from her hands and set it down on the coffee table as well.

It seemed the most logical thing in the world to push her down against the sofa cushions then, to feel the warmth and the curves of her body. She let out a startled little gasp, but she didn't try to stop him, only wrapped her arms around him and pulled him even closer. Levi could feel himself responding, sense how his body reacted to the way he lay on her, felt his groin touch hers. They were both fully clothed, but in that moment he began to understand what would come next...if she let him.

He cautiously moved one hand up under the T-shirt she wore, again marveling at the exquisitely soft texture of her skin. Would she tell him to stop now, or even move away slightly, thus signaling that she didn't want matters to progress any further?

But no, Hayley didn't say anything, only sighed softly as his hand moved upward, finally grazing the edge of her bra, fingers touching the lace of the garment. Here he paused, because he knew if he reached up to cup her breast, to feel her in such an intimate way, that he would have crossed over a boundary, one he couldn't easily retreat from. Was he ready for that? His body told him that he was, but even so....

"It's all right, Levi," she whispered. "I—I want you to. I want you. Is—is that okay?"

Oh, it was definitely more than okay. He nodded, replying, "It's more than I'd hoped for. You are more than I could have hoped for. But…."

"But what?"

"Do you mind if we go to the bedroom? It seems that it would be more comfortable than this couch."

She chuckled. "You're probably right."

Then her delicate features went quiet and still, as if she had just realized what she'd agreed to. Would she demur now that the situation had become so much more real? Levi forced himself not to say anything else, knowing that this was her decision to make, and if she decided to stop now, he would have to abide by her choice. Perhaps it was all too soon….

A smile spread over her lips, and she reached up to brush the hair away from his forehead. Still smiling, she asked, "Are you going to show me your bedroom, Levi?"

Was she really doing this?

Yes, she was really doing this.

They got up from the sofa and walked back to

Levi's room. The layout of the flat was almost identical to her brother Brandon's, only mirrored, so here the larger bedroom occupied the same position as the room Hayley was borrowing at her brother's place. Like the rest of Levi's apartment, the room was conspicuously neat, with a queen-size bed in a simple oak frame, and an oak bedside table and low dresser. More black and white photos of Sedona and Jerome hung here as well.

She didn't pay much attention to the decor after that, because Levi was kissing her again, and then they fell onto the bed, his weight on her as he kissed her over and over, his hand once again slipping up under her T-shirt. This time, however, his fingers did close around her breast, and she gasped aloud, her entire body thrilling at his touch, his skin so warm, even through the lacy fabric of her bra. To help him out, she grasped the hem of her T-shirt and pulled it up and over her head. In response, he buried his face in the valley between her breasts, both hands now closing on her, caressing.

Oh, Goddess, that was good. It would be even better without the bra in the way, though. She reached back and undid the clasp, since she figured Levi might have a difficult time managing that task. He pulled the bra away, and his eyes widened.

"You are so very beautiful," he whispered.

A warm thrill went through her. Hayley knew she'd never had a man gaze at her the way Levi did then, as though she was a goddess, and deserving of his worship. Not that she wanted him to worship her—she wanted him to make love to her.

And she also wanted to get his T-shirt off as well.

Her fingers curled around the edge of the garment and tugged it upward. At once he reached down and grasped it as well, so in less than a second it was up and over his head, and tossed somewhere on the floor.

Oh, dear lord, he was amazing. Never in her life had she seen a man so perfectly sculpted, so, well…godlike. She wanted to run her hands over the muscles of his chest and stomach just so she could convince herself that they were real.

Which was exactly what she did. His skin was smooth, with only a light sprinkling of golden hair at the center of his chest. The muscles underneath that skin were so rock hard, she was sure she could've bounced a quarter off his stomach.

And speaking of rock hard….

She grasped his belt buckle and pulled his belt through the loops, loosening it so she could undo the button and zipper of his jeans. He made a small, shocked sound, as if he hadn't guessed that she would be quite so bold. Well, she was going to be bold. They were here now in bed together, and she needed him. Wanted him. Needed to feel his skin against hers, wanted to feel him in her. Maybe then she'd be able to forget how that demon had come flying out of nowhere, how she still didn't feel quite safe, despite the wards Levi had set.

Her fingers slipped under the waistband of his jeans, and the briefs he wore underneath. A couple of tugs, and he was free, completely naked, the pants kicked off to land somewhere beyond the foot of the bed.

Oh, dear Goddess, he was definitely human. Every inch. Her fingers closed on his erection, and she began to slowly move her hand up and down. His head rocked back, and a moan escaped his throat.

Careful, she told herself. *He's never done this before. You don't want to make him come before you're ready.*

That was for sure. Yes, she could always wait for him to bounce back, so to speak, but she'd rather not. After caressing him a few more times, she let go so she could undo the zipper on her own jeans and slide them off. Eyes gleaming, he took hold of her panties and tugged them down as well. And then they were both naked, bodies clasped together, as he kissed her throat and worked his way to her breast, his mouth closing on her so his tongue could glide over her nipple.

A jolt of heat went through her, almost as electric as the bolts he'd flung at the demon earlier. No, she didn't want to think about that. She only wanted to focus on the exquisite sensations flooding through her body as he suckled on her, even as one hand moved down to slip between her legs.

This time she cried out, glad that no one was around to hear. Because she couldn't stop the gasping moans that escaped her lips as Levi stroked her. How did he even know to do that? Instinct? Had he studied human sexuality?

Right then, she realized she really didn't care. All that mattered was the way he made her feel.

She came hard, clamping down on his fingers as the orgasm rushed through her, the moan that accompanied it really more of a scream. And when she opened her eyes, she saw him watching her with a surprised tenderness, as though he was happy he'd been able to evoke such a response from her, even if he wasn't quite sure how it had all happened.

Time to return the favor.

Hayley reached down and stroked him a few more times, then wrapped her legs around him and pulled him close, felt him brush against her entrance. He gasped, but still seemed to hesitate.

"Yes, Levi," she whispered. "It's all right. Please."

He apparently didn't need any encouragement beyond those words, because she felt him push against her, and then into her, sliding so deep she let out a gasp of her own. Good Goddess, he was big. It had been a while for her, so it took a moment for them to find their rhythm, for them to begin moving together in unison. Once they did, though, every stroke seeming to drive him deeper, she shut her eyes and focused on the sensation of him filling her, of realizing she felt even closer to him now than she did when she mingled her powers with his.

His breathing began to speed up, and she knew he was probably going to come soon. That was fine—she could feel the spreading heat within her, the orgasm building. All she could do was cling to him as he thrust into her, faster now, starting to lose his rhythm as the moment approached.

And then he groaned, and she cried out, and they rode the wave together, her fingers digging into the muscles of his shoulders as his hands clasped her by the waist. The world roared in her ears, and she clung to him, needing to feel him, to have him anchor her to this spot, to make sure she didn't dissolve into a being of pure ecstasy.

The glow began to fade after a moment, and

Hayley pulled in a breath, made herself repeat the charm to Blessed Brigid, the one that would keep her from conceiving. Her love for Levi was fragile and new, and the entire clan was facing an enemy the likes of which none of them had ever seen. As the charm itself said, now was not the time.

His hand passed over her tumbled hair, and he breathed into her ear, "I love you, Hayley."

"I love you, Levi," she said. Yes, she did. She knew that now, knew she could never be with anyone else. Maybe in the future their relationship would cause some problems with her parents, but for this blessed moment, she could only revel in her closeness to him, could only breathe in the warm scent of his skin and feel the welcome weight of his body against hers.

"I never," he began, then paused. Very gently, he kissed her cheek, and, just as gently, eased himself out of her.

She knew that in a minute she'd need to head to the bathroom to get cleaned up, but for now, she only wanted to be in bed with him. "You never what?" she asked softly.

"Intellectually, I knew what making love what supposed to be like." He sat up and ran a hand through his tousled blond hair. "But I never realized it could be like that. No wonder it occupies such a large space in people's minds."

"Well, it's not *all* we think about," Hayley teased him. "Just mostly."

He grinned, his blue eyes lighting up like sunlight on a mountain lake. "I can see why."

Her body still thrummed from their contact, from the way he'd filled her. In fact, the mere thought made her think that maybe they should fall back into each other's arms, and go for another round. After all, they had this precious time alone together, without worrying about whether her brother would wonder exactly what they were up to. They might not get this chance again for a while.

In the next moment, though, Levi's pants began ringing. Or, to be precise, the phone in the back pocket of his jeans, still lying on the floor, started to ring.

Hayley wanted to tell him to ignore it, but she knew that wasn't a very good idea. Not with everything that had been going on. So she gave him a reluctant nod, and he slid off the bed and went to retrieve his phone. At least his doing so gave her a chance to get a good look at his ass, which was just as sculpted and perfect as the rest of him.

He'd been smiling, but his expression went flat and still as soon as he answered the call. "Yes, Angela. Yes." A long pause. "No, it's not a problem. We can be up there in a few minutes. All right. We'll see you then."

No point in asking who it was, not when Hayley had heard Levi say the *prima*'s name. It sounded like Angela and Connor were back home…and they needed to talk. She watched as Levi gathered up his underwear and jeans, and began to put them back on.

"They want to see us," he said, his tone somewhat apologetic. Had he picked up her thoughts about wanting to make love again, or had he simply been thinking the same thing?

"I kind of got that." Hayley pushed herself off the bed. "Give me a couple of minutes to get cleaned up, okay?"

"Of course."

She picked up her own discarded clothing and retreated to the bathroom. A few careful dabs of cold water on her face, a quick wipe-up to get rid of the aftermath of their lovemaking. That was about all she had time for before she pulled on her clothes. Yes, she'd grab the brush from her purse and tidy her hair, and put on some fresh lip gloss, but she wasn't sure whether that would be enough.

No matter what she did, Hayley had a sinking feeling that Angela would look at her and Levi and know exactly what they'd been up to for the past hour….

17

"Tricia called me," Angela said briskly, once Levi and Hayley were seated on a couch facing her and Connor. "She told me what happened. But I wanted to hear it from you, too. Are you absolutely sure the wards will protect us now?"

Levi wanted to shrug, although he knew such a gesture would only make it appear as though he was not terribly concerned about the situation, and nothing could be further from the truth. It was more that he couldn't tell Angela with any confidence whether or not the town was safe. Yes, he'd put everything he could into those wards, and with Hayley's extraordinary gift lending them strength, they certainly were an order of magnitude beyond anything that had protected the town before now.

Even so, he didn't know whether it would be enough.

It was hard not to turn toward the woman who sat next to him, to once again drink in her beauty. He couldn't forget how it had felt to touch her, to bury himself in her glorious body. The only thing he wanted was to be able to do that again…and again.

Somehow he managed to force his thoughts back to the matter at hand. "How can I say that I'm absolutely sure? The wards are very strong. Hayley and I made sure of that. But because I can't know the actual extent of Joaquin Escobar's powers—or his son's—I also can't know for sure that this last demon was the most powerful one they're capable of summoning."

Angela and Connor exchanged a glance, one that Levi couldn't quite read. From time to time, he'd wondered whether they were somehow capable of communicating without speaking. He didn't have any true evidence of such a gift, but they did seem to share an extraordinarily strong rapport. And when a *prima* and *primus* were joined as those two were, something that hadn't happened in all the recorded history of witch-kind, who knew what they might be able to do?

"Tricia said it was strong, that at first it looked like you had trouble destroying it."

"I did," Levi said simply. He didn't see this as a

failing on his part. One could only work with the hand one was dealt, nothing more. "I could only be glad that there was just the one. Perhaps it was beyond the Escobars' power to send more than a single demon of such strength. We can hope, anyway."

Neither Angela nor Connor looked very hopeful. In fact, they appeared more tired than anything else. It had to have been difficult for Angela to see the woman who'd raised her now brought down by the Escobars' machinations. Levi wondered where the twins were, because the house was quiet, with not even the low murmur of a television on in the background. Possibly they were still being watched by the woman Levi had spotted playing with them earlier, and the *prima* and *primus* had put off bringing the children home until after this interview was concluded. It made sense.

"Where does it end?" Angela asked then. "I mean, it sounds as though we've shored up our defenses as much as we possibly can. We were lucky this time that at least the demon came into our territory at a point where not many people were around—and they won't remember it, thanks to your Jedi mind trick—but we can't go on like this, always worrying whether another demon is going to appear and attack someone else in the clan."

"Or create a disturbance that's impossible to hide," Connor added. He rubbed at his forehead, as though a sudden headache pained him. "This town has more than a million tourists pass through it every year. All we need is the hordes of hell to descend on the Haunted Hamburger or something, and the next thing we know, Jerome's on the front page of the *National Enquirer*."

Which of course wouldn't do at all. The witch clans survived by being discreet about their powers and abilities. They couldn't afford that kind of exposure, even if it didn't also involve personal pain and injury for those they loved.

"I wonder if that's part of Joaquin Escobar's game," Hayley said then, her tone thoughtful. "I mean, it's obvious he's out for revenge, but he could have gone after Rachel in a more subtle way than having a car with no driver crash into her store right in front of everybody. Luckily, it drove away right afterward, so I don't think any of the civilians who were around saw much of anything, but—"

"That's true," Angela said. Her face was pale, but she didn't try to refute Hayley's words. "If we're put off balance by trying to keep everything on the down-low, then we're wasting energy we might otherwise be spending on trying to keep our people safe."

"But how do we stop him?" Connor asked.

"We've gone into his territory once and lived to tell the tale, but now that Joaquin Escobar knows that Levi has the power to teleport in and out of a place, he must be even more on his guard. I don't think we can manage that kind of trick again."

"Plus, we're not exactly the sort of people to send assassins after someone," Angela responded. "Even if he might deserve it. I think a lot of us were willing to settle for a kind of—well, not a peaceful coexistence, but if he'd just allowed us to take Lucinda and cut his losses after that, we might have let the rest of it go."

"But didn't he enslave their *prima*-in-waiting?" Hayley asked. "Kill the former *prima* and her consort? How could we possibly let *that* go?"

Again Connor and Angela were silent. Levi could almost see them wrestling with the moral dilemma Hayley had put in front of them. At last Connor said, "I don't know if it's that simple. The witch clans, in general, don't interfere in the business of other clans, even if that business happens to be dirty. Right or wrong, that's just how it's been for centuries. Things have gotten muddled around here lately, simply because there's been so much recent intermarriage among the three witch families here in Arizona, but we still didn't have anything much to do with clans outside the state."

"In this case, it's Matías who started things, though," Levi said. "If he hadn't come here and stirred up trouble by kidnapping your witches and murdering one of them, then none of us would be here having this conversation. It seems logical that we'd need to do something about it by finishing what Matías started."

"By doing what, exactly?" Angela demanded. "Going to California and attacking the Escobars there? None of us are equipped for that sort of thing—even counting the feud between the Wilcoxes and the McAllisters, there hasn't been outright warfare between witch clans for more than a hundred years. And for good reason. Those sorts of conflicts never turned out well."

It was a difficult problem. The McAllisters were not warriors. Levi didn't know as much about the Wilcoxes, or the various talents of that clan's numerous members; it was possible that they had more among them whose gifts were suited to magical battle. The same for the de la Pazes. And yet, he didn't want to contemplate what such a conflict could do to the Arizona clans. They were not warlike people. But unless they did something, those demons would keep coming.

Unless....

A thought struck him, one so audacious that he honestly contemplated for a moment whether he'd lost his mind. It wasn't possible...

...unless it was.

Perhaps it wasn't feasible to have the McAllisters and Wilcoxes go charging into Pasadena and openly attack Joaquin and Matías Escobar. However, the rogue warlocks' ability to raise havoc would be greatly reduced if they were suddenly unable to call any more demons to do their bidding.

And the easiest way to do such a thing?

Close the portal that connected the demons' world to this one.

"What are you thinking, Levi?" Hayley inquired. Her tone wasn't precisely suspicious, but it sounded as though she guessed that he was contemplating a notion she wouldn't very much like.

"Yes, Levi," Angela put in. "If you have an idea, we're all ears."

Curious expression. However, Levi knew this was not the time to delve into the idiosyncrasies of the English language. "These demons must travel to this world, because obviously they're not part of it. To come here requires stepping through a portal that a warlock has conjured. All I have to do is make sure that the portal is closed."

"'All you have to do'?" Hayley repeated in incredulous tones. From the way she stared at him, it was clear that she didn't like his idea at all. "This isn't exactly like installing a new deadbolt, you know."

"I do know," Levi said calmly. He reached over

and laid his hand on top of hers, hoping that simple touch would be enough to offer some reassurance. Perhaps it would have been better to take her in his arms, but he didn't know if such a display of affection in front of the *prima* and *primus* would be appropriate. "I know because I came from outside the world as well. I know where these demons come from."

"So you came from there, too?" Angela asked. She'd taken Connor's hand, as though seeing Levi offer comfort to Hayley had led her to seek it from her own husband. "The place of the demons?"

"Not exactly. Our planes touched, but they are not the same. A good thing, too, because if the Escobars had ever learned of my existence, they might have set about finding a way to exploit my powers." Levi hesitated, trying to think of the best way to explain a concept that had no true analogue in the physical world. "I was a being of no substance, of pure spirit, if you will. That's why I'm able to use all the powers that manifest in human witches and warlocks, rather than being confined to the one or two most of you have to work with."

Connor shook his head, his expression showing that he was not entirely convinced. "It sure seems as if Joaquin Escobar has more than a couple of different talents at his command. My brother did as well. And even Angela and I can step outside our native-born gifts if the situation calls for it."

All true, of course. Levi paused for a moment, doing his best to think of a way to explain concepts that were not easily grasped by the human mind. "Your situation is different, because you and Angela use your powers to bolster one another. As far as your late brother's gifts are concerned, it seemed his talent was magic itself, a very rare thing. It could be that Joaquin has a similar gift, or that his powers as a null allow him to draw other people's magical energies to him so he can exploit them at will."

"Sort of like a human black hole," Hayley offered. The phrase sounded vaguely amusing, but he could tell from the grim set of her lips that she wasn't joking.

"Yes, something similar to that," Levi said. "Anyway, the demons all come from the same plane, the same world, even though their individual strengths and weaknesses vary among them, just as they do among witches and warlocks. Jack Sandoval told me that as many as twelve were summoned to cast the terrible magic that returned Matías Escobar's powers to him. I can believe this, because to reverse a spell cast by a *prima* and *primus* working together is no small thing. I have to wonder if the summoning of so many demons at a single time was the work of his late daughter, her special talent, because otherwise, why wouldn't Joaquin have done the same this time around?"

Angela shuddered. "Thank the Goddess that he didn't."

"Yes, but we know he is unscrupulous to the extreme. If he could have, he would have—which means we need to seize the moment while we can, while he's recovering from this latest defeat." That was one thing Levi had noticed—these attacks did not come immediately on the heels of one another, but were spaced apart by hours or even days, intervals that could be based on how much time Joaquin needed to regain his strength following his newest summoning. Because the demon Levi had just vanquished was very strong, it stood to reason that its conjuring must have sapped a good deal of the Escobar warlock's strength. But recover he would, and try again… unless they did everything they could to stop him.

"And by 'seizing the moment,' you mean closing the portal to the demons' plane," Connor said.

"Exactly. I know where to find it, I think."

"You think?" Hayley said. She shifted on the couch so she faced toward Levi. Even now her mouth looked faintly swollen from his kisses, and he had to force himself not to think about how beautiful she was, how much he would miss her if…

…well, if things didn't turn out as he hoped.

"It's not as though a map exists of these things," he replied, making sure he kept his voice level, patient. While he understood her concern, he also knew that they didn't have much time to waste. "It's more that I will need to rely on my instincts. They've served me well enough so far, which means I need to trust them in this. Besides, it's the only way. If I don't close that portal, then the demons will keep coming…and sooner or later there will be too many, or one so powerful that even I can't stop it. What Joaquin is doing… it's somewhat like exercising a muscle. With more exercise, that muscle gains strength. Each time he successfully summons a demon to this world, he also gets stronger and better at what he does. Eventually, he'll be impossible to beat."

That pronouncement only made Angela and Connor look at each other again, the strain in their faces clear enough, even though the afternoon was beginning to shade toward evening, and the light in the living room had started to fade. Sitting next to him, Hayley was pale and mute with worry, her fingers now twined with his, their sudden chilliness telegraphing her fear.

Was he afraid? Levi didn't know for sure. He had lived each day in this world as a gift, knowing that he had never been created for this purpose, that in the grand scheme of the universe, he wasn't supposed to be here. And he had known that someday he might have to return whence he came, although he'd always hoped that wouldn't be the case, that the world where he lived now could be his permanent home. Now the thought of leaving pained him far more than it would have only a few days ago, because of Hayley. He knew he loved her. He wanted to spend each day with her, wake up beside her. Perhaps, if the Goddess the McAllisters believed in was merciful, he and Hayley might one day have a family.

But he would risk all of that to ensure she was safe from the depredations of the Escobars' demon minions.

After a long moment, Angela said, "What do you need from us?"

There really was nothing they could do, unfortunately. Their magical gifts were prodigious, but even Connor and Angela could not go where he needed to travel. He had heard that she had once walked in the otherworld, had helped to heal the rift between hers and Connor's long-dead fore-bears, but the afterlife frequented by human spirits was very different from the plane the demons haunted.

Nothing human had ever ventured there. Levi

would only risk the journey because, while his body was human, his soul was not.

"Very little," he said. "I'll go with Hayley and get something to eat, because I might as well make sure I'm fortified for the ordeal. You can sit with me when I 'go,' if you like, but it won't make much of a difference. If something goes wrong, you won't be able to bring me back."

"Are you sure?" Angela asked. Her mouth had set, and a spark of defiance flared in her green eyes. "I've had experience walking in the otherworld, too."

"This isn't precisely the otherworld," he replied. "Your world of the spirits is still connected to this world, because everyone there was once human. This…this is entirely different."

The *prima* swallowed, suddenly looking rather pale. "We'll be with you—even if you say it won't make a difference."

"All right. Then let us all meet at my flat in an hour. I think we can risk that much of a delay." Levi squeezed Hayley's hand gently, then untangled their fingers. "Let's go get something to eat."

She stared at him, stricken. "Do you really think I can eat at a time like this?"

"Well, I need to, and you might as well have something. I'm not sure how long this will take, and you might be sitting up with me well into the night."

Her lips pressed together, and she nodded, then got up from the couch without saying anything else. Levi took that as his cue to stand as well. "We'll see you in an hour."

"We'll be there," Connor said, while Angela murmured her assent.

There was nothing else to say, so Levi headed for the front door and opened it for Hayley, then closed it behind them once she stood on the porch. From the stiff set of her shoulders, it seemed clear enough that she didn't feel liking talking right then.

Very well.

On to his last meal.

18

THIS HAD TO BE A NIGHTMARE. SURELY AT some point she'd wake up—hopefully, next to Levi—and realize she had been asleep this whole time, that all this talk of demons and portals and travel to other planes of existence had only been a dream conjured by a brain with far too much weighing on it.

But no, there was Levi calmly eating a piece of pizza, occasionally pausing to take a sip of water. While she'd thought there had never been a better occasion to have a drink, he'd demurred, saying that the wine might ruin his focus when it came time to walk in the demons' dimension.

How in the world was she supposed to reply to a comment like that?

Basically, she didn't. She forced a piece of Greek pizza with feta and Kalamata olives down because her body had started to feel hungry, even if the thought of food seemed repellent to her. Should she have another? No, that would surely lead to disaster. One piece would get her through…whatever was coming next.

Voice pitched low, so the civilians at the booth across from theirs wouldn't be able to hear anything, she said, "There has to be another way."

"There isn't. At least, not one with as little risk to the rest of the clan—or clans, since this affects everyone in Arizona." Levi set down his half-eaten piece of pizza and gazed across the table at her, his expression pleading. "I have to try. If I'm not successful, then you may have to attempt a more head-on sort of confrontation. But let's hope it doesn't come to that."

Talk about your understatements. He might have been a part of her life for only a few days, but Hayley knew she couldn't face the consequences if he should fail. How could she even think about a world with no Levi in it? No, it wouldn't happen. He'd faced down the Escobar-summoned demons three times now, and had been successful each time.

Yes, but that was only a few at a time, she thought then. *He's going to a full plane occupied by those things. How in the world can he possibly survive that?*

Of course she had no idea. Levi seemed confident as he sat there and ate his pizza and drank from his glass of water, but how much of that was false bravado put on so she wouldn't worry any more than she already was?

No, she wouldn't accept that. Bravado was not a concept she could associate with the man she loved. If he thought he could do this, it was because he'd mentally weighed the risks and found them acceptable. He wouldn't do anything crazy, not when he had her to come back to.

Oh, that sounded terrible. She knew she wasn't Levi's reason for living, or anything like that. He was doing this because he wanted to save all of them, not just her. But…

"I love you," he said softly. "I want to survive. Of course I do. Tell me you understand."

Hayley wasn't sure if she did. Selfishly, she wanted to grab him by the hand and run, run far away from the Escobars and their scheming. Problem was, once they'd suborned the entire Santiago clan, would they be satisfied, or would they want to keep going, pulling more and more witch clans under their spell? All her family, and the Wilcoxes and de la Pazes as well?

No, this wasn't Levi blindly throwing himself away. He knew what was at stake. His decision had more than a hint of "it is a far, far better thing I do now, than I have ever done" about it, but she couldn't fault him for that. She had to allow him to do this, no matter how much it hurt.

"I understand, Levi," she replied. "And I love you, too. More than anything in the world."

He smiled at her, but she couldn't find much reassurance in that smile. Actually, it hurt to look at him, to see his beauty and his brilliance, and worry that it was about to be taken away from her forever.

They finished their meal, and had the leftovers boxed up so they could take the extra pizza home with them. And wasn't that an irony, pretending that Levi would even be around to eat those leftover pieces of Greek pizza with white sauce.

No, he would be. Hayley knew she had to believe that, or she'd break down sobbing right then and there.

They walked down to their building, and climbed the stairs to Levi's flat. No sign of Lucinda and Brandon, and Hayley couldn't tell if she was annoyed or relieved. She supposed it was good that they'd stayed in Cottonwood for dinner, because that meant they were still enjoying one another's company, and yet, right then she wanted her brother to be there so she wouldn't have to go through this alone. Yes, Angela and Connor were coming over, but Hayley didn't know them very well. If the worst happened, she didn't know if she'd be able to hold it together in front of the *prima* and *primus*.

Levi was calm and matter-of-fact as he went about the apartment, turning on a lamp here and there, before he headed into the bedroom so he could straighten the rumpled bedclothes they'd left behind. "It's best if I lie down in here," he explained as he smoothed away the last traces of the lovemaking they'd shared in that bed only a few hours earlier. "I could lie on the couch, I suppose, but the bed is more comfortable, and I need as few distractions as possible."

"I understand," Hayley said. Did she? It somehow hurt to watch Levi make it appear as if nothing had happened in that bed, as if those ecstatic moments they'd shared were being erased forever. Tears pricked at her eyes, and she swallowed, telling herself not to be an idiot. Nothing could change the time she'd spent with Levi in that bed. She was only starting to lose it because she feared she'd never be able to lie in his arms again.

He came close and touched a hand to her cheek, then bent and kissed her very gently. "Don't cry, Hayley. I need you to be strong for me."

"I'm not sure I'm very good at that." She reached up and brushed away her tears with her fingertips, knowing that she didn't want Angela and Connor to see her all weepy and fragile.

"Oh, yes, you are. You stood with me against the demons. You never left my side. You're stronger than you think. You just need to keep on being strong."

She nodded, not trusting herself to speak. At that moment, a knock came at the door, and Levi passed a caressing hand over her hair before he went out into the hallway so he could answer the knock.

Hayley took a deep gulp of air and followed him. *Be strong,* she told herself. *Be strong for him, even if you can't do it for yourself.*

Levi had already let the *prima* and *primus* into the flat. They offered Hayley a pair of awkward smiles, as though they knew all too well how hard she was working to stay calm.

"Would you like some water?" Levi asked, and they both shook their heads. "All right," he said, then continued, "I will lie down on my bed, and you'll keep watch on me as I 'travel.'"

Angela frowned slightly. "Your body stays here?"

"Yes. We are all spirit on that plane—the demons only become corporeal when they enter this world, since it is a world of matter. Much as I only took on a body once I arrived here, although of course my form is very different from theirs."

The *prima* appeared to absorb that explanation, and nodded. "I guess it makes sense—that sounds sort of like when I did my spirit walk. Do you have chairs we can bring in?"

"I have one in the bedroom already, and we can get two more from the breakfast set by the kitchen."

Some time was taken up fetching the chairs and squeezing them into the bedroom, which really didn't have the space for extra furniture—the chair Connor sat in ended up halfway in the hall. Once that task was done, however, Levi climbed onto the bed and lay down, his legs straight in front of him, his hands folded on his chest.

"How will we know if you're successful?" Hayley asked.

"I'll wake up and come back to myself. If I don't awake…then you'll know my soul was defeated on the demons' plane, and doomed to remain there forever."

She swallowed, and willed the one piece of pizza she'd eaten to remain where it was. "Oh, is that all?" she responded, trying her best to make light of the situation. Unfortunately, her voice cracked on the last syllable, and she could feel the tears start to her eyes once more.

He lifted one hand from his chest and extended it so he could touch her fingers. Briefly, just enough for her to feel the warmth of his flesh. He seemed so real. He was more real to her than anyone she'd ever met. Surely she couldn't have been lucky enough to have him come into her life, only to lose him when she realized how much he meant to her.

"I'd best go now," he said. "We really don't know when Joaquin Escobar will make his next attempt to summon more demons."

"We'll be here," Angela promised him. "May the grace of the Goddess go with you."

And before any of them could say anything else, he'd shut his eyes. His body went so still, Hayley couldn't even see the rise and fall of his chest as he breathed. She wanted to reach out to him, to place her fingers on his wrist and feel his pulse, reassure herself that he was alive. But she stopped herself, because she didn't know if even that light a touch might wake him from his trance.

"Now what?" she asked.

"Now," Angela replied, after a quick glance over at Connor, "we wait."

Darkness swirled around him, darkness given shape and form, like a heavy fog black as tar. Levi pushed through that darkness, even as he felt its negative energy, its desire to thrust him back to the world he'd come from. It knew he was not supposed to be here.

But he willed himself to keep moving forward, to break through that dark fog. It relented at last, allowing him to appear on a vast, empty plain, the ground beneath his feet stony and gray, mirroring the sky above him. Iron-hued clouds rushed overhead at unimaginable speeds, looking like the time-lapse images he'd seen in the human world. This was no time lapse, however; they truly were moving that quickly.

The portal he'd used to come here was not the same one utilized by the demons, because each portal had to resonate with the particular energy of the being it was transporting. That was something of a relief, because at least then he wouldn't have to worry about those dark beings using the very doorway he'd traveled through to get back to the world of the living.

He stood there for a moment, letting his senses range out and away from him, seeking the other portal, the one Joaquin Escobar had conjured to allow the denizens of this realm to escape and wreak their own particular havoc. Yes, there it was—a dark, gaping maw, one which had a strange, glittering lightness at its heart, an enticing glimpse of the world beyond. No wonder the demons would be drawn to it, would seek to travel to find that light, which was the warmth and life energy of the human world.

In this world, he did not need to walk; he had a body here, although it was only a construct of his mind, was still pure spirit. But all he had to do was visualize that portal, imagine himself standing next to it, and he was there. This close, the portal's energy was far more apparent; Levi's hair was tousled by an unseen wind, the opening in the world pulling everything in its vicinity toward it. He stood fast, though, would not allow himself to be drawn through. True, everything he loved was on the other side of that portal, but he could not use it. His flesh was human, and would be destroyed the second he attempted to go through.

Besides, he could not return to that place until he was done with his work here.

He paused for a moment, thinking of the best way to heal the tear in the world. Then he recalled how Rachel would sometimes sit during quiet spells at the store with a piece of embroidery, the sharp needle flashing in the sunlight as it moved in and out of the cloth, pulling the fine silk floss with it. He did not have a needle with him, but he didn't require one. This gash would be sewn up with magic.

Magic lived in his core, was a part of him the way it could never be with human witches and warlocks, because they were human first, and magic second. Magic was not like air to them, as it was to him. All he had to do was breathe in, and ask the power to come forward.

The ground beneath his feet rumbled, and the portal began to shrink in size, slowly at first, and then with increasing speed. It had started out wide enough to drive his truck into, and now it was barely the size of the silver basin Allegra Moss used to cast her spells of healing and unity under the light of the full moon.

A beating of heavy, leathery wings and a wash of foul-smelling air told Levi that he was no longer alone. He had to leave off the spell of mending, and throw up a wall of protection around himself. This was accomplished with barely a second to spare, because as soon as he was surrounded by that shimmering barrier, a trio of demons appeared above him, wings churning at the thick air. Their eyes flashed scarlet with rage, rage at his trespassing here in a realm that wasn't his own.

"You have no place here, mortal," said the demon in the center of the trio. He seemed somewhat larger and bulkier than the other two.

"I will leave as soon as my work is done," Levi replied.

"Your work?" retorted the demon on the left. "Your only work is to leave before the life is squeezed from your throat."

The third demon narrowed its blood-colored eyes. "This one smells human, but I do not think he is entirely mortal. He has a whiff of the other-world about him."

"That makes sense," the largest demon remarked. "Otherwise, I do not see how he could have come here. Only—"

"It doesn't matter what he is," the demon on the right said. "It only matters that we keep him from doing whatever it is he planned to do."

That was the only signal Levi required. Demons could be talkative, but their sometimes chatty nature never prevented them from attending to the matter at hand. He had to strike first, while they were otherwise occupied.

Neither flame nor lightning would affect them here on their home plane. Those sorts of attacks worked in the human realm, because the demons' bodies were made corporeal there, and so could be destroyed by natural elements. Here, he could only use the power of his mind and his magic to disrupt them, to go inside and destroy their very being from within.

The effects were instantaneous. The demons' eyes bulged, and then they writhed in midair before their wings seemed to collapse in on themselves, and they fell to the stony ground. A few more shudders, and then they were gone.

Levi's mouth compressed. He did not like

what he had just done, even though it was necessary. True, the demons would not have scrupled to destroy him if their roles had been reversed, but all the same, it was never good to take a life. However, now he had bought a little time. He could only pray that it would be enough.

Once again, he turned all his strength, all his focus, on making the portal close. It had begun to expand while he was distracted by confronting the demons, but now he was able to regain the ground he had lost. Yes, now the portal was less than a yard wide…now only a few feet…down to the width of one hand….

The blow knocked him sprawling. Levi went down on his knees, his right ear ringing. Had another demon blindsided him? Entirely possible, he supposed, since his attention had been fixed on the portal, and he had to assume that more demons would come to replace the ones he'd destroyed.

But as he pushed himself to his feet, he realized the source of the blow hadn't been a demon.

No, the being who faced him now was as human in appearance as he was.

For a second, Levi could only stare at this apparition, at the man who seemed to be roughly his same age, and who had coal-black hair and dark eyes that danced with a mocking light. He was far too young to be Joaquin Escobar, and so that meant….

"Yes, my father sends his regards." The stranger made a waving motion with his hands, and it was as if an unseen fist collided with Levi's jaw.

He staggered back a few feet, then collected his magic in order to steady himself. At once an invisible wall went up around him, one that even an Escobar's powers would find difficult to penetrate. "Matías."

"You look surprised." Matías Escobar still held his fists up, as though he was a boxer readying himself for the next assault from his opponent. "Didn't expect to see me here?"

"I'll admit I'm surprised. I didn't know you had the power to travel between worlds."

A slight lift of his shoulders. "I don't—but my father does. What I do have is the power to summon demons."

This revelation did startle Levi. He—and Angela and Connor, and everyone else who had knowledge of the matter—had thought Joaquin Escobar must be the one who'd sent the demons against the McAllister clan, although abetted by his son. But then Levi remembered how it was Matías' half-sister who'd been the witch behind the demon attacks in Scottsdale, who'd killed more than one person and planned to kill more, until she was shot to death by a civilian, of all people…how it had been Matías who'd called the demons to him to assist in the slow murder of Maya de la Paz. Perhaps the power of demon-summoning existed only in this younger generation.

"Not a talent to be proud of," Levi replied.

"I don't know. It's been useful." Matías eyes narrowed. "Why did you take her?"

Levi didn't bother to ask who the warlock meant by "her." "Because she was not your property. She deserved to be free—just as all the others in the Santiago clan deserve to be free."

That comment only elicited a sneer. "The Santiagos will finally be a power to be reckoned with, instead of a weak clan with an invalid at their head."

"Oh, so a *prima* whose mind is completely enslaved by your father is a better alternative?"

"It is the perfect solution." The curl of Matiás' lip translated into something that looked suspiciously like a leer. "Besides, she doesn't seem to mind being with my father. And why should you care? You're not even human."

"I am as human as you are," Levi said calmly. At the same time, he wondered how the Escobar warlock had been able to tell that the man he faced wasn't strictly a man at all. None of the McAllisters—save Angela, who had special powers of her own—had ever mentioned that his energy felt different from the others in their clan. Not that it mattered at the moment.

"Keep telling yourself that," Matías replied. "But let's stop dicking around, shall we? Step away from the portal."

The inflection of this final command was different from that conversational tone Escobar had previously used. The vowels and consonants blended together in one sonorous wave rolling around in Levi's head, strangely persuasive. Of course he needed to move away from the portal. The portal needed to be protected.

No. Levi dug his heels into the ground and shook his head, feeling like a dog trying to shake water out of its ears. The violent movement helped to clear some of the brain fog he'd begun to experience.

So that was what it felt like to be under the spell of Matías Escobar's talent. Levi had been able to resist it, but only because his magical nature made him less susceptible to that treacherous gift than an ordinary mortal would have been. He could see why it was so difficult to fight—Matías' power made his suggestions seem like the only logical thing to do.

"No, I don't think so," Levi said, and once more sent his energy toward the portal, causing it to shrink by a few more inches. All he needed was a little more time—

"Cute trick," Matías returned. "I think you just proved you're not really human, *pendejo*, because there's no witch or warlock in the world that can withstand me."

"Are you sure about that? I seem to recall that Caitlin McAllister was able to escape you fairly easily."

The dark warlock's black brows drew together. "Only because I was focusing on the other two, and Jorge and Tomas weren't paying attention. If she was here now, it would be a different story."

"Lucky for her that she isn't," Levi remarked. "But I am, and I have a message for you and your father. Leave the McAllister clan alone."

"Give me Lucinda back, and maybe we'll talk."

From the way Escobar's gaze shifted away from Levi as he spoke, it seemed clear enough that he would never hold up his end of such a bargain— even if the McAllisters would stoop so low as to barter with someone's life. Besides, Levi somehow doubted that Matías had the authority to make such a promise. Yes, his powers were quite prodigious, but it was still his father who ruled the Santiago clan now, who had made a slave of their *prima*.

"No, I don't think so," Levi said. "I can't agree

to that, and I'm sure neither Angela nor Connor would accept such a deal, either."

Hatred blazed in Matías' dark eyes at the mention of the two people who'd stolen his powers away from him. Clearly, it didn't matter that he'd recently regained them. The insult and injury would linger for a long time. "Then I don't think we need to say anything else."

A wave of his hand, and the charcoal-gray sky turned black overhead. Could it be that a storm was coming in? But Levi knew that the weather never changed on this plane—a ceaseless wind blew, and it was always cold and dry. Nothing lived. Nothing grew.

Then the darkness began to take on shape and form. Those weren't clouds moving overhead. They were armies of demons, moving in an unholy murmuration that took up the entire sky.

Levi's ears rang with Matías Escobar's laughter, even as those demons began to dive toward him.

19

"He's been away for a long time," Hayley said anxiously, her gaze moving toward the clock on the far wall. She'd been counting the minutes; Levi had been in his trance—or whatever you wanted to call it—for almost forty-five minutes now.

"Time can move differently on other planes," Angela replied. She had been watching Levi almost the entire time, but now she shifted her weight to the back of the chair where she sat, and looked over at her husband. "How long was I gone when I went to the world with the shining river?"

Connor tilted his head to one side. Unlike the other times Hayley had seen him, his longish dark hair now lay loose on his shoulders, and it seemed to make the Navajo blood in his features more apparent, accentuating the high cheekbones and the long, sculpted nose. "A little over an hour, I think. I know it felt longer, because I was sweating bullets the whole time, wondering what the hell I was going to do if you didn't come back."

Sweating bullets. Yes, that was exactly how this felt, as if every excruciating moment was somehow being carved out of her flesh.

Angela took Connor's hand, squeezed it lightly. "But I did come back." Her gaze shifted to Hayley. "And Levi will be back, too. We just have to trust in his talents. He knows what he's doing."

The *prima* sounded so confident. She'd known Levi longer than Hayley had, so maybe she was only telling the truth, wasn't trying to create hope where there should be none. Hayley prayed that was the case. And since Levi had told them all not to disturb him while he was away on this journey, there wasn't much any of them could do.

She looked back over at him, at his still features, so perfect, so calm and handsome. There was still color in his cheeks, so even though she couldn't see his chest rising and falling, she had to tell herself that of course he was alive, that he didn't move because he was in a trance deep enough to send him far from the very borders of this world. Once he had accomplished what he'd set out to do, he'd return to her. He'd be safe. The McAllisters would be safe.

If she kept telling herself that over and over, maybe she would believe it. For now, all she could was nod and tell the *prima,* "I hope you're right."

~

Striking out against so many foes seemed impossible. Instead, Levi raised a barrier of shimmering light all around him, not unlike the protective shield that Alex Trujillo was able to conjure as part of his talent. The demons screeching down from overhead slammed into it, black blood spattering everywhere, even as their limp bodies slid to the ground.

Standing a few feet away—but untouched by the demon horde he'd summoned—Matías scowled. "Again," he called out, and another phalanx of the black creatures dived from the sky, sacrificing themselves against the barrier Levi had conjured.

He felt that one. It was not unlike having multiple mallets swung into his skull, all at the same time. Wincing, he pulled in a deep breath and willed the sensation away as best he could. The barrier held, but if he allowed himself to be distracted by pain, then it might fall away entirely, and he would be unprotected.

"Still feeling invincible?" Matías taunted him, walking in a circle around the little bubble of glowing light. He made a sweeping motion with one hand, and the bodies of the fallen demons were flung off to one side, to be heaped like so much garbage. Obviously, he had little care for how many of his servants he killed, so long as he was ultimately victorious.

Invincible was the last thing Levi considered himself right then. His ears rang, and he ignored that as well. He might not have been born in this body, but he knew how much punishment it could take, and he still had a ways to go. "Your servants should have been warned that they serve a cruel master."

Matías shrugged. "What, you're worried about demons now? They exist to serve. And right now their only duty is to take your sorry ass out."

Those words were followed by another strafing run. Once again the demons thudded into the magical barrier and slid away, their dark lives forever extinguished by the shock of their black energy hitting a construct made entirely of light. The pain was so intense, however, that Levi was driven to his knees, where he knelt on the rocky ground and pulled in deep, searing breaths of air, forcing himself to maintain the barrier, although the agony of compelling the magic within him to keep functioning was only slightly less than the physical pain he was experiencing.

Another one of those blows, and he very

much feared he wouldn't be able to hold the barrier any longer. When that happened, the demons would fall upon him and tear him to pieces.

The mental image was so clear, Levi couldn't help wincing. At the same time, though, another thought came to him.

Matías was obviously confident in the power he held over these demons. But what if Levi could manage to turn them against him?

How, though?

The realization blazed into him like the sun coming up over the horizon. Matías had said the demons existed to serve, but that wasn't the precise truth. It was more that their natures didn't allow them to rebel if the correct spells were used to harness their energy. All Levi had to do was wrest that control from Escobar, even for only a minute. That would be long enough. Yes, the other warlock possessed some unique skills, but Levi was fairly certain that he didn't have the power necessary to protect himself the way Levi had.

One small problem, though—he would have to lift the barrier to cast the spell. It protected him, but at the same time, it kept his magic trapped inside.

That was all right. He was willing to take that risk.

A blink of his mind, and the barrier was gone. As Matías' eyes widened in surprise, Levi thrust himself to his feet. The words of the spell tumbled from his lips.

Dark above
    Dark below
    Demons fly
    Demons fall
    Take the one
    Who enslaved you all.

As one, the swirling mass of the demons dived from the sky, aiming toward Matías Escobar with the precision of an army of guided missiles. He swore and began to run—but there was no place for him to run, not with the portal he'd used to reach this plane many yards away. The demons descended, and Escobar screamed, high-pitched shrieks of pain that, mercifully, died away soon enough.

Feeling very weary, Levi turned back toward the portal that had allowed the creatures access to the human world. His head throbbed, and red flashes appeared before his eyes, but he made himself finish the spell, closing off access—if not forever, at least until someone with the requisite skills and raw talent was able to open it once more.

With any luck, that time would not come again for a very long while.

As Levi began to move toward his own portal, the one that would return him to the life he'd left behind, one of the demons descended in front of him. He was very tall, nearly half again Levi's height, with the same leathery wings of all his kind, but also with a mane of heavy black hair that fell to the center of his back. His true name was older than time, but Levi knew better than to say it out loud. Besides, he wasn't sure if his human mouth could even form the syllables.

"You have freed us," the demon said. "Are you not going to make us your army now?"

"I wish for no army," Levi replied, then added, using the demon's human-given name, "I only wish to go home, Lord of Chaos."

"'Home'?" the demon repeated. "That place is not your home."

"It is now." Lifting his head so he might look more or less into the demon's blood-tinted eyes, Levi went on, "And if you come there again, you will find a new war on your doorstep."

"It is not a place we would choose to go." The demon paused, and looked past Levi so he might focus on his otherworldly cohorts. "But it seems that those who would call us there are now dead."

"You know of no others?" Was it too much to hope that the talent for calling these beings to earth had died with Matías Escobar and his sister? Even now Levi feared that Joaquin still might possess enough of that sinister talent to carry on his dark crusade.

"No. There are none who now walk the earth who can do such a thing." The Lord of Chaos smiled. With those pointed teeth, and those glowing, blood-red eyes, his visage was not exactly a reassuring sight, and yet Levi still couldn't help but experience a rush of relief.

"Then may you and your kind live in peace here," he said.

"I am not sure of that, but at least you will not have to worry about us troubling you."

Levi could not ask for much more than that. He bowed and walked away, still not sure that the demon lord might not reach out to tear him open with his claws as soon as his back was turned. But the blow never came, and there was the portal, a strange, shimmering fog that beckoned him to return to the world he now called his own.

Back to Hayley.

He stepped into the fog, and left the demons' otherworld behind.

〜

She knew she shouldn't cry. It had only been two hours, after all. The Goddess only knew what Levi was going through, in a world she couldn't begin to imagine, except to do her best to understand that it lay in a universe completely separate from this one.

Problem was, Hayley could feel her eyes stinging, could feel a tear begin to slide from the inner corner of her lower eyelid and slip down the side of her nose. She reached up and wiped it away, then shot a surreptitious look at the *prima* and *primus*. Luckily, they were both gazing down at the phone Angela held; Hayley had the impression that they'd been quietly texting with Tobias, who was still at the hospital, keeping watch on Rachel.

She shifted in her chair, trying to ignore the way the hard wood of the unpadded seat had begun to bite into the backs of her thighs. As she held in a sigh, she shifted her gaze back over to Levi.

Hayley's breath caught.

Had she imagined it?

No, that was definitely a flutter of the dark gold eyelashes that lay against his cheeks. He sucked in a gasp of air, coughed, then laid his hands flat against the bed and pushed himself up to a sitting position as he stared wildly around him, as if not entirely certain of his surroundings.

"Levi!"

She didn't care that Angela and Connor only sat a few feet away, didn't stop to think that Levi might need a little longer to get his bearings. All that mattered in that moment was her arms around him, the sensation of his warm body next to hers. A single second of hesitation, and then he was returning the embrace, his arms encircling her and holding her close.

"Hayley," he murmured, his lips against her hair, and then her cheek. At last his mouth touched hers, strong, hungry, reestablishing the connection between them. Clearly, he wasn't concerned about displaying that sort of intimacy in front of the *prima* and *primus*.

They both got up from their chairs, their words tumbling over each other. "Did you do it?" "Are we safe?"

A long pause, and then Levi gently let go of Hayley, although he kept his fingers clasped with hers so she couldn't rise from the bed where she sat. "The demons won't trouble us again. The portal has been closed."

Angela's eyes shut, and she whispered, "Thank the Goddess."

Connor didn't speak, but from the way he nodded, his entire expression one of grim satisfaction, it was clear that he was relieved as well.

"There's more," Levi added, and Hayley

stared at him, worry starting to overtake the sensations of relief that had begun to flood through her.

"What else?" she asked quickly. "You're not hurt, are you?"

"No. That is, I suffered a few blows in the otherworld, but they haven't traveled with me here." He let go of one of her hands so he could trail his fingers over her hair. Such tenderness in that touch, but also a sort of wonder, as if he'd feared he wouldn't be able to do such a thing ever again. His gaze flickered from her to Angela and Connor. "Matías Escobar was there."

"In the otherworld?" Angela inquired, her tone sharp.

"Yes. He was the one summoning the demons. Like sister, like brother, I suppose. We…fought."

"And?"

"He's dead. He won't trouble any of us again."

Angela reached over and took Connor's hand. Her expression was difficult to read. Was that happiness in her eyes…or doubt?

"It's true," Levi added. "I set his own demons upon him."

That must have been something to see…from a safe distance. Hayley wondered what had gone through Matías Escobar's mind during those last few moments, when he saw the creatures he'd been using as his own servants suddenly turn on him. Had he recognized his defeat, or had he been defiant to the end?

"It's not that we don't believe you," Connor said. "It's more that…can you think of anything more guaranteed to piss off Joaquin Escobar than killing his only son?"

A long silence followed that question. It wasn't that they didn't all know the answer—it was that no one wanted to acknowledge such a bleak reality out loud.

"I had no choice," Levi told him.

"We all know that. And believe me, I'm sure everyone will be relieved to know that Matías Escobar has departed this mortal coil…or whatever coil he was on when he died. But we also have to be prepared to face the consequences."

Hayley gripped Levi's hand. "Well, can we do that after Levi has had a chance to recover? It's not like he just got back from a walk in the park."

"Of course," Angela replied, giving her husband a significant look. "We need to go and let the elders know what's happened. Why don't you two get some alone time, and then we can all regroup once Levi feels like he's up to it?"

"I'm fine—" Levi began, and Hayley shook her head.

"Swear to the Goddess, Levi, if you don't let me baby you for at least five minutes, I'm going to be seriously annoyed."

He chuckled then, and lifted his shoulders, as if to indicate defeat. "All right. I promise I'll allow a little pampering…but not too much."

"I think that's our cue." Angela smiled, some of the care erasing itself from her delicate features. "Just text us when you're ready."

"I will," Levi said.

The *prima* and *primus* left the bedroom, and a moment later, Hayley heard the front door quietly shut. At once she bent down and kissed Levi on the lips. To her relief, he kissed her back with even more fervor than he had the last time they'd embraced, a fierce need communicating itself to her, as though he had to know that nothing had changed between them. After the kiss ended, she asked, "Do you want to tell me about it?"

"Not really," he replied, then went on before she could interrupt, "but I will. Not now, though. It is…a difficult thing, to take a life."

"Even when that life belonged to Matías Escobar?" Hayley had never considered herself a vengeful person, but the thought of what Matías had done to Lucinda…had done to Danica Wilcox and the Goddess knew how many others…made her blood run cold. As far as she was concerned, the Escobar warlock had gotten exactly what he deserved.

"Even then." Levi's tone was very gentle, and he reached up to touch her hair again, as if marveling at its texture. "I suppose I'd like to think that he had a core of good in him somewhere. Perhaps if he had had a different life—"

"A different father," Hayley interrupted, and Levi tilted his head to one side, apparently considering her words.

"Perhaps. It's hard to say. His father's blood ran in his veins, but he wasn't raised by the man. But if he'd grown up among the McAllisters, if he'd been accepted as all of you have accepted me...possibly then he would have been a different person."

"We'll never know," Hayley said.

"No," Levi said, the word tinged with sadness. "We'll never know."

He got up from his bed soon after that—against Hayley's protests, although she subsided once he promised he would sit down on the sofa in the living room. After admonishing him to stay put, she went into the kitchen and got him a glass of water, and also brought a plate of cheese and some grapes he had in the refrigerator.

"I didn't know if you'd want any wine, after all that," she said as she sat down next to him.

"Not right now. Maybe later." Truth be told, he was experiencing a weariness that seemed to have settled into his very bones, and he honestly didn't think that drinking alcohol would help with that at all. It was good to sit here by Hayley, to steal a glance at her, to watch the light from the lamp across the room shimmer over her golden hair. During the time he'd been on the demons' plane, night had fallen here in Jerome.

Levi didn't want to admit there might be any particular significance to that observation.

"I understand." She waited until he'd picked up a slice of cheese and slowly eaten it before she went on, "So…what happens now?"

"I don't know." He reached for his glass of water and took a sip. There, that helped. His throat had been dry ever since he'd awakened back here. Perhaps the acrid air of the demons' world had settled in his lungs. "That is, Matías died in that other world, but he would have died here as well, in the very instant that his soul was extinguished. I'm sure his father knew immediately, because he must have been with him when he traveled to that plane, just as you were here, keeping watch on me."

Her lips pressed together, and Levi could see the fear that flared in her eyes. He couldn't blame her; Joaquin Escobar might not have turned out to possess the demon-summoning abilities of his offspring, but he still had a veritable arsenal of other nasty powers at his disposal. However, she only said, "Well, at least Matías wasn't alone when he died."

Such evidence of compassion—especially unlooked-for as it was—made Levi love her that much more. Many would have said Matías Escobar was a monster…and Levi wasn't sure he could refute such a statement…but perhaps even monsters deserved to have someone who cared about them nearby when they passed on.

He reached over and took Hayley's hand. Her fingers wrapped around his, warm and welcoming, but also so slender, so fragile. That very fragility told him he needed to be here for her, to protect her against whatever might be coming next. Yes, she was brave and strong and true, but her magic on its own could not save her. And he thought then of all the McAllisters, so many of whom had abilities that any civilian might marvel at, and yet who still wouldn't be able to do much when it came to the fight ahead.

His expression must have altered, because she said, "What is it?"

"Nothing." At least, nothing he wanted to say in that moment. Very soon they would have to all come together and decide how to face the storm that was approaching, but for now he wanted only to sit next to her and breathe in the sweet scent of her hair, bask in the comfort her mere presence here provided him. "Will you stay with me tonight?"

"Tonight, and all the nights after that…if you want me to."

He pulled her close and kissed her then, needing the fierceness and the fire in her lips as she returned the embrace. She held on to him, pulling him close. Ah, yes, that was better; the warmth of her body seemed to dispel the chill that had settled in his bones from his brief sojourn in the demons' world.

After the kiss ended, however, and they had pulled apart, an expression of dismay passed over her face. "Oh, damn."

"What's wrong?"

She glanced toward the door, in the direction of her brother's flat. "It's Lucinda. We still really haven't figured out what we should do about where she's staying—at least, until Rachel is back home and able to take over again. I'd started to toy with the idea of having Lucinda stay in my room while I slept on the couch. If I stay here with you, it feels like I'm kind of abandoning her."

"She can still take your room," Levi said. "You won't be using it."

Hayley sent him a skeptical look. "Don't you think it will be strange, to have her staying alone with Brandon?"

"I don't know," Levi replied. "Why don't you ask her?"

"I—" She broke off there, because at that very moment, someone knocked at the door. Her eyebrows lifted. "How did you know?"

Levi's body was human, but his senses were just enough sharper than most people's that he'd been able to hear Lucinda and Brandon coming up the stairs. "I told you I had many powers."

Hayley made an exasperated noise and got up from the couch, moving quickly, thus making it clear that she expected him to stay put while she answered the knock. As she opened the door, she said, "Hey, Brandon, Lucinda."

"Hey," Brandon replied. He peered past his sister's shoulder into the living room. "We're not interrupting anything, are we?"

"No," Levi said. Ignoring Hayley's frown, he got up from the sofa and came to the door. "But we were discussing accommodations."

From her spot on the landing just behind Brandon, Lucinda shot him a puzzled glance. "Accommodations?"

"Well, it's definite that Rachel won't be coming home from the hospital until tomorrow," Levi said. "And Hayley mentioned how she thought she could offer you her room."

"She really doesn't need to do that," Lucinda protested. "I mean, it should be okay for me to stay at Rachel's by myself, as long as Rachel and Tobias don't have a problem with it."

"I don't think anyone's asked them," Hayley said. "The thing is…I really won't need the room, because Levi wants me to stay here with him. But if you think it's weird to crash at Brandon's place, then we can put that off until Rachel comes home."

This revelation made Brandon's eyebrows work overtime. It wasn't difficult to see that he wasn't terribly thrilled about his little sister moving in with his next-door neighbor, especially since they'd only known each other for a few days. However, he remained quiet, seeming content to allow Lucinda to make the final call, since Hayley had been addressing her.

The Santiago witch appeared somewhat flummoxed by the offer. She glanced from Hayley to Brandon and then back again, her dark eyes troubled. "I—I'm not sure—"

"Or we could find someplace else to put you up," Levi said. "Maybe one of the rooms at the Mile High Inn, or at the Connor Hotel?"

"I wouldn't want to cause anyone any trouble," Lucinda said hastily. "If Brandon is okay with me staying in Hayley's room, then I'm okay with it, too. Besides, it should only be for tonight, right?"

"Probably," Levi replied. "Maybe two nights at

the most." He paused, wondering whether he should tell her of what had transpired in the demon world, how Matías Escobar was no longer a threat to her. Probably more than anyone else, she deserved to know. "And Lucinda—"

Her head tilted to one side, her gaze sharpening slightly. Perhaps she had caught the shift in his tone, or his own expression had altered enough to signal an important change of subject. "What is it?"

"Matías is dead. You won't need to worry about him coming after you."

This pronouncement made her hand go to her throat. She seemed to stumble, as if her knees had begun to give way under her. At once Brandon had a hand on her elbow, steadying her. "You're sure?" she gasped. "How can you know that?"

"Because I was there. I saw it."

With her warm complexion, it was difficult for her to go completely pale, but Levi could still see the way the blood drained from her cheeks. For a few seconds, she didn't reply. Then she glanced up at Brandon. "I think—I think I would like to take Hayley's room. If it's all right."

"Of course it is," Brandon said, sounding more solicitous than Levi had ever heard him. "Do you want to sit down?"

"I think I'd better." She paused for a second,

then looked back at Levi. "Thank you—thank you for telling me."

And then she was letting Brandon help her across the landing and into his flat, his hand on her elbow the whole time. The door shut behind them, and Hayley looked up at Levi.

"That's got to help, doesn't it?"

"I think so," he replied. He closed the door and went back over to the sofa, glad of the chance to sit down again. Damn, he really was more tired than he'd thought.

Hayley followed him and resumed her seat as well, only this time with one leg tucked under her, so she might face him. "I'll need to go back over in a little while and get some of my stuff, but I figured it was better to give them some time."

"Probably. Lucinda has to allow herself to understand that the thing she feared most can no longer trouble her."

A nod, but from the way Hayley looked down, seemingly preoccupied with turning the ring on her middle finger around and around, it appeared that she was troubled, indeed. "And what about the rest of us?" she asked. "Matías is gone, but…."

"But Joaquin Escobar still controls the Santiago clan. I know." Levi glanced past her, at the window that framed the rising moon, now only a few days away from full. Somewhere beyond these hills and mountains, beyond the dry deserts that surrounded Phoenix, almost all the way to the ocean, a man grieved the loss of his son.

And Levi knew that grief could bring about their downfall.

EPILOGUE

Somewhere in the background, a woman was weeping. Joaquin wanted to tell her to be silent, that he needed to be alone with his thoughts, but he stopped himself. He would not show any outward grief over Matías' death, and so he supposed he might as well allow Olivia to cry now, for the brother she had lost. His son deserved that much.

A black wreath hung on the door, and some of the Santiago women had come to the house to drape cloths on all the mirrors. Tomorrow would be the funeral, with a line of hundreds of cars going to St. Andrew's in Old Town Pasadena, so all the Santiagos could grieve for the son of their *primus*.

Olivia's tears irritated Joaquin, though. They had been estranged the last few years of Matías' life, mostly because Olivia could not see past her own weaknesses to understand how truly great her brother was destined to be. What a waste of skin, his only remaining child. Such an irony the universe had cast before him, that the only one to live would be a *nunca,* a witch whose true powers had never developed. Indeed, for many years, he had barely thought of her as his daughter.

No, all his hopes for the future now lay in the child Marisol carried. With his runaway coward wife Isabella long dead, the Santiagos no longer had a healer. However, modern-day pregnancy tests were as good as healers when it came to confirming that a woman was with child. It was very early yet, so early they had not yet bothered to find a doctor, but Joaquin knew he must do so soon. The thought grated on him, that an Escobar should be brought into the world by a civilian physician. Better that, however, than the child be unhealthy in any way. No, this heir of his must be perfect.

Would he—or she, although Joaquin had already begun to think of the child as a son—also carry the Escobar gift of command? He must, or he would not be able to continue ruling this clan after his father was gone. The Santiagos would accept him for a while, because he would be the child of their *prima,* but such a grasp would be tenuous if he did not have the means to keep them obedient, like a pack of hunting dogs cowed by their master's voice.

Well, the child's birth was still months in the future, and his days as the ruler of this clan further off still. In the meantime, Joaquin knew he must seek vengeance for the death of his son. He must extend his reach beyond the Santiagos, so his enemies would have no hope of victory. They must be crushed utterly, beyond any means of recovery. All of them—the Wilcoxes, the de la Pazes.

And yes, the hated McAllisters.

Yes, a storm was coming…and soon it would sweep all of them away.

The End

The Witches of Cleopatra Hill series will conclude with *Darktide*, releasing in January 2018. A spin-off series, The Witches of Canyon Road, will release in March 2018.

THE ARIZONA WITCH CLANS

The McAllisters (Jerome, Arizona, and the Verde Valley)

Angela McAllister (Wilcox) – *prima*, or head witch, of the McAllister clan

Rachel McAllister – Angela's aunt

Bryce McAllister – one of the McAllister clan's elders

Allegra Moss – one of the McAllister clan's elders

Margot Emory (Wilcox) – formerly one of the McAllister clan's elders, now married to Lucas Wilcox

Sylvia Emory – Margot's mother

Ruby Lynch – former *prima* of the McAllister clan

Henry Lynch – son of Ruby McAllister and Patrick Lynch

Tobias Miller – fiancé of Rachel McAllister

Sonya McAllister – Angela's mother, deceased

Boyd Willis – a McAllister warlock

Micah Landon -- an absentminded artist

Floyd Barnett – lives above the store next to Rachel's

Rosemary McAllister – lives on the other side of Rachel's store above the tea shop

Susan Callery -- an artist with a studio in the same building as Tobias' flat

Efraim Willendale -- runs the post office

Wyatt McAllister -- owns a B&B on Paradise Street

Dora McAllister – Great-Aunt Ruby's caretaker

Jocelyn Riggs -- the clan's strongest medium

Kirby McAllister – a cousin of Angela's and one of her "caretakers"

Tricia McAllister -- the new clan elder after Margot Emory steps down

Richard McAllister – Tricia's husband

Caitlin McAllister (Trujillo) – daughter of Tricia and Richard; a seer

Michael McAllister – Caitlin's older brother, a chef

Roslyn McAllister -- Caitlin's first cousin; youngest sister of Jenny and Adam

Marcus McAllister -- Tricia McAllister's older brother, father of Jenny, Adam, and Roslyn

Lysette McAllister – Marcus' wife and mother of Jenny, Adam, and Roslyn; a civilian (non-witch)

Jenny McAllister – eldest daughter of Marcus and Lysette McAllister

Adam McAllister – only son of Marcus and Lysette McAllister

Roslyn McAllister – youngest daughter of Marcus and Lysette McAllister

Evan McAllister—a distant cousin of Angela's; the clan's "fixer"

Levi McAllister — an otherworldly being adopted into the clan

Hayley McAllister—a witch from the Payson branch of the family

Brandon McAllister—a warlock from the Payson branch of the family; Hayley's older brother

The Wilcox Clan (Flagstaff, Arizona, and the northern third of the state)

Connor Wilcox – *primus* (head warlock) of the Wilcox clan

Damon Wilcox – former *primus* of the Wilcoxes, now deceased

Lucas Wilcox – a cousin of Connor's, now married to Margot Emory

Mason Wilcox (McAllister) – Connor's cousin and a friend of Angela's; now married to Adam McAllister

Danica Wilcox – Mason's younger sister

Joseph Wilcox – Mason and Danica's father

Olivia Wilcox – Mason and Danica's mother

Andre Begonie – Angela McAllister's father

Marie Wilcox (Begonie) – a cousin of Connor's, the Wilcox clan's seer

Eleanor Garnett – the clan's healer

Darrell Wilcox – a Wilcox warlock gifted with heating the area around him

In the 1880s:

Jeremiah Wilcox – the Wilcox clan's *primus*

Nizhoni – Jeremiah's second wife, a woman of the Navajo

Jacob Wilcox – Jeremiah and Nizhoni's son

Samuel Wilcox – Jeremiah's brother

Edmund Wilcox – Jeremiah's brother

Nathan Wilcox – Jeremiah's brother

Emma Garnett – Jeremiah's only sister; children are Louis, Susan, Marcus, and Jeffrey

Aaron Garnett – Emma's husband

Grace Wilcox – Samuel's wife; five children are Benjamin, Addie, Esther, Clay, and Dorothy

Lida Wilcox – Edmund's wife; their three children are Kathleen, Annabelle, and Wyatt

Jennie Wilcox – Nathan's wife; their four children are Oliver, Calvin, Levi, and Victor

The de la Paz clan (Phoenix, Arizona; Tucson, Arizona; and the southern third of the state)

Maya de la Paz -- *prima* of the de la Paz clan up through *Protector*

Alex Trujillo -- Maya's grandson

Diego Trujillo -- Alex's older brother

Alicia Trujillo – Alex and Diego's little sister

Letty Trujillo – Diego's wife

Luz Trujillo – Alex and Diego's mother and Maya's daughter; *prima* of the de la Paz clan after the end of *Protector*

David Trujillo – Luz's husband and father of Alex, Diego, and Alicia

Valentina de la Paz – the de la Paz clan's healer in the Tucson area

Alba de la Paz -- the healer in the Phoenix area

Zoe Sandoval – the de la Paz clan's *prima*-in-waiting

Zander Sandoval – Zoe's little brother

Luis Sandoval – father of Zoe and Zander

Andrea Sandoval – mother of Zoe and Zander, Alex Trujillo's aunt (Luz and Andrea are sisters)

Luis de la Paz – Alex's cousin; works at the family's store

Jack Sandoval -- Luis Sandoval's youngest brother; a detective with the Scottsdale P.D.

Miguel de la Paz -- a private detective

Oscar de la Paz -- with the Tucson P.D.

ALSO BY CHRISTINE POPE

THE WATCHERS TRILOGY

(Paranormal Romance)

Falling Dark

Dead of Night

Rising Dawn

THE WITCHES OF CLEOPATRA HILL

(Paranormal Romance)

Darkangel

Darknight

Darkmoon

Sympathetic Magic

Protector

Spellbound

A Cleopatra Hill Christmas

Impractical Magic

Strange Magic

The Arrangement

Defender

Bad Blood

Deep Magic

Darktide

THE DJINN WARS

(Paranormal Romance)

Chosen

Taken

Fallen

Broken

Forsaken

Forbidden

Awoken

Illuminated

THE SEDONA FILES

(Paranormal Romance)

Bad Vibrations

Desert Hearts

Angel Fire

Star Crossed

Falling Angels

Enemy Mine

TALES OF THE LATTER KINGDOMS

(Fantasy Romance)

All Fall Down

Dragon Rose

Binding Spell

Ashes of Roses

One Thousand Nights

Threads of Gold

The Wolf of Harrow Hall

Moon Dance

The Song of the Thrush

THE GAIAN CONSORTIUM SERIES

(Science Fiction Romance)

Blood Will Tell

Breath of Life

The Gaia Gambit

The Mandala Maneuver

The Titan Trap

The Zhore Deception

ABOUT THE AUTHOR

Christine Pope has been writing stories ever since she commandeered her family's Smith-Corona typewriter back in the sixth grade. Her work includes paranormal romance, fantasy romance, and science fiction/space opera romance. She fell under the Land of Enchantment's spell while researching her Djinn Wars series and now makes her home in Santa Fe, New Mexico.

To be notified about new releases by Christine Pope, please go to www.christinepope.com and sign up for her newsletter.